Skank

Heart of the Assassin

...some defects we hide in our hearts...

SKANK

Heart of the Assassin

This is a work of Dark Fiction, with occasional bad language. Any similarity to persons living or dead is purely coincidental.

This book is dedicated to Nancy Zuidema, who put up with every 2000 word increment during NaNoWriMo and the tedious editing process that followed.

With Special Thanks to Allie Long for correcting my atrocious grammar

...and to Mike FitzGerald for getting me started and NaNoWriMo for keeping me going.

Cover art: R.W. Zuidema
Title Page art: Allie Long

1

I was sitting in a squeaky wooden chair in the hallway next to a spindly, doily-topped table. While through the double doors in front of me lawyers decided my fate. It wasn't that they were specifically talking about me or cared at all that I existed; no, if I couldn't be sold for money either whole or cut up for spare parts, I was useless. They were cutting up those pieces of what was left of my father's life, weighing the value of houses and cars against what was owed to the bank. What was clear was that my life would be forever changed.

I stood up and stared into my face in an oval Victorian styled mirror that hung over the small table. In high school I was labeled "Skank" because my single parent father could not teach me to look and act like a proper girl. I was voted most likely to be locked away in a mental institution. Staring back at me through plain grey eyes was a 19 year old girl with a thin short nose, small mouth with thin lips and a pointed chin that was a bit too small. All of my workouts hadn't added any woman like shape just slightly more muscle definition, making me look more like a boy in B cups. I fussed with my straight mouse brown hair trying to get the top layer to stay in the clip that tied it back.

The sound of chairs grating against the wooden floor startled me back to reality signaling the end of the meeting in the next room. A hand grasped the door handle with much more force than necessary, rattling the frosted glass before yanking it open in a show of masculine strength. The smell of cologne preceded the troop of money-eating vultures out of the room, each in their dark grey suits and power ties that draped from their necks like the throbbing penis display of a male baboon. They didn't say a word as they marched from the room, jaws clenched, muscles rippling on clean-shaven manly faces, not even looking in my direction. I watched the procession go down the steps and out the side door before I looked towards the open door of the meeting room. Markus Philter, a short, round, balding man who was the lawyer for my father's estate, was standing there gazing at my breasts. "You can come in now, Millicent." He said.

I walked into the converted Victorian parlor, now dominated by a simulated wood grained conference table that extended almost to the bay window on the far end. I slowly slid into one of the fake leather swivel chairs, still warm from its previous occupant. I felt somehow soiled. With his eyes still firmly fixed on the open buttons of my Henley T-shirt, Mr. Philter passed me several sheets of paper. "As you most likely know Millie, can I call you Millie?" He continued, without waiting for an answer. "Much more was owed on your father's estate than it was worth. Therefore, there is not really anything left besides what was specifically in your name, which means only the $5,328.63 in your bank account."

"What about my car?"

"I'm afraid, Millie, that the car is still in your father's name."

"Not the Pontiac, the Volkswagen, don't I get to keep that?"

"I'm afraid not Millie, officially that was still in your father's name. There are certain items, however, you are entitled to, meaning clothes and personal effects, but you will need to be out of the house by the end of the month."

I was about to pee my pants as reality was finally getting a grip on me. "Well Millie that's a list of the terms and items you may take from the premises. If there are no more questions, you may go." He stood jogging the papers he still held, and ushered me out of the room. The old wood and glass door rattling behind me as it closed. Still staring at the papers, but unable to focus on the words, I stumbled down the steps and out the side door, just in time to watch my white VW, with the rainbow Apple sticker on the back window, trundle after a tow truck out of the Law Office driveway and down Hampton Street.

My dad always thought tyranny would come with uniformed soldiers marching in step down Main Street with guns, forcing everyone to submit. No, it came with more stealth, from men in dark suits, picking us off one at a time.

I wandered dazed down Hampton Street, a two-block road behind the town green of Winfield Connecticut. Isn't this the part where Prince Charming comes galloping up on his white charger to whisk the ugly duckling princess away from her disastrous life with the dead end job to live happily ever after? Shit, the hell with Prince Charming, I'd take the ugly duckling's old dead end job. I started walking towards home, at least home for the next 15 days.

When I was in high school I was afraid to walk down Main Street past old drug store, where all the gang kids hung out, but now it didn't even register on the panic meter. Their turf, a small alleyway between shops was now occupied by a homeless man, sitting cross-legged behind his cardboard sign with crayoned words that told a sad story, wanting a handout. Another victim of the creeping greed machine that ground flesh into money, but like a consuming fire had moved on to China, India or other country where cheap meat was still available. I dropped all the coins in my pocket into the box that supported the sign. Why had I done that? I'd never done

5

that before, when I had money I never noticed him, now that I had none he was the only person I saw. I turned back, looking at my 85 cents sitting in his box. I might need that back, because I was next on the list of the lost if I didn't choose the same path my father chose. Why, why did my father leave me? Didn't he know I still needed him, with or without a job?

Still looking back, I collided with a woman feeling the softness of her body and sensing the sweet incense smell from the Neo Pagan shop she'd just walked out of.

"I'm so sorry." I said, trying to untangle myself from her beads and layers of dark dyed Indian cotton clothing. The look in her eyes told me that everything was okay.

"Your spirit is troubled." She said, as she was leading me into the Enchanted Moon Magik Shop. I didn't really think of myself as intolerant but the store did make me a little uncomfortable, not wanting to totally give up on the whole Christian thing. "Maybe we can help." She continued.

"I don't know," I answered," do you have any lawyer repellent?" The woman, caught off guard, barked out an involuntary laugh.

"Most women your age have issues of the heart, not of lawyers."

"I don't think there's an age limit on lawyers." I answered, looking around at the silver and jade jewelry, and dark colored gauzy cotton clothes. I was feeling out of place in my LL Bean Sage colored cinched cord jacket, white Henley T shirt and double L jeans. My eyes locked on Robin "Raven" McCardy working behind the counter. Robin had been in my class in high school. Although we weren't really friends, we did at least share a similar outcast status as decreed by the "normal" kids. She's a hauntingly beautiful black Irish girl with shiny dark hair large green eyes and porcelain perfect white skin, wearing a deep indigo long dress with a silver necklace.

"Skank, sorry, Millie?" She corrected herself.

"Hi Raven," I answered.

"Millie, was that your dad that…" she trailed off. Up to this point I had not cried, still in the denial stage. Now it was coming as sure as a tsunami after the water drains away from the shore, and there was nothing I could do about it. I was only able to nod as the wave crashed into the shore. I clamped my mouth shut trying to hold back the flood, but it came leaking from my eyes. The woman, who had led me into the store, was struggling to understand what was happening, but I was becoming completely incoherent, so she turned to Robin for an explanation.

"Her dad killed himself last week." Robin answered the non verbalized question.

"Oh no," the woman said, hugging me closer. I could see the concern in her eyes.

"I'm sorry," was all I could say before melting into a complete mess, crying openly. She led me into a back room, holding me even tighter.

Robin followed us in, the woman asked her. "Do you know her?"

"She was in my class in high school, her name is Millie Willard, I hadn't seen her since then, but I think she was going to Manchester Community College. I read in the paper that a man named Mark Willard committed suicide after losing his job. I wasn't sure if it was really her dad until now."

"Poor thing." She said, turning to me she continued, "Please just sit here as long as you need to." She sat me down on a low counter between the inventory of bright colored pillows and scented candles. She then led Robin out of the room. "You called her skanky?" She asked Robin in a low voice thinking that I couldn't hear her.

"Skank," Robin answered, "That's what everyone called her in school."

"You know that's not a very nice name."

"I know, there were a lot of not very nice people in school," Robin answered. The cruelty in high school was such a contrast to the caring I was seeing now, I didn't deserve such kindness from a woman who had originally pulled me into the store only to make a quick sale.

This is all too confusing, I thought, hugging my arms around myself rocking back and forth as my future swirled before me like an open drain.

"Maybe I should just follow my dad and ask him what he was thinking." I looked up into the woman's shocked face not realizing I'd said that out loud.

"No, child," she set down the cup of water she was holding. "Everything will be okay, even if it's not now, it will be." What she said was somehow whacked enough to make sense. Did she really know me that well? She sat next to me, stroking my hair, hugging me to her warm, comfortable body. Is this what it's like to have a real mother, someone who could hug away all the problems of the world? My dad told me I had a mom once, at first gentle and caring. I don't really remember her. The woman I have vague memories of was an obnoxious shrill woman who would seem to visit once in a while. She talked mean to dad and wouldn't set down her beer and cigarette long enough to hold me. After a while she didn't come to visit anymore. I found out later that she found the "real man" she'd been looking for. I was just glad she never came to visit anymore.

"The universe will take care of you." She added. There were things about the universe that didn't make sense to me. Just when I was basking in the comfort of making that final decision, this happens, giving me just enough to keep me hanging on by fingertips. I guess despite what Einstein told us, God is under no real obligation to have the universe make sense. I looked up into her eyes hoping to find an answer in her caring. She looked down and took the little olivewood cross that hung around my neck that was usually tucked under my shirt so that no one would see it. "I thought Christians weren't supposed to commit suicide." She said.

"I don't think I'm a very good Christian" I answered.

"No, I mean..." she stopped, but I knew what she was going to say. I'd always considered myself Catholic like my grandmother, although I hadn't actually been to church since she last took me when I was seven. My dad was an evangelical atheist because he so hated hypocritical Christians. He always thought of the universe as a vast complicated machine.

"I guess he knows the truth now." I answered.

"What?"

Looking up at her again I answered, "My dad, I guess he now knows what happens after you die." She hugged my head against her shoulder and stroked my hair. I sat there soaking in the loving kindness, flashing back to when I was that 7 year old girl in church remembering a drawing they had in the Sunday school room of Jesus carrying a lamb in his arms surrounded by children.

I don't remember exactly when the woman left and gave me the cup of water, but now I was holding the water and Robin was asking me if I was going to be okay. Behind her was a man dressed in layers of all black with long hair and a beard. He looked like someone who became a wolf during the full moon but his eyes were kind.

"I'm going to be okay, I'm so sorry about all of this, I should be going." I said, as I finished the water and started to get up.

Robin looked at the man. "I should take her home, daddy." she told him. Wow, I envied her even more now.

"Are you sure, Raven?" He asked.

"It's okay, I don't live far. I can walk." I said.

2

I watched Robin's bright blue Toyota Echo drive away, its back window displaying decals of mythical forest creatures, and then I turned and faced the late 50's Cape Cod style house. No family room, master suite or bath with jetted tub, no granite counters with stainless steel appliances. It was a leftover wooden box built as a place to stuff post war families. It had weaned a crop of baby boomers that had grown up and grown old before my dad bought it. Even though I'd grown up in it, I didn't recognize it anymore. My dad's G6 was gone and there was a lock box already hanging from the front door, luckily my key still worked. I walked in and went to the refrigerator, but after looking in I didn't want to touch any of the food inside, so I got a glass of water instead and wandered into the living room.

Down the hall, I could still see the trails of yellow police tape that had covered the door to my dad's office. Emotions churned in my stomach as I started a slow cautious walk towards the closed door. A swirl of images played backwards in my head, the nights at the motel that the police provided, the smell of the patrol car that had taken me from class to the morgue, the community college differential equations classroom that I was pulled out of by an officer with the crackling radio. As if in a slow motion video the scene burned into my brain, incomprehensible math scrawled on the marker board, the door at the front of the classroom opening the contrast between the officer's dark blue uniform and the off-white painted concrete block walls. The officer calling my name, "is there a Millicent

Willard here?" the fear that gripped my stomach, the crushing weight of every eye on me as I stood up to go with him, under the instructor's stern gaze and the words from the officer's mouth.

"I'm sorry Ms Willard, but something's happened to your father, could you come with me please?" I looked back into the classroom; the class that only seconds before I wanted to drop was now the last scrap of the "normal" world I would ever see. It slid away like a lighted portal in the wall of a great dark abyss.

Standing before the closed door to my father's room, I remembered the argument over that very differential equations class. After going through all of the engineering math and physics I was failing differential equations. The night before his death, I had a huge argument with my father, I told him I didn't want to be an engineer; I had never wanted to be an engineer. He only wanted me to be one because that's what he wanted to be, but had only a two year degree in Computer Aided Design. I told him nobody wanted engineers from this country anymore; they were all from China and India. The very next day he and his whole engineering department gets let go because the company was contracting all engineering functions off shore.

I backed away from the door as if it were the gate to hell itself. My hell, with the realization that he didn't leave me, I left him, trampling his whole life's ambition, only to be validated by money gluttonous business men. My father didn't commit suicide, I killed him!

I jumped at a hard knock on the door, "Police! Open up!" And they were here to arrest me for it. I rushed to the front door slopping water from the glass I still held. "What are you doing here, this is a crime scene!" he demanded as I opened the door.

"They told me they were done, that I could come back home." I said, still holding the door half open. My eye caught movement as he pulled his gun.

"What?" Wait a minute, why would a cop have a gun with a silencer?

This was my opportunity, I could passively stand here and let this fake cop end my life, go find my father, tell him I'm sorry, with no guilt of having to do the deed myself. Or not! I threw the glass into his face and kicked the door shut, bracing my back against the stair wall and pushing the door with both legs. His hand holding the gun was still inside keeping the door from closing all the way. He screamed in pain, bashing against the door from the outside, opening a large gap. I kicked with both legs again, smashing his hand in the door. He left go with the loudest "FUCK!" I ever heard in my life as the gun dropped to the floor. Someone else told him to keep it down, he wasn't alone and I was dead for sure. He slammed into the door one more time, and was now able to pull his hand free. I fell to the floor as the door slammed closed, and scrambled for the gun. I was still fumbling with it when the door exploded inward, propelled by his kick. I pointed the gun in the direction of the opening and yanked on the trigger; there was a loud pop, the gun jumped, and he screamed.

"That fucking bitch just shot me." Suddenly bullets fired from outside came through the front wall, not up high through the window like in the movies, but down low where I was, smashing right through the side of the house as if it were paper. I scuttled across the floor as stuffing exploded out of the chair next to me. Around the corner I clawed the cellar door open and rolled down the stairs like a full hefty bag. Scrambling around the cellar, I hid under the shelf next to the washing machine. I heard two people race into the house, thundering across the living room

13

floor over my head. "You find the computer; I'm going to kill that bitch." I heard one go straight to my father's room, and the other began ransacking the other rooms on the first floor indiscriminately firing as he went. Finally he started down the cellar stairs. I fired the gun I still held, the step he was about to put his foot on blew apart. "Damn bitch!" he screamed as he jumped back, and then started firing through the floor above me, blasting chips from the concrete at my feet. I tried to tuck them up under me as I pushed myself farther under the small shelf.

"I can't find it, I can't find another computer." The other guy was yelling.

"It's got to be there somewhere, the cops don't have it."

They were looking for my father's work computer the one he did his CAD work on. Looking up at the beams under my father's office, I could see the self that he had built with the computer still on it.

"Quiet!" The other guy said. "The cops, I hear the cops coming, we need to get out of here."

"We need that computer." The shooter yelled back.

"We'll get it later, come on."

"Hey, little girl, I hope you're dead, bitch, or bleeding to death."

Heavy footsteps ran to the door. A minute later, I heard a large engine start and a heavy car tear away from in front of the house. As the sound faded, I heard sirens approaching.

The siren stopped out front. I didn't start to unfold myself until I heard two people enter. "What the hell? This is a war zone. Dunley, call this in." I could hear their cautious crunching over the shambles of the rooms and hallway, each calling "clear" as rooms were checked.

"Baker, the sergeant says there should be someone home, teenage girl, Millicent Willard."

"You've got to be kidding, Millicent?

"Millie? Are you here, are you okay?

"I'm here," a shaky voice answered. "Down here in the cellar." I walked to the stairs and started up as one of the officers started down.

"Whoa, Millie, drop the gun." I looked down at my hand surprised to see I was still holding the dark grey automatic. I dropped it like it was covered with spiders, and it bumped heavily down the steps and clattered on the concrete floor. Unlike in the movies, it didn't go off.

I put my hands up saying "Sorry." Both of the young officers stared at me wide eyed as I emerged from the doorway into the living room.

"Are you okay," one said as he led me by the shoulder into the middle of the room. I looked down at myself as if checking for bloody holes. Finding none, I answered. "Yeah, I think so."

"What happened here?" Baker asked.

Words started flooding incoherently out of my mouth. "My father didn't kill himself, they murdered him, they were looking for his other computer, but they didn't find it. It's downstairs, you have to get it before they do. The one guy tried to kill me, he shot up the house and shot holes in the floor, and he said he hoped I was dead. They're coming back to get the other computer, it's down under my father's room."

Just then, an older man, large and balding, wearing a sports coat and dark tie, walked through the front door and gave me the evil eye asking, "Did you do this?"

"What? No, this guy dressed as a cop came to the door and tried to kill me, they were after my father's computer, the one down in the cellar."

"And you stopped them bare handed? Right! Baker, put her in the squad car."

"But sir?"

"JUST DO IT!" Baker started leading me out the door.

"You have to get my dad's other computer, down in the cellar." I pleaded, "Before they come back for it."

"BAKER!" The plain clothes man barked, "What is she, your girlfriend or something, cuffs, put the cuffs on her."

I could tell Baker was pretty exasperated, and put the cuffs on loosely, leading me outside. The darkness was punctuated by flashing blue and red strobes reflecting off the light colored bath robes of the neighbors across the street. I was surprised to see their faces showing more concern than accusation. Officer Baker was gentle as he tucked my head into the back door. I sat there for what seemed like hours listening to the official sounding female voice on the radio talking in numerical code between staccato bursts of static. Most of it I couldn't understand, but heard my address at several points and my description as a white female teen, unharmed and, in custody. I leaned my head against the door, and was awakened, not sure how much later, by the front car doors opening as Baker and Dunley got in. As we drove away, I noticed that there was now a dark van parked on the front lawn.

Dunley was driving, and Baker looked back to check on me. I gave him a tight lipped half smile to hopefully let him know there were no hard feelings, and I wasn't going to try anything desperate. He turned and spoke into the radio. I went back to looking out the window, watching the people on the sidewalks in lit pools created by the street lights. Clumps of teenagers out later then they should be turned wary faces towards the car as we passed by, some staring, others averting their eyes.

There was a time I thought about my future, trying to furtively chart a rational course between changing events. Now the future seemed totally irrelevant as I hunkered down in the crack between the seat and the door as if it could provide shelter in the chaos. A few minutes later the car bumped into the lot in front of the brightly lit police station.

Inside was a well lit large room filled with beige metal desks and people milling around between them. I was not the only one being towed around in cuffs. I was plopped into a metal office chair next to one of the desks and left there. It seemed no one was watching me, and if I wanted to I could have gotten up and walked out. What I really needed, however, was to pee, but was unable to get anyone's attention. Looking around, I spotted the ladies room and got up to go not thinking of exactly how I was going to accomplish the feat with my hands behind my back. I was halfway there before I was spotted.

"Hey, hey where are you going?" a voice blared.

"I need to pee," I yelled back, suddenly the room was quiet and every eye was on me, there was laughter rippling in pockets and corners. One female officer rolled her eyes as she got up to escort me the rest of the way. She removed the cuffs long enough for me to finish my business. By the time I was heading back, the sports jacket man was standing by his desk railing about his missing prisoner. "I'm here!" I called as the officer towed me back.

"You are one pain in the ass, aren't you?" he said looking me up and down as I was dumped back in the chair. "Now, no more bullshit, what the hell did you do?"

I started, "I answered the door, there was a man there dressed like a cop who pulled a gun with a silencer on me."

"This gun?" He asked as he tossed a zip lock with the gun in it on the desk.

"Yes"

"So you just overpowered him and took it from him?"

"No, he dropped it after I slammed his hand in the door."

"What was he some wimp or something that you were able to push the door on his hand, or did he just stand there and wait for you to get a running start?"

"No, he was tall, with a long thin face and a big chin, I don't think he was expecting me to kick the door closed, and I was using my feet to hold it."

"What like some flying in the air Crouching Tiger thing?"

"No, no! Look did you get my dad's other computer? You need to get his other computer before the bad guys get it"

"STOP, STOP, I don't know what fantasy you're living in, but it doesn't make sense and if it doesn't make sense it's not true, so now let's try this again."

Another man in a suit interrupted him, pulling him aside, saying something I couldn't hear. He gave the man an annoyed answer, "Yes, fine, I'm not getting anywhere with miss ninja warrior here anyway." Tuning to a uniformed officer he said, "Maitland take Miss Willard here and lock her up, I'll talk to her again tomorrow, and hopefully she'll be more rational after she comes back from whatever planet she's living on." The officer took my arm; I thought this kind of stuff only occurs in badly written movies.

"I'm not crazy, they wanted my dad's computer, he didn't commit suicide, he was murdered." The man gave me a dismissive wave. I turned to the officer leading me hoping he would be more sympathetic. "You need to listen, they tried to kill me!" He continued towing me into the cell block area. "Those two guys were the ones that shot up the house." Another officer unlocked one of the cells. I was getting frustrated, "I couldn't have done that much damage with that one little gun." The other officer removed the hand cuffs; with my hands released, I brushed them along the side of my jacket, my finger caught on something. "A bullet hole? Look I've got a bullet hole in my jacket!" I shouted after the officer as he was walking out. The guard closed and locked the door, "and this is my best one." I said mostly to myself looking down at my finger sticking in the hole.

I looked up to see three pairs of wide eyes staring back at me. Two women dressed in evening wear, possibly girl's night out gone bad, and a large woman dressed in clothes that were several sizes too small. All of the women skittered to the far side of the cell as I tucked myself onto the bench in the corner, folding my knees up into my chin and wrapping my arms around them.

The frustration subsided, there was something about the realization that my dad was murdered and did not commit suicide that made me feel better. I didn't kill him, he didn't leave me, he had no choice, and maybe he died a hero, obviously not giving them what they were after. The knot in my stomach relaxed and I slept better that night, tucked into the corner of the cell, than I had in a week.

I awoke briefly when the two "night on the town" women were collected by a rather grumpy looking older man.

"I'm so glad you're here," one was saying. "I can't believe they put us in here with that crazy girl." The door slammed shut, the other woman was staring at me with a look of abject fear on her face. I gave her a slight smile, hoping it would calm her if it was me she was afraid of.

She quickly looked down studying the floor. I should have told her I was sorry, I wasn't really that crazy, but I didn't, instead I just went back to sleep in my cozy corner.

3

The next morning I was awakened to the clanging door, as a trench coated redhead came for the other woman, to her great relief. "Oh Carol, thank God, they put some crazy girl in here with me, she had some kind of shoot out with the police, I couldn't sleep a wink wondering when she was going to strangle me in the middle of the night." I sat there still folded in the corner watching Carol's face as the woman continued on about her jail cell adventure. I gave her a palms-up shrug hoping to convey that her friend really wasn't in any danger.

As they were leaving, an officer entered and spoke to the guard who was starting to close the door. Before it shut, he pulled it open again. "Ms Willard, come with me please." I stood up as he guided me out of the cell, no cuffs this time. We walked into the main room.

"Here she is, Detective." The officer told the man who had me locked up last night. He looked like he was still dressed in the same clothes.

He plopped a plastic covered photo on his desk. "Is this the guy?" he asked. I picked it up, turning it around. There was his face staring at me with numbers across the bottom and without the uniform.

"Yes, that's him," I said breathing a big sigh of relief.

"Ms Willard, you talked about another computer last night?"

Finally, "Yes, my dad mounted his work computer on a shelf between the beams under his office. All of the drawings he did for work were done on that computer."

"Well, we didn't find one."

"I can show you where it is," I offered.

I could tell by the look on his face that he thought I was crazy, but finally he said. "Show me." He stood up and started for the door, I rushed after him, amazed that I was no longer treated like a criminal. Something must have happened last night that changed his mind, but he didn't seem likely to tell me what that was. He pointed to the passenger side of a large dark colored Ford. I got in, and he was backing out of the space before I had the door closed.

My house was surrounded by rings of yellow tape, vans, patrol cars, police officers and neighborhood spectators. The Detective piloted the huge Ford through the obstacle course one handed, sliding to a stop on the lawn next to the driveway. Several uniformed officers approached as we got out of the car. I looked out at the neighbors who had gathered, finding more accusation than comfort in the once familiar faces in the crowd.

"Hey ninja girl!" The detective called, "This way." I followed him into the house.

Inside there was plastic and tape everywhere, several people in white lab coats appeared to be studying several of the numerous bullet holes. We tramped over the plastic on the floor and down the cellar steps. In the cellar there was another lab coated man studying the floor beams under dad's office. The shelf had been torn away. The man looked from the floorboards to us. "There's a cut cable here, but no computer." he said.

"That's where dad's work computer was, it was still there last night," I said, looking from the cellar ceiling to the detective.

Don't get me wrong, I loved my father, but he was a little nerdy, and as a single parent didn't really know how to teach me how to act like a proper girl, but evidently that

"I told you so" look is genetically encoded into all women, because I'm sure that's what the detective was picking up right now. "Just get out of here!" he barked at me as our eyes connected. I was just as glad to obey, and quickly went up the stairs past the lab people crackling across the plastic.

Once out of the house, I slowed my pace but continued across the street towards the people who were standing on the Morgan's front lawn. The murmurs stopped and most of the people began to back away as I approached, all except for the Mrs. Morgan. They were an older couple of about sixty or seventy who had lived across the street for as long as I could remember. Actually they had also looked to be about sixty or seventy for as long as I could remember.

"Oh Miss Willard, Miss Willard?" I heard someone calling from my house, turning I saw a distinguished looking gentleman approaching from across the street. He was wearing a tweed jacket and bow tie under his white lab coat and spoke with an educated accent. "I'm afraid I'm going to need your jacket Miss Willard," He said as he walked up to where Mrs. Morgan and I were standing on their front lawn.

Turning to her he continued. "It seems our young Miss Willard here had a rather close call last night." He said as he lifting the left lower side of my jacket. "What you see here," he went on explaining to Mrs. Morgan, "is what looks like two bullet holes. However, it was actually created by a single shot that passed through the side of the jacket. You can see how these threads are puckered in as these in this side pucker out," pulling my jacket up to show what he was talking about. "It's a good thing this shot wasn't an inch closer in or it would have hit our young girl in the hip joint, disabling her, allowing the bad guy to easily finish her off." I rotated myself out of the jacket while he was still holding it, lest he start demonstrating the forensic scenario on my body parts. Mrs. Morgan reacted to the news of my close call with death by asking me...

"Have you eaten yet?"

"Huh, no," I answered, "I haven't eaten since breakfast yesterday." She got a very determined set to her jaw.

"Come with me." She said. Now jacketless, I followed her across the street back to my house. On arrival she told me, "You go right up those stairs and you pick out a change of clothes for yourself." I wasn't about to disobey her. Upstairs in my dormer bedroom I picked out my gray cargoes, red Celtic design T-shirt, denim jacket and underwear, and headed back downstairs. By the time I got there the 85 pound, 70+ Mrs. Morgan had the 250 pound intimidating police detective backed into a corner and was, as his generation is so fond of saying, tearing him a new one with her little pointing finger going like a sewing machine for emphasis.

"That poor little girl has been through a terrible ordeal, then you arrest her, keep her in some dirty jail cell with who knows what kind of people, drag her back here without letting her get cleaned up or have anything to eat? You should be ashamed of yourself." She looked up at me as I came down the stairs. "Come with me Millie, let's get you washed up and something to eat."

I was hoping her choice of words was just a figure of speech and she wasn't planning on sitting me in the tub and scrubbing me herself. Thankfully, I got to do my own scrubbing.

Ever noticed that you're never comfortable being naked in someone else's bathroom? I mean, your own could be as dirty as the Titanic's bulge and theirs squeaky clean but you're still afraid to touch anything. But the warm water felt good and it was nice to put on clean clothes. By the time I got downstairs, Mr. Morgan was playing his big old Wurlitzer electric organ and Mrs. Morgan had toasted cheese sandwiches and chicken noodle soup made.

"Thank you so much Mrs. Morgan." I said as I sat down at the table. She smiled and stroked my arm.

"You know, you should dry your hair better than that or you'll catch yourself a cold."

"Sorry Mrs. Morgan, I will." I smiled at her.

All the time growing up she always seemed to disapprove of me. How I would play in the woods with the boys instead of jump rope and play hop scotch with the girls. It didn't matter that there were no other girls around and no one played hop scotch anymore. She disapproved of me working at the chicken farm instead a nice retail sales job, and disapproved of my jeans and T shirts instead of dresses. And especially disapproved of my riding my dangerous little moped everywhere. But maybe it wasn't me she disapproved of, maybe it was because they never had any children of their own, and I was the closest thing they ever had to a daughter.

I remembered they had an old dog named Butchie, kind of a funning looking low rider cross between a basset hound and who knows what else. When I was maybe seven or eight, I'd come over to their house and ask if Butchie could come out and play. We'd go off into the woods between the housing projects, me exploring, and him smelling the ground and barking at everything else. As I got older, other things took center stage, when I was 12, poor old Butchie passed on. It was my first real encounter with the whole death thing, and I'd somehow gotten the idea that it was my fault because I'd forgotten to play with him. You know, the Puff the Magic Dragon thing. I went over to the Morgan's and told them I was sorry, they were nice and explained that it wasn't my fault, that he was just getting too old and too stiff to go running around in the woods anymore. We had a little memorial service for him that made me feel better.

I understood death as not getting a second chance, if you messed things up you didn't have a do over to fix them later. However, I couldn't buy into my dad's idea that we were just errant chemical reactions that ceased to exist when that reaction stopped. I just couldn't get my head around being nothing, forever.

I crunched on the best toasted cheese sandwiches I'd ever had in my life and spooned up the chicken noodle soup feeling it warm my lonely belly. Mrs. Morgan came back in to check on me and was pleased to see me with a spoon in one hand and a small piece of sandwich in the other. I smiled up at her and she smiled back. There was a knock at the door and she went to answer it.

"She's not done yet." I heard her say.

"Could you have her come back over to the house when she's done?" Came the reply from a voice I didn't recognize.

"I'll tell her." She answered. She poked her head into the kitchen.

"I heard," I told her, she smiled again and left as I finished the soup and sandwich. When I was done I got up and took the dishes and spoon to the sink and began rinsing them.

"Oh no, I'll get that," Mrs. Morgan said as she came in. "I think they want you back at your house, there's someone new." I thanked her again, she hugged me then watched as I left and walked across the street. Most of the other neighbors must have gotten bored and moved on.

There was indeed someone new; a big black Lexus was parked on the side of the street, looking out of place because it was the only vehicle that was not parked at a skewed angle. As I started towards the house, a man with a briefcase in a dark, very expensive suit and got out and came towards me. "Ms. Willard?" He called, snapping open the black case.

"Yes?" I said.

"You've been served."

"What's this?" I responded holding the paper gingerly on one corner like the rest was covered with cooties.

"It's for the damage to our property, Ms. Willard." He answered over his shoulder.

Written on the paper in suitable legalese were the charges and a court date for tomorrow in Norwich. I wondered if that were enough time get to Tibet. Probably not far enough, does the US have an extradition treaty with China? I wondered back into "Their property."

The police had let me pack the rest of my clothes and put me back into the flimsy motel I was in before. I left my stuff there and walked to the library to see about legal representation. Although they didn't directly have anyone there who could help, they pointed me towards Hampton Street where there was a paralegal office next to the Botanicals flower shop.

4

"Hey Skank!" It was Reaper. His real name was Reilly, but everyone in my high school class knew him as Reaper. He was always talking fondly of death, mostly everyone else's, but had his own fantasies about being rewarded with a legion of demons if he managed to die violently. We had history, no not that he was ever a boy friend or anything like that.

There was a girl in the class, Terry Banneau, who wanted to be a chef. Also, unlike me, she wanted to be normal, have friends, sleepovers, go to the prom, but she was very overweight. Not that that would have kept her from any of those things, the problem was that the other kids teased and bullied her terribly because of it. One day after school I caught Reaper playing his knife in front of her face and body threateningly because it got such a terrified reaction from her. I walked up to them and said,

"What are you going to do Reaper, cut her up right here in the hallway?" Terry panicked worse than ever, thinking this was not the time to call his bluff, but I got the intended reaction. He turned his attention to me. I was hoping once that happened she would make her escape, but she just stood there, her eyes fixed on the knife he now pointed at my left breast.

"Maybe I'll just cut your heart out first, Skank." He said. I made no effort to protect myself but instead leaned closer and said...

"That's not my heart." I could tell by the expression that flashed in his face that I'd won. The knife quickly disappeared as voices approached.

He said, "This isn't over, Skank," as he walked away. I turned towards Terry, ready to rag on her about not escaping when she had the chance, but before I could she said…

"You ARE crazy." Somehow that gave me a warm triumphant feeling inside.

"Hi Reaper," I said as I tucked my hands behind my back and moved in close enough to infringe on his personal space. I wanted to give him every opportunity, to remember just how crazy I still am.

"Sorry about your dad." That answer took me totally off guard. I looked down, taking a slow breath.

"Thanks." I answered, and then looked up again, backing away. He went back to fiddling with his butterfly knife; I turned to continue on to Hampton.

"Oh Skank," he said looking up at me again with a slight smile, "I still fantasize about killing you."

I looked back, "I hope it makes your dick hard whenever you think of me." Then turned and walked away.

The paralegal office was in an old store front. There were two people in the office, both hunched over computers. It took a minute for one of them to look up at me.

"Is there something I can help you with?" a mid thirties woman with dark curly hair asked.

"I hope so, I received this notice about a court date, and I'm being sued for damage to the house caused by two people who attacked me."

"You shouldn't be sued for that, let me see that." I showed her the summons.

"I want to know what I need to prepare for this."

"This is for tomorrow, when did you receive this?"

"Today."

"That's kind of dirty pool; you say you didn't do the damage?" I told her the whole story. "They just don't seem to have a real case if you can get a copy of the police report."

"I'm not sure if I can, the investigation is still ongoing."

"Boy that is dirty, here, I'll give you this on legal letterhead, with it you should be able to get you a copy of a preliminary report dealing with just the pertinent issues." She clicked out a letter on her computer and sent it to print. She walked over to the printer, brought it over, signed, dated and notarized it. "The police report should be everything you need. That will be thirty dollars."

I handed her my student visa card, she ran it, then looked funny at the machine, ran it again. "This card has been declined." She said.

"What, that can't be right, it was just paid off."

"Do you have another card?"

"Just this, it's a debit card, will that work?" she tried it, and the machine beeped ominously again.

"This one is declined also; you're being straight with me, right?"

"Yes, there should be plenty of money in the bank account."

"Wait a minute," she said, "Let me check something." She looked at the card and made a call.

"This is Annie Jens at Jens and Davis Paralegal; could you tell me if there has been a hold placed on an account? The person is Millicent A. Willard. Yes? Could you tell me who placed the hold? Commerce Bank. Thank you." She hung up the phone. "Those sons a bitches, they're being downright nasty."

"Why, what's going on?" I asked.

"These guys know they don't have a case, so they're doing everything they can to keep you from being able to make a case against them; the quick date, the court site being in Norwich when it could have been done here, and freezing your account so you can't get legal representation. I'm going to give you this for nothing, and I think I know someone who can help, hang on." She made another call, "Stacy this is Annie at Jens and Davis, do you have an opening to help someone who's really being screwed over by Commerce Bank? Millie Willard, good, good... When? Now, I'll send her right over, thanks." She hung up. "I called Stacy at legal aid; she can help you nail those guys. She's at 121 Front Street, it's a house but you'll see the legal aid sign in the window, just knock on the door."

"Thanks," I said.

"Let me know how it goes."

"Thanks again, thanks so much."

Front Street was only a few blocks away, and it only took minutes to make the walk. The house was a large white garrison colonial; there was a small printed cardboard sign in the window next to the door. I knocked using the brass knocker in the center of the green door. I waited for what seemed two or three minutes, not wanting to be too impatient with the person who was, hopefully, going to get me out of this mess. I was about to knock again when the door opened with jerks and starts. Soon I saw why, standing in the hall was a short round woman with short blonde hair who walked with the aid of aluminum forearm crutches. She backed away from the door as it swung in.

"You're Millie?" she asked.

"Yes, that's me."

"This way," she turned and led the way as I closed the door and followed. There was something that seemed familiar about her but I couldn't place it. She turned into a room off the center hall; I saw that glint of recognition in her face also. Somewhere we had seen each other before. She walked around the large wooden desk and sat, stacking her crutches in a corner, and then motioned to the chair in front of the desk. I sat down and caught sight of a picture behind her. A wave of fear reverberated through my body; I looked down quickly, as if final confirmation were needed, the name plate on her desk read Stacy Banneau. The connection clicked with her at the same instant. The last time I'd seen her, she was in a wheelchair at her daughter's memorial service. I was able to rescue her daughter from Reaper. His weapons were only knives and guns, the worst he could do was send you to the kingdom of heaven early. I was unable to help her with the popular kids of the class, the ones that welded weapons of words and could ruin the rest of your life with a wag of the tongue. Terry Banneau, whose picture was on the wall, had a life and a dream, a dream that was well on the way of coming true through her hard work and the support of a loving family. Her senior year, she was accepted to the New York Culinary Institute of America, and her parents bought her a set of Wusthof knives as a reward for her hard work. After Megan and Rea got through with her during the days leading up to the prom, she used one of them to slit her carotid and bled out in under a minute.

I wanted to crawl into a crack in the floor.

"I know you, you were in my daughter's class, you're..."

"Millie." I finished for her, not sure if her daughter ever knew my real name.

That was two years ago, but it was a pain that did not go away with time. Tears filled the corners of her eyes.

"She talked about you," she looked down as if shuffling through memories. Even through the tears, a quick smile flashed as if the memory could bring her back to life, if only for that fleeting instant. Shaking her head, she said, "My daughter said you were scary crazy, but also you were the only person in that whole school who ever stood up for her. I told her she should try to talk to you."

"I'm afraid talking to me wasn't very good for anyone's reputation." I answered.

"Reputation, like anyone would want to be friends with those evil children, they came to her viewing you know, they looked down at her and laughed. You were there too, weren't you, I remember you, you sat in the back, and you were the only one from her class who was actually sad."

The wrong person died that day, she had everything to live for, a dream, a future... Me, I had no plan, no purpose for being, I was just trying to stay out of everyone else's way as much as possible. "I'm sorry I didn't help her, I wish I could have traded places with her."

"You're not the monster here Millie, you lost your dad, and now monsters I can do something about want to gloat over his body. Millie, I will do everything I can to make sure their heads are hoisted on a pole." My crazy scary was nothing compared to the just plain scary that was in her eyes.

"Thank you Mrs. Banneau."

She reached out across the desk, and I met her halfway with my hand. "Call me Stacy."

She went to work, calling the police station first, convincing them to fax a copy of the report of the attack. Then she called my bank, threatening them with legal action for being party to malicious prosecution by freezing my account, reading them the details of the case. It was the first I'd heard that the neighbor's testimony backed up my story, and that the tall fake cop had been found murdered in an abandoned dark-colored Ford, the same type used as patrol cars. She asked me for my version of the attack, going over it several times, being quick, stern, even hostile. It didn't take too many episodes of Law and Order to realize she was prepping me for the hearing. "Do you have any way to get to the Norwich courthouse?" She asked.

"If my account is unfrozen tomorrow, I can get there." I answered.

"Don't worry about it, if you don't mind going early, you can ride with me." She said. She stood up, "I think I have everything I need from you, there are a few other calls I need to make, but you don't need to be here for them."

"How much is this going to cost, because I can't afford very much."

She smiled. "Even if this wasn't no cost legal aid, I'd still do it pro bono if for nothing else than to see those bastards twist in the wind." I left able to breathe again.

I stopped at the ATM and found that my account was still frozen; I also found that I no longer had a room at the Motel. The police had finished with the house again and my stuff had been moved back there. Instead of going back to the war zone of a house, I returned to the library. A little research revealed that there were few jobs in town that I would qualify for. Even the chicken farm I worked at had burned down last year. I wrote down the few possibilities. I also found that the closest temp agencies were in Manchester and New London; without a car, I had little chance of getting there.

The jobs were bank teller, grocery checker, and waitress. Without experience at any of them, I was turned down rather quickly. My grumbling stomach won out and

I spent $4.98 of my last ten dollars on a premade burrito at the grocery store while I was there.

Returning to the house there was no reason to worry about keys with the damaged doors and broken windows. After barricading myself in my bedroom, I was able to get a good night's sleep.

5

The next morning my room seemed warmer than usual, but when I opened the door and came downstairs to take a shower I realized why. The rest of the house was very cold because of the missing front window and the heater was trying to compensate. I turned it down to not waste more energy, and took a hot shower in a very cold bathroom. Back upstairs in the warmth of my bedroom, I was trying to decide what to wear to court today. I had a nice fitted white shirt, but the thing that went best with it was my dark pleated skirt that was a little too short. The only pants I had available were either the cargos I wore yesterday or jeans.

I was still pondering the situation, wearing only the white shirt and stockings, when I heard the front door open and two guys walk in talking. It was a rather casual discussion about knocking out the front window to make cleanup easier. What? I still had rest of the month before I had to be out, they couldn't be tearing the house apart yet. I padded down the steps in stocking feet yelling.

"Wait, wait, I'm still living here!" Two very surprised construction workers in stained jeans and t-shirts stared open mouthed at my bare thighs. I became very aware of a cold draft wafting up the lower half of my body. The taller of the two checked the papers he was holding.

"We were told this house was empty, we got a dumpster and crew coming in an hour to clear this place out, and you'll need to be out of here by then."

"What? I have a legal document from dad's lawyer saying I have to the end of the month to live here. My stuff is still upstairs in my room, you can't do this to me!"

Just then, Stacy Banneau pushed open the front door with one of her crutches. Her eyes did a survey of the room then settled on my lower half.

"You're going to want to wear a little more than that to court, Millie." She said.

"They're going to gut my house while I'm still living here," I answered.

"No they're not, just finish getting dressed, everything will be fine."

"Jeans or short plaited skirt?" I asked.

"Do the jeans have holes or swear words on them?"

"No?"

"Jeans then, you don't want to do the naughty school girl look."

I went back upstairs and slipped on the jeans and shoes and finished with a brown cord blazer style jacket. I gathered my keys, wallet, and papers from the original settlement and went back downstairs.

Stacy was waiting at the bottom when I came down, and the workman was on his cell phone.

"Come on Millie, I'll take you to breakfast."

"What about the house?" I asked.

"For the unflappable crazy person my daughter described, you sure worry about the details." We made our way to her SUV type BMW and headed out, stopping at the Cozy Cabin Restaurant and parked in a handicap spot. She ignored the "please wait to be seated" sign, and chose a table by the window. A waitress came by asking if we wanted coffee, and Stacy answered for both of us. As I opened the menu she said, "Order the most expensive thing on there, the town of Winfield is buying."

It wasn't the most expensive thing, but it was what I wanted.

"Two eggs sunny side up, bacon and an English muffin" I told the waitress. Stacy had oatmeal and fruit.

"Didn't anyone ever teach you how to be a proper girl?" Stacy asked.

"What, why?" I objected.

"Girls are supposed to be all about sugary fruity things, that's a truck driver breakfast."

"I guess my dad wasn't very good at girly things."

"What happened to your mom?"

"She left us for another man."

"And she never fought for custody of you?"

"Well, she might have, if her new more manly man hadn't beaten her to death" I said just before shoveling in a piece of muffin.

Stacy looked at me, setting her spoon down on the plate under the bowl. "You're kidding."

"Nope, she was always nagging my dad about him not being man enough, so she set off to find a real man. His solution to her nagging was a little different than dad's."

She didn't say anything, just shook her head and continued eating. Finally, she said in a quiet voice, "I wish you and my daughter had gotten to know each other better."

"What ifs" always seem to float around, coupling and uncoupling like errant DNA into strings of "didn't happen" possibilities. Would I have liked Terry as a friend? She was very different from me, but why is that such a problem? I imagined coming to her house, Terry talking about mirapoix and me talking about two cycle moped engines.

"I think I would have been a disaster in the kitchen." I answered.

38

"I could have put up with the mess." She responded.

It was a little before 10 when Stacy parked front and center in the Norwich courthouse lot. Our case wasn't until two.

"Sorry to leave you like this, but I've got another case. There's a park down towards the river, and the downtown shopping area is just a block north.

"I'll be fine, don't worry about me, I'm the crazy girl, remember? And, thanks."

"Oh yeah, I forgot, anyway I'll see you at one." She said, smiling, then turned and headed off in a determined four legged gait, her shoulder bag following behind her. I wanted to run up and hug her.

I thought I should test to see if my card worked, so I set off to find an ATM machine, figuring the shopping district would be the most likely direction. True to easy flow consumerism, there was an ATM guarding the gates to the shopping district. A quick check of the card indicated that it was not going to disgorge any money. Therefore, even if an overpowering need for new shoes should descend upon me, shopping was out.

I headed back towards the courthouse. On the side entrance to the police station was a small sign indicating a military recruiting station was inside. I stood there for too long; this was an option I had not thought about.

"Any questions?" I turned to see a young man in a crisp Marine uniform standing as straight, as if at attention.

"No," was my first response before thinking, then, "Wait, yes, yes I do have some questions."

"Well come on in then, I promise not to hold a gun to your head and force you to sign anything." I followed him to the door, which he opened for me. Inside was a small room with military posters from all of the different branches represented.

"So this is not just for the Marines?" I asked.

"No, I can represent any of the branches, is there some career path you are specifically interested in?"

"Not really, I was going to a community college studying to become an engineer, but I didn't do well in differential equations."

"That's pretty heavy duty; there are a lot of things you could do in technical fields that don't require that much math."

"I'm not sure what I want to do; how does this work?"

"The military does try to put people in positions where they are best suited; with so many different jobs we are in a unique position to have many different kinds of careers."

"So how would I know which one was right?"

"There is the ASVAB that tests your aptitude in a wide range of disciplines."

"Is that something that happens after you join?"

"No, you can take the test at a number of scheduled places and times; you can take it with no obligation to join. Then if you do decide, you can take the results to a recruiter, they can let you know if there is something in that field you can sign up for."

"When and where is the next test?"

He checked his computer, "Monday, 9:00 AM, New London unified school. Should I sign you up? Don't worry; it's not a commitment to join."

"Okay, how can I find out how I did?"

"You will be notified by mail, then you can call here and I can go over the results with you." He said, "Name and address?" I gave him the information, and then glanced up at the clock.

"Is there some place you need to be?"

"I have a court appearance and need to meet with my lawyer at one."

"Trouble with the law?" He asked.

"I'm being sued by the bank that owns my dad's house because it was damaged when someone tried to kill me."

He did some typing on his computer.

"Here you are. You spent a night in jail, in protective custody, after fighting off the attacker?"

"Well, I mostly hid in the corner of the basement."

"Wait, your father just passed away, this isn't a last resort decision, is it?"

"I guess that could be part of it, but tell me, how were you sure this is what you wanted to do?"

"Hum, good question, but after the test we'll talk about it, no decisions under duress, okay?"

"Okay."

I met Stacy at about 10 minutes after 1 when she came out of the court room area; we went down to the cafeteria and had cokes. I started to ask her about the case, and she held up her finger, "No talking about the case before the hearing, cramming makes you nervous."

We got to the open doors of the court room about a minute early, but she stopped and didn't go in. She was listening to the bank lawyers, and smiled as they were already salivating over their perceived victory talking over how they would convince the judge to rule in their favor after I didn't show. With 30 seconds to spare, she led me in.

"Oh look, she did show, and she brought her mommy. "

"Stacy Banneau, attorney for the defense." she told the bailiff.

"All rise, called to order, Commerce Bank Vs Millicent Willard." the bailiff called.

The dark suited, spit polished lawyer started with a smirk.

"We seek damages, for the willful destruction of bank-owned property by the defendant. On April 14, 2010 at 8:34 PM, the defendant did willfully, cause damage to 126 Sunnybrook Lane. We enter into evidence the following photos of said damage. The defendant, one Millicent Willard, was subsequently arrested and held for perpetrating the damage."

The judge viewed the photos with raised eyebrows, and then turned to Stacy, "You may proceed."

"The defense would like to submit the police report for the night of April 14, 2010. The report clearly indicates that the defendant was placed in protective custody after being attacked, witnesses confirmed her testimony, and no charges were filed against my client."

The bank's lawyer stood, "This is an outrage, your honor, the child was clearly in the house at the time of the damage and is therefore liable. "

"Does the attorney for the bank suggest that my client somehow invited the attack that almost took her life?" Stacy answered.

"She did nothing to protect our property."

"So the counselor suggests that she should have allowed herself to be killed so as to minimize the damage to the house."

"Objection!"

"On what grounds, councilor?" the judge demanded.

"That is a misleading and emotional plea that ignores the facts of the case." He answered.

"The facts of the case appear to be that the young lady did not cause the damage and is no more liable than the owner of not providing sufficient protection of your own property." Mrs. Banneau countered.

"Your honor, by her own testimony to the police, she fired a weapon inside the house, causing the damage."

"Is that true, Miss Willard?"

"Yes, your honor, I did fire a single shot damaging the second step on the cellar stairs."

"So noted, and you, Ms. Banneau, have a counter claim."

"Yes, your honor, we claim that agents of Commerce Bank did maliciously freeze Miss Willard's account in an attempt to keep her from seeking legal aid, and did specifically hold the hearing away from her home town in an effort to prevent her from attending these proceedings, indeed she was unable to obtain transportation, or even basic necessities, leaving her with only the five dollars in her pocket."

"That was to protect our interests; she could be a flight risk."

"She is a nineteen year old who just lost her only remaining parent; the bank had already confiscated her only transportation, and as they have already testified, she was incarcerated when the hold was placed. How could she possibly have been a flight risk?"

"She is known to be mentally unstable, who knows what she is capable of?"

The judge motioned to Stacy to hold, "I am aware of your tactics, Mr. Fallow, and this indeed borders on malicious."

"You can't prove that."

"Sit down, Mr. Fallow. As to the case against Miss Willard, the court orders her to pay for the damage to the house, the sum of $5 for the basement step. "

"That's outrageous!"

"Sit down Mr. Fallow, I'm ruling. As to the claim against Commerce Bank, the court orders the bank to release Miss Willard's accounts and pay punitive damages in the amount of $1000 a day for each day the account is frozen retroactive to the day it was placed. Therefore, Miss Willard, would you please give the bailiff your five dollars?" I pulled the crumpled bill from my wallet.

"Mr. Fallow, if you would give the bailiff your $1000 dollars."

"That's ludicrous; I don't carry that kind of cash."

"The court will wait as your assistant goes for the money. There is a bank nearby."

"This is an outrage!"

"Mr. Fallow, you are not leaving until Miss Willard has your $1000, if you prefer you can be a guest of the town of Norwich until the sum is produced, and I can easily order your assets frozen as well. After all, you are a flight risk."

Mr. Fallow turned to his assistant. "Go!"

"Mr. Fallow?"

"Just go!" the muscles in his jaws quivering with rage.

6

Unfortunately we didn't get to see Mr. Fallow's incarceration, but I did receive $1000 in an envelope. That much cash in my pocket made me nervous. Stacy declined to let me buy her dinner; I told her that she didn't have to drop me off at my house. I wanted to spend some time in town. The first stop was at my bank. It took a while to talk to the manager, who told me that my account was still frozen and that there was nothing they could do about it until they received a release order from the holding bank. Somehow I wasn't surprised. Of course, as long as the $500 a day order was in place, and I had money in my pocket I could live on; I didn't mind that they were taking their time. The next stop was the library to use a computer, thinking I would look for more jobs. Instead I looked up information on women in the US military. There was actually a lot of information, from babes in red white and blue bikinis holding M16s to issues with harassment, and the vague line between combat and non-combat situations pertaining to the no women in combat rule. There was only one article I found on the really big issue I needed answers on. What about my hair? Up to this point I'd gotten away with lying to myself that I didn't care about my appearance.

The truth was, I actually liked the way I looked and put some work into cultivating a cute grunge appearance, and my hair was a big part of it. Now I was considering a career where my clothing choice would be made by someone else, and that someone, the US government, wasn't noted for being particularly fashion forward.

Therefore, instead of looking up the articles dealing with chances of getting blown to pieces by mortar fire, I looked up pictures of military women in uniform. After skipping the ones that were obviously wrong, they all showed the women, with their hair in a bun style hairdo. Quite honestly, this was my least favorite style. I was trying to picture myself dressed in army fatigues with all the equipment. I was glad staff sergeant Bennett couldn't see me now after his little lecture on good and bad reasons for joining the service. Try as I might to deny it, somewhere in the irrational section of the three pounds of wetware in my head, the decision was already made and no amount of logic seemed to be changing my mind. Well, the test would apply more fuel to the decision process.

I vacated the library and stopped at Tony's for a grinder for supper. Murdock was there with a friend. He tried hard to not acknowledge me, but I didn't let him get away with it, and sat down next to him. I thought about planting a big wet one on him, but decided to only embarrass him, not ruin his life.

"Hi Murdock, how's UCONN?" I asked. When I was a sophomore, he was a freshman. At that time, before both of us were clued in on how the high school social structure really worked, we were invited to the same party. What we didn't know was that it was for entertainment purposes only, not ours, but everyone else's. Not to go into all of the details, it culminated in a video of him feeling the crap out of me. The video, besides getting flagged as inappropriate by the Youtube users group, helped earn me my Skank nickname. I didn't harbor any ill will towards him, actually felt bad about the damage to his own reputation.

"It's okay" was his answer, "This is Larry."

"Hi Larry,"

He turned to Larry, "and this is, ah..."

"Millie," I finished for him.

"Hi Millie," Larry said.

"I thought you were living at UCONN?"

"Spring break." He answered. Juan, who was working the counter, motioned that my grinder was ready.

"That's great, have a good break," I said, getting up and paying for my grinder.

There were no workmen at my house when I arrived, however, there was a dumpster in the front yard, the front window had been covered with plastic, and the front door had been somewhat fixed. The problem, however, was that my key no longer worked. I spent a few minutes wallowing in frustration while standing on the front step, but finally decided to just pry up a corner of the plastic and climb in through the window. Inside the house, all of the downstairs furniture and mess was gone. A quick panic check of my bedroom upstairs revealed that my stuff was still there, and appeared to be untouched, a reasonable compromise, I thought. I came back downstairs and ate my supper, standing at the counter between the kitchen and the small dining area.

I grew up in this house, now I no longer belonged here anymore. Did I do this whole life thing all wrong? Why can't I just reload life from a previously saved version, and if I could, where did things start to go wrong? At what point would I not be Skank, would Murdock's reputation not be ruined, and Terry would not have died? If I'd done things differently, would dad still be alive? What if I was home that day? Is the future already written? Do I have a destiny I can't escape, or is every mistake I make sending the universe off in a different direction? That's too much power in the hands of a confused little girl, and two months from now someone could be handing me a deadly weapon.

I didn't want to stay in the house, even if it was just to get out and take a walk. I went to look for the garbage can in its usual place, but didn't find it. Instead, there was a copy of today's Harford Current open to the headline. "Teen Survives Home Invasion Attack," with a picture of the police cars surrounding my destroyed house. I read through the story, most of the facts were at least close. However, there was no mention of my father's death, let alone that he was murdered and his computer stolen. They made it sound like a random act of robbery gone badly. On the next page continuation, there was a very large picture of me standing next to a police car in front of the house with my usual confused expression on my face. With a caption: "Young woman miraculously survives shooting rampage." It must have been taken when they brought me back to the house after spending the night in protective custody. Would I have made the paper if I wasn't a young woman who's ugly face couldn't be hidden with a blurry picture?

Just then the phone rang. It was Murdock.

"Millie, I didn't know, I'm sorry, did you know you made the national news?"

"I what, made the national news? Oh shit, no, I didn't know I don't have a TV anymore."

"You got to come over and see this."

"I don't have a car anymore either."

"I'll be right there." He hung up before I had a chance to object. Well, I did want to get out of the house tonight.

He lived in a newer housing project in town, not far away from where I lived, so it wasn't long before he pulled up in his Honda civic hybrid. I left the house through the door, making sure that it was unlocked. He got out of the car to get a better look at the house.

"Those are all bullet holes?" he asked, as I jogged to the car.

"Yes, they shot right through the house, trying to kill me."

"How did you ever survive?"

After getting in the car, I told him the whole story, from the fake cop, the struggle at the door, running to the cellar and hiding.

"I even had a bullet hole in my coat."

"Where?" He asked.

"Down here towards the bottom." I tried to show him, but he was too busy driving.

It took only a few minutes to get to his house, a nice contemporary two story.

"Is Larry still around?" I asked, as we exited the car and walked up to the house.

"No, he had to go home after we finished at Tony's. I can't believe this are you really okay?" he asked, holding the door open for me.

"You know, I'm not really sure anymore." I answered, and gave him a kiss, "that's for caring." I said.

Inside the house we were met by his mom. "It is her!" she exclaimed. "How could such a thing happen right here in our town?"

"I think the same people who killed my father were trying to kill me, for something that was on his computer."

"What! Killed your father?" Murdoch said.

"You didn't know that my father is dead?"

"I thought," He paused, "You know…"

"Killed himself?" I finished. "No he was murdered."

"The news didn't say anything about that."

"I don't think the police want to release that information yet." I lied. He led me into the large living room in the back of the house. He had the news recorded on the DVR connected to a large flat screen. He picked up the remote and started the playback.

"A 19 year old Winfield woman, home alone was attacked by two men dressed as police officers. She managed to escape and hid in the basement as the two attackers ransacked the house."

The video was showing pictures of the front of the house. Next, an actual video of me exiting the police car and going into the house as the announcer continued. It was really strange seeing myself on the news.

"The police were called by a neighbor, and the woman was found unhurt and taken into protective custody. No motive was given for the attack."

He stopped the recording, and we sat next to each other in silence for a few minutes.

"What are you going to do now?" He finally asked.

"I'm not sure the bank is taking the house by the end of this month, so I won't have any place to live. I think I'm going to join the Army."

"The Army? There is no way you can stay in school?"

"I don't think so, I was in the engineering program and I don't think my math grades are good enough to get accepted anywhere."

"How about one of the other sciences?"

"I don't think so, the only courses I have are physics and math, besides biological anthropology."

"Well, it may be worth a try. If you wanted to check it out, I could give you a ride up there."

"Thank you." I said. I put my hand on his and said, "Thanks for showing me that."

"You're welcome," he said, giving my hand a little squeeze, then moving off.

He seemed to have matured a lot, and survived the trauma of high school relatively unscathed given how bad the other kids had treated him.

"Going into the service seems pretty hard; I hope you'll be okay."

"I think so," I said. Unlike me, Murdock was the kind of guy who was going to make it in engineering, smart and focused.

I ended up spending the night at his house in the guest room; I woke up to sunlight streaming in through the window. Although the room was uncomfortably clean and neat, I slept well. My clothes that I had tried to pile as neatly as possible on the chair next to the bed were gone, and a white bathrobe was in their place. There was a door to a Jack and Jill bathroom. I knocked to make sure it wasn't occupied, then went in and showered. By the time I got back to the bedroom, the bed was made and my clothes were washed, dried, and neatly folded at the foot. I dressed and headed downstairs to the large open kitchen and family room. Murdock was there with his mom who asked, "Hi Millie, are you ready for breakfast?"

I was going to say that she didn't need to go through all that trouble, but saw that it was already laid out. "Thank you," I said instead.

She stood beside the table like a waitress and said, "There are more cereals if you like."

"These are good," I said sitting down next to Murdock and choosing Cheerios and milk. She also set out grapefruits with all the segments cut. I reached for the sugar, but his mom said.

"Oh, I'm sorry, that's real sugar, do you want no calorie sweetener? I'm not used to having girls in the house, we have all boys here."

"Oh, no, this is good, thank you so much," I answered, "Where's your dad?" I asked Murdock.

"He's up and gone to work already."

"So your dad worked last night, and now he's at work again on Saturday?" I asked.

"Yep," was his answer as he crunched on more Frosted Flakes.

His mom asked, "Is there anything else you want?"

"No thanks, I'm good," I answered. Actually, it's probably a good thing I didn't have a mom like her, I'd get way too used to it.

I told Murdoch that I should get going, but he insisted on taking me home. Before I left, his mom gave me a big hug and told me it was nice to have a girl in the house. I think she was trying to get Murdoch and me together. Murdoch was a great guy and was going to be a great engineer, but I flashed on an image of him being like his dad, gone to work 24/7 and me being like what I remember of my mom, a cigarette toting bar dwelling lush, aka skank, and shook the image out of my head.

We pulled up in front of my construction site house, "If there is anything I can do let me know." Murdoch said.

"No, I don't think so, well, maybe, are you going to be around Monday?" I asked.

"Yeah, I've got the whole week."

"Could you give me a ride to New London? I'm supposed to take a test for the military. It's at 10."

"Sure, not a problem" he answered.

"Thanks." I gave him a little kiss on the cheek and got out of the car. I suddenly felt very alone as I watched him drive away.

7

On Sunday, I actually went to St. Luke's. It was the first time I'd been inside a church in twelve years. I sat in the back, trying not to be noticed, and felt out of place. When I was a kid, it didn't seem so complicated. I'm not sure why I was there or what I expected to happen. A light beaming down from heaven with angel choirs and a voice telling me to either join or not join would have been nice, but that didn't happen. After the service, I had almost made my escape when a young man in a suit and tie came up to me.

"You look familiar, is your name Millie?" he asked.

"Yes?"

"You're the girl who was on the news; do you want to talk? There is nothing like a near death experience to get you thinking about God."

"It's not so much death," I said, "It's life that's scary." We sat on a bench in a little garden area on the side of the church building.

"Death is a scary thing," he said, "But with faith, you…"

"Why?" I interrupted. "Why should death be scary, I mean, if there is a God, isn't it being forgiven that is important?" I looked him straight in the eye and asked, "Can I be forgiven?"

I was met with a blank stare, "Only God can answer that question, but don't underestimate His capacity to forgive."

"I don't think I'm a very good person," this was not what I wanted to talk about, so I did a mid stream correction. "I'm thinking about joining the Army, will God hate me? I mean they're going to train me to kill people."

"Unfortunately, war is a fact of this life, and many who offer their lives in service of our country are cared for by God. I imagine a hallway on the way to heaven, where soldiers from both sides who previously fought each other meet. What we see here and now as important will not be so in God's kingdom."

"Then why do we get so caught up in all this, shouldn't we be doing what God wants?"

"That," he said, "is a very good question. Besides, I don't think women are called upon to go into combat."

Walking home, I turned all this over in my head. I'm not sure it made sense to my brain, but it seemed to make sense to my heart, because the little butterflies were gone.

I didn't think I was ready to make this kind of decision, but then, was this about choice, or survival? Does a wildebeest sit and ponder its situation; should I eat grass today, or run from lions? Am I special and cared for by God, or am I just another animal fighting for survival? I was struck with just how much protection from the outside world my father had provided all those years. If God wasn't with me, then I was in trouble, because I didn't feel particularly well suited for survival in the wild.

That night, I was lying on my bed looking up at the ceiling, imagining the hallway the minister talked about, thinking, what I would say to the person I just killed, or to the person who just killed me. Would I be upset about it, would I say I was sorry, or would it be completely irrelevant?

I had a very strange dream that night. I was sitting in a court room watching the proceedings. Terry and Reaper were on trial, and the lawyers and the judge were talking back and forth trying to determine who was guilty of killing me. I tried to say something, but was prevented. As the arguments progressed, they seemed to fade away.

I turned around and found myself standing in a hospital hallway looking into a room. I saw my dad lying in a bed with all the equipment around him. I suddenly felt very guilty for neglecting him, leaving him there all alone and not coming to visit him.

I woke up to the sound of the workmen downstairs. I jumped up to check the time, and relaxed to see that it was only 7:30, and I had not missed my test appointment. I got up, gathered my distressed jeans and navy t-shirt to wear today, but wore yesterday's clothes to the bathroom. There were a couple of guys punching out the sheetrock around the bullet holes.

"Hey guys, can I take a shower before you knock out the bathroom walls?" I asked.

I got a funny look, but one of the guys ushered me in without saying anything. As nice as the shower felt, I tried to hurry it up, being a little nervous with all the workmen waiting to rip out the walls. I put on the clean clothes and left the bathroom. "OK, I'm done," I told the two waiting and padded back upstairs.

As I went up I heard, "Boss, that girl is still here."

"Shit." was his only reply as I gathered the rest on my stuff, put on my denim jacket and headed back downstairs. I was met at the bottom by the tall guy I spoke with before. "You can't be here, it's not safe."

"I don't have anywhere else to go."

"That's not my problem."

"Well it is somebody's problem, because I have a court order that says I can live here until the end of this month."

"How are we supposed to get this house fixed up with you here?"

"That's not my problem."

"I'm making it your problem, because everything still upstairs has got to go and all these walls are being demoed."

"You can't do that!" I gave up trying to reason with the guy because he obviously didn't care about court orders. I walked over to the phone and called the police.

"What is the nature of the emergency," said the voice that came on the line.

"There are workmen here tearing my house down."

"Please say again?"

"There are people in my house telling me I have to get out because they are tearing it down."

"Do they have a court order to do that? You know you can't stay in a place that has been ordered vacated."

"No, I have a court order saying I can stay until May first. Would you please send someone to work this out?"

"Just stay there, we're sending someone." The workman was watching me with his hands on his hips, waiting for the outcome.

"They're sending someone," I said.

"I hope they can work this out, because I'm paying these guys a lot of money for this." Lawyers and money, I felt crushed in the cogs of the greed machine again. I looked up at him. I don't think he was a bad person, I'm sure someone in a suit somewhere was yanking his chain about getting this done, and there was probably someone pushing him. I wondered if there was actually anyone driving this train, or we were all pulling on useless handles as it continued screaming out of control towards the end of the line.

"I'll wait outside for them," I said "where I won't be in the way." I walked past him, making sure I had my court paper safely tucked in my jacket pocket.

I sat down on a convenient pile of lumber and waited. While I was there, a guy came over. I thought he was picking up wood so I stood up to get out of his way, but he motioned me to sit. I recognized him as the other person I saw that first day. He lit up a cigarette and said, "Sorry about your dad, are you doing okay?"

"Well, yeah I guess, I just don't know what I'm going to do, I had to drop college, I don't have a place to live, and I can't find a job. About the only thing I can think of is to join the army."

"My son's in Afghanistan," he said with some concern in his voice, "he says he's doing okay, but that doesn't keep me from worrying."

"He's lucky he has someone who worries about him, I think knowing that helps keep him alive."

"You know, I think you're right." As he was speaking, the police car showed up, and I stood up to meet them.

A uniformed officer got out of the car; he wasn't someone I'd met before. I walked over, "These guys are redoing the house and say I have to be out, but I have this court order saying that I can stay until the end of the month." I showed him the paper; he took a minute to read it, and then headed toward the house. The man in charge came out with his own paper, and the officer read that one.

"You are Miss Willard?" he asked me.

"Yes?"

"It appears that his court order supersedes yours."

"How can they do that without telling me, and how am I supposed to find another place to live so quickly? My stuff is still in there."

It was then that Murdoch arrived. "I need to go, but please don't throw my stuff away." I said, and then headed for his car.

I had him drop me off at the test location and told him he didn't have to wait, that I could find my own way back. I wasn't sure exactly how I was going to do that but I didn't want him to have to wait for me to finish.

As it turned out after I handed in the test and walked out, Detective Walter Harvester was waiting in front of the school. He motioned me over and opened the door.

"Get in," he said, handing me a cup of coffee. I wasn't a coffee drinker, but I was afraid to turn it down. "I wanted to talk to you about your father's case." Harvester said, I felt a little burst of fear. "You said there were two people who entered the house, did you get a look at the second guy?"

"No, he was outside and didn't come in until I was already down in the cellar, I only heard him speaking. He sounded young, that's all I could tell. They left before I came back upstairs." I answered.

"Do you have any idea what could have been on your dad's computer that was so important? Did he do anything for the government?"

"No, he worked for Scitron, they made scientific instruments for schools and universities mostly, and he never said anything about doing anything for the government. Why, what's going on?"

He didn't say anything, just started the car and surged out of the lot deftly piloting the huge Ford like it was a BMX bike. We were flying along Route 2 towards Winfield before he spoke again. "To answer your question, some heavy duty feds came in and took everything. I haven't heard a thing since."

"That doesn't sound good."

"An understatement." he replied.

"Oh shit," I said. He turned and gave me a stern look.

"I put my old address on the test and I don't live there anymore."

"Don't worry about it, if you did well enough, they'll find you." His phone rang and he illegally answered it while driving and drinking coffee; he didn't say a word before snapping it shut. "We got you in the same Motel, but you'll have to pay the bill."

8

He dropped me off in front of the motel and drove away. I went into the office, picked up the key, and gave them some cash, but instead of going to the room, I headed to town, stopping at Henry's Drive In to get something to eat. I got a southwest soft taco, although I think the closest these ever got to the southwest was Cincinnati Ohio, and a vanilla milk shake.

Sitting at one of the picnic tables, I watched Winfield's next crop of twelve and thirteen year old bullies terrorize a scrawny Harry Potter look alike. The bullies were snorting and pawing like young male herd animals. In a few years, they will be butting their heads in testosterone fueled dominance displays while harems of skinny, squeaky girls came flocking to the winner and ignoring the loser just like so many generations before them.

I used to watch Animal Planet with my father before it went to all crab fisherman and animal cops. I would sit there and think how nice it was to be human, and not subject to such illogical behaviors. How young and stupid I was, for despite our two extra pounds of brain matter, we are still blathering slaves to our chemical urges. There is nothing that proves the existence of a divine creator more than the human brain. With all of its higher functions and complexity it makes no evolutionary sense. All of the most successful life forms on the planet in terms of biomass, range, and diversity have no brain at all. A brain only seems to cloud the issue of sensible survival with confusing conflicts of conscience doing battle with our internal chemistry.

It seems that the most successful among us human animals are the ones who ignore the burden of intellect in favor of the ignorance of chemistry. Little Harry was on the ground crying, setting the mental stigmas that will shape the rest of his life. While I finished my taco and concentrated on the milk shake. I couldn't help wondering how many Albert Switzers turned into Adolf Hitlers in parking lots just like this one. The bullies got bored and left poor Harry on the ground; I finished my milk shake and headed towards the library.

I'd promised myself that I would try one more time to find a job and put a "normal" life together. On the way, to the library I dreamed up all sorts of chick flick fantasies about finding the perfect job in Hartford, getting it, moving there, and living happily ever after. That dream ended as I stood, staring at the library doors reading the sign that said "Closed on Mondays".

I turned and leaned against the large oak doors. I didn't want to read too much into this, but maybe someone was trying to tell me something. I grew up in this town and it was supposed to feel like home, but now it was fading into the distance. I'm not home anymore and I needed to find a new one. I turned and headed back towards the motel.

By 5:30, I could not stand waiting any longer, and started heading for the house that was not mine anymore. By the time I got there, the workmen were gone; I lifted the corner of the plastic and went inside. All the sheetrock on the walls had been stripped. I headed upstairs, and found it completely cleared out. At this point, I was done being angry, I felt like they tilted the world to dump me off, I'd missed my appointment with death and was now just a fragmented loose end that had been left behind by the reapers scythe. I slowly walked down the stairs, went outside, and climbed into the dumpster and found my stuff dumped in piles between broken pieces of sheetrock. I salvaged dust-covered clothes, papers, and all the little treasures that one collects over the course of their lives. Memories personified in trinkets and artifacts. I pulled a dusty duffle bag from the mess and began to stuff things into it. What I still needed to find was a little locked box. I spent what seemed like an hour searching and finally found it, except it had been pried open, and there was nothing inside. Some special photos, a few old coins, and my birth certificate, and they had to take them? More searching turned up a few pictures, my high school diploma, and my birth certificate; at least I still had proof that I was a real human being. I brushed them off, stuffed them into the bag and climbed out of the dumpster.

I woke up the next morning staring at the ceiling, I had no reason to stay in Winfield anymore, I could find cheap hotels anywhere. The most logical choice was Norwich; I could look for work and be near the recruiting center. The next step was to find the bus schedule. Life without the internet sucked, but perhaps they would know that information at the Motel office. I pulled open the door and stood face to face with Sergeant Bennet, who was just getting ready to knock on the door. Who says Prince Charming no longer exists?

"Hi," I said, "how did you find me?"

"You seem to be well known at the police station."

That can't be good, I thought.

"I'm assuming you wouldn't come all the way out here to tell me I failed the test."

"Good test scores and deductive reasoning, good combination. Can we go somewhere to talk?" He said.

"Do you want coffee, breakfast or a dark alley?"

He cracked a wide, strong-jawed smile. "Coffee will be fine."

"There's a Coffee Cat in the center of town on Main Street."

"That works, are you ready?"

I gathered a few items, and walked with him to his government Chevy Impala. We parked along the side of the building and walked around the corner into the shop. I ordered a cool cat, and he got a regular coffee.

"Well," he asked, "How are you feeling about this?"

"I'm feeling very good about this, to be honest, I don't know if all of my motives are as pure as they should be, but I can't think of anything else I'd rather do."

"Well, here's the story, you pretty much aced the test, the highest score I've ever seen. The MI people want you."

"MI?" I asked.

"Military Intelligence." he responded.

"What happens next?" I asked.

"Next is MEPS."

"How does that work?"

"I make you an appointment, are you sure about this?"

"I'm sure."

9

I think that was the last decision I would ever get to make on my own. Sitting on the bus to Fort Knox, I was staring out the window watching the sky lighten. Two months before my twentieth birthday, and I couldn't tell if those last 19 years were actually real, or if I was born yesterday. Every point of reference I'd ever known was gone like I'd just jumped off a cliff and was enjoying the exhilarating ride down but I knew I would soon smack head first into reality.

After the bus stopped, it didn't take more than 10 seconds for us to realize that we were now in the army, rousted from the bus and lined up outside. The first three days in the initial entry battalion was all about forms, regulations, vaccinations, and uniforms.

The next cheery face that we saw was the DI, "mom" for the next 9 weeks. Basic training was physically challenging in the same way that Antarctica is chilly and Fort Knox was like a 10,000 acre jungle gym. First thing in the morning, you get inspected. You have to be spotlessly clean, crisp, and perfectly even. But within thirty minutes, you are so covered with mud it's difficult to tell if you are human. There are log piles, towers, ropes, ladders, and trenches that you get to know like a long lost boyfriend, and the whole thing is coed.

Army regulations indicate that your hair be above your neck, but not be too masculine, meaning very short. Therefore, all the women wore it up, something I just could not get mine to do. This constantly earned me extra pushups and latrine duty, thankfully, Soldano, one of the guy recruits, showed me how to put it up and make it stay. His explanation was that he was from a large family, and had a lot of sisters.

When I was in school, I used to hate it when the instructor would say break into groups, or find a partner. Well, every bit of BCT is that way. You are responsible for everyone else. I soon learned to run my ass off over the obstacle courses to make sure little 5'5" 120 pound me wasn't stuck in the back helping all of the 200 pound plus guys, over the obstacles. It was so pervasive that during mess, I had to fight the urge to cut up the meat for the guy sitting next to me. The bullying thing was less of a problem because there were less women, and we just didn't have the time. However, it wasn't nonexistent. There was a woman named Sasha Wells; a meaty, trash talking, hip hop dancing African American who took a hate at first sight attitude towards me. And, of course, we were constantly paired up for hand to hand and pugil stick training because we were close to the same size, although she outweighed me by twenty pounds and consistently kicked my butt. What she wasn't was mechanically inclined, she couldn't assemble a single piece jigsaw puzzle with numbered pieces, and in true BCT fashion we were paired for anything mechanical, which included chemical, radio, and especially M16 training. For me, the M16 training was the bright spot, especially shooting. Even before being shot at, I was no big fan of guns, however, they held no special metaphysical status. With 3 semesters of college engineering, I knew they were just Newtonian physics, no special relativity required. And machines made the best marksman; therefore I just had to learn to become part of the machine.

Within the first week, it became obvious to the DI that Sasha and I were polar opposites, therefore, his solution was to make my graduation contingent on her shooting performance, and her graduation on my hand to hand and pugil performance. The thing that saved one of us from ending up buried under an obstacle course mud pit was dancing. For her hand to hand combat was just dance steps, these she taught to me. I built on what I called the robot dance, she called it pop and lock, to teach the mechanics of shooting, stripping, cleaning and reassembling the M16. This worked wonders for both of us.

It was near the end of the second week. I attempted to buy shampoo in the PX. It was the first time I'd tried to use my AMT card, and found that it had still not been released from the hold that had placed on it almost four weeks ago. Actually, it was not a big deal. I did have cash to live on, but I was still pretty upset that the bank never honored the court order. I told the DI about it, not expecting much to happen right away. I was wrong, I was called into a meeting with the battalion captain that day. Two days later, I was called to a meeting between the DI, the captain, and a Navy JAG officer; a total hunk dressed in an immaculate white uniform. He asked me the details, although he already had all of the court documents in front of him. The next day the DI escorted me into a large meeting room. Inside were the JAG officer and Mr. Fallow. Mr. Fallow was explaining how he wanted to settle out of court, and assured the JAG officer it was an oversight and had already been corrected. If the JAG officer just signed a few papers everything would be fine, and no additional action would be necessary. The JAG looked it over and pushed it back asking, "Where's the $12,500 dollars you owe her?"

Mr. Fallow did his usual jaw clenching, "We can't be held to that, it was not our fault, she never followed up on her own account." I knew better than to say a word, continuing to stand at attention. As it turned out, I didn't need to. JAG Commander Harris narrowed his eyes, but said in a cordial but commanding voice that it was his job to make sure that it was done, not mine, and that their oversight was going to cost them $12,500 dollars as the court order stipulates. Or they could go to court, and court costs and punitive damages would be added to that amount.

Mr. Fallow shot me a "wait till I get you alone" evil look. In the time that it takes electrons to change valence levels, the DI was in Fallow's face.

"Don't you ever look at one of my soldiers like that again, do you hear me..."

Commander Harris was quick to respectfully pull him away. What I saw in that instant was the embodiment of the basic values that was part of our training: That we are all a part of one team and watch out for each other, a lesson I would never forget.

Once Mr. Fallow was sure that he still had control over his bladder, he continued trying to talk his way out of the bank having to pay the full amount. Harris was not budging. Finally, a verbal promise to pay the full amount, but it would take time for him to work it out with the bank. Commander Harris made it very clear that he wasn't leaving without the account unfrozen and the $12,500 deposited. Mr. Fallow's face was red with rage. Between his teeth, he said, "You can't hold me here where that ape," referring to DI Cochrane, "could slit my throat in my sleep." I shot Fallow a look, but the DI put his hand on my shoulder. I returned to attention, looking straight ahead.

The DI walked calmly over to Fallow, and said in an even, slow voice, "Don't worry, I won't touch you, I'll let recruit Willard kick your ass in a fair fight in broad daylight in front of the whole company."

Fallow sneered. "Put your money where your mouth is, sergeant, double or nothing."

DI Cochrane looked him up and down with a slight smile curling the corners of his mouth. "You're on."

The Commander raised an eyebrow.

"Can you work that out, commander?" the sergeant asked him.

He glanced over at me, "Gladly."

The next morning, after exercises, breakfast, and maneuvers, the company was assembled at the combat course at 09:30, I stood at attention in regulation workout clothes and protective headgear, holding a pugil stick. Fallow showed up in the same headgear, wearing a burgundy Harvard t-shirt, heather gray shorts, and a similar stick. He was whipping the stick around, bragging about iron man, triathlons, and never accepting defeat. This was an important test for me, I knew with complete confidence that I could not beat him, but I also knew with total confidence that the US Army could. I didn't need trash talk intimidation, I didn't need to be psyched up, I didn't need to go over the fight in my head, all I needed was to remember my training. DI Cochrane's voice was heard through the company, "At ease." Everybody who had been at attention broke from soldiers to spectators.

Even Commander Harris was there in his Navy dress whites, casually talking with Captain Benforth.

The DI announced, "First one off the mat on the ground is the loser. Begin!" I moved up and took a fighting stance. Fallow approached, bobbing and weaving, but clearly not well versed in pugil combat.

1.4 seconds later, I was standing at attention, $25,000 richer, and Fallow was just figuring out he was on the ground. Don't get me wrong, I didn't mind the money, and I enjoyed kicking Fallow's ass, and the cheers, with Hip Hop's being the loudest, but the satisfaction on the DI's face was priceless. The DI motioned to recruit Hernandez, and he helped Fallow to his feet. Fallow started hemming excuses, but when Commander Harris asked if he wanted a rematch, he shut up. We were given a ten minute break, then normal life resumed. There was a realization in all this, not only had Fallow been beaten, but also Skank was a new person.

That evening, Hernandez, himself a former amateur boxer, came to complain about my fighting style, saying that although he enjoyed watching Fallow receive two well placed hits before he knew what happened, he said that I knew nothing about pleasing the crowd, who was hoping to see Mr. Fallow receive a much lengthier pummeling. "Sorry," I said. "I guess I was a little nervous." My relationship with Hip Hop had also changed. Although we would still trash talk each other, we were now friends, not enemies.

10

I'd come to the conclusion that BCT was like the prom, an event that would come and go at a constant rate no matter how much you worried about it, and there were only two possible outcomes: you would live though it, or you wouldn't, so there was no reason to worry about the small stuff. I did live through the first milestone, the transition from Red Phase to White Phase. During this phase, we needed to qualify with the M16. Also, we were introduced to additional weapons, grenades, and the shoulder launched rocket. As in the first phase, regardless of whether women were allowed in combat, we went through the same training as the men, including combat situations.

Since joining, I started going to chapel services. At first it was a little scary, because the priest or minister was Evangelical, and I always thought they were pretty turn or burn judgmental, and they hated Catholics. However, the army required that the services be relatively non denominational, and therefore there was little chance I'd be dragged out of the building and stoned to death. There were some differences in mechanics, and in the Lord's Prayer we owed God money instead of squatting on His land, but the services were essentially the same. The one marked difference that I did notice was that unlike the lay minister I talked to at St. Luke's, this guy appeared to be sure of God's forgiveness for all of us. It seemed a bit presumptuous, but to be honest I wouldn't mind being sure, so I made a mental note that if I ever got the chance, I would ask about it.

The big deal during this phase of BCT was weapons qualification; it used to be a relatively straight forward affair of 40 shots at pop up targets in three different positions. However, recently it was changed to a more "real world" scenario of complex simulations, and Hip Hop was getting pretty nervous, I had to keep reminding her of pop and lock. To be honest, she was actually getting very good, and we were constantly pushing ourselves to get better. She just suffered from test anxiety. We ended up having a rather high volume discussion about thinking like a machine. "Machines don't get nervous," I told her.

"I'm not a machine," she said. Up to this point, I'd been doing fairly well at controlling my innate unbalanced nature, however, not being a particularly social creature, I have a tendency to have strange things fall out of my mouth before I'd had a chance to really think them through. This was one of those times.

"How," I said, "are you going to do this against people and not be a machine?" There was a "twisting a knife in her heart" look on her face as she backed away. "Wait, wait, I'm sorry!" I pleaded, not really sure where to go from there.

"I don't think I know you." She said.

I'm fairly certain that like baseball, there is no crying in the army, however, two minutes later I was in the far corner of the latrine breaking that regulation.

Mid day the next day, I was pulled out of formation by the DI and taken to headquarters. I was sure that after my little outburst, I was going to be found too psychotic to be in the army. I was brought to a room that looked way too much like an interrogation room, and placed in the chair without explanation. After a very long wait, a man in a dark suit came in an announced that he was from the FBI, showing his identification. He sat in the chair opposite, opened a file folder, and asked, "You are Millicent Abigail Willard?"

"Yes, sir."

"Your father was Mark Lenard Willard?"

"Yes, sir."

"What happened to your father?"

"He was murdered, sir."

"This says that he committed suicide."

"I believe he was murdered, sir."

"Why do you believe that, Private Willard?"

"Because men broke into the house and tried to kill me, looking for my father's computer."

"What was on that computer that was so important?"

"I don't know, sir."

"Come on, private, if you think there was something on his computer worth killing for, you must have some idea what it was."

"What I know is that someone came to the door, tried to shoot me, and took my father's work computer. That led me to believe there was something they wanted very badly on that computer."

"Your father worked for a government contractor?"

"He worked for Scitron."

"And what do they do?"

"My father told me they made scientific instrumentation."

"Your father told you, you don't know for sure?"

"Yes, well, no, I never had any reason to doubt him. Do you think he was doing government stuff and didn't tell me?"

He ignored the question, "So there could have been anything on that computer, and you would never know?"

"What are you saying; my father was a spy stealing secrets?"

"If he were, you would never know, would you?"

"If he were, why didn't he just give them the right computer in the first place, or better yet, just give them the files? Instead he died trying to protect them."

He looked at me for a minute, not saying a word, then got up and left the room. Although he didn't really say much about what was going on, just the fact that he was here asking these kinds of questions meant it was big. Could my father have been working on things he didn't or couldn't tell me about? I could believe he was actually working on top secret stuff, I could understand him not telling me about it, but I just couldn't believe he was involved in stealing secrets. We didn't get much time to surf the internet, but next time I got a chance, I was going to look up Scitron.

I never heard any fallout from the FBI investigation, and eventually I did get a chance to use the internet in the base PX. What I found, however, was nothing at all, not just that Scitron was what my father said it was, or that they didn't say what they did, but when I did a search on Scitron, there were thousands of hits but absolutely nothing at all about the company my father worked for. I returned to the barracks in a daze, trying to figure it out.

Later that same day both Hip Hop and I qualified at the expert level. That day before lights out, I was surprised when Hip Hop came over.

"You look like you just lost your mom," she said.

"My dad, actually." I answered.

"What?"

"He actually died back in April, he was murdered, and the FBI is investigating, but I don't think I knew who he really was, the company he told me he worked for doesn't exist."

"Wow, what do you think it means, and why is the FBI investigating?"

"They think he was doing something illegal, I don't know what to think, he was obviously lying to me and I don't know why."

She changed the subject. "Listen, I'm sorry about the other day." she said, "It's just, you made me think about things I didn't want to face."

"It's okay; I should warn people I'm not really normal." I answered.

"We have a leave coming up between phases, and my grandfather is very old. He means a lot to me, I would like to be able to visit him…"

"If you need money for plane tickets, I can give it to you. After all, you're the one taught me how to kick Mr. Fallow's butt."

She smiled, "Thank you, but I'd like you to come with me."

I wanted to ask if she was sure that she wanted to bring someone like me home, but instead I said, "I would love to come with you."

11

It was a three-day leave, so it was going to be a pretty whirlwind trip to Cincinnati and back. After living the previous 7 weeks on an army base, the civilian world seemed very alien, and evidently we seemed pretty alien to the civilian population. In McGhee Tyson Airport, most people only stared, but some people actually thanked us for our service and some people cursed at us, saying things like blood for oil. I wanted to ask them what kind of car they drove, but Sasha just wanted to kick their ass. I told Sasha, "Isn't that what we joined up for, to defend their right to say whatever they wanted?"

She thought about it, and then said, "Yes, you're right, but I still want to kick their ass once I'm out of uniform."

"Oh, well, that's okay then." I answered, "Because we're defending our right to disagree with them."

"I sure missed your crazy philosophizing," she said.

The Delta flight was boarding. It was a smaller aircraft and a relatively short flight. Sasha wanted to know my life history, so I gave her all of the gory details from mom's rejection to dad's murder, and as much as she could stand in between. Her only comment was, "No wonder you're so screwed up." I gave her the "Duh" look.

Her brother Mendelssohn met us at the arriving flight area outside the terminal. He was a little peeved that he had to use the family minivan and couldn't bring his Honda, which was my fault because he'd taken the back seat out to put in amps and speakers. Sasha was happy because she still wanted have some hearing left by the time she got home.

Her house was a beautiful old townhouse on a quiet street in an older city neighborhood. There was a ton of people out front waiting to greet her when she got there. She tried her best to introduce me to everyone in between all the hugging, but there was no way I was going to remember all the names anyway. The assemblage moved into the living room to meet with her grandfather, Jeremiah Wells, who was looking forward to seeing her in her uniform. He'd served in the 92nd Division in Italy during WWII.

Sasha rushed in, dancing in front of him with a big wide smile and proudly showed him her expert marksman badge. She dragged me over to let him know that I was the one who helped her to qualify. He got all teary eyed with pride, but the war stories were cut short by the dinner bell.

It was as if I were a member of the family, given a place next to Sasha at the long table in the large, wood paneled dining room. I was amazed at all of the complexities in the interaction going on around the table; there were multiple conversations at once, in several different dialects according to age group. But they all seemed to think it was normal. There was tons of good food that all looked like it was made from scratch. Mrs. Wells, who was the mid generation mom, as far as I could tell, asked,

"Is everything OK? Millie, do you need anything?"

"Everything is wonderful," I answered, "When it was just my dad and me, I actually did most of the cooking, but it was usually something from a box with three step picture directions."

"So it's just you and your dad then?" she asked.

"Ah..." I struggled, "My dad died." That seemed to create a hole in the conversations.

"Oh, I'm sorry." she said, "What about your mom?"

Luckily Sasha rescued me, "I think we're embarrassing her, mom." I mouthed a thank you to her and the table chaos returned to normal. I'd become ridiculously full by the time dessert, rhubarb pie, was brought out. After that, the crowd started filtering to the living room, and I tried to start clearing the table, but was informed that was the job of the younger brothers and sisters. Sasha's mom was still concerned as to why I wasn't spending the leave with my mom, so we had to fill her in on all the gory details.

After the kids finished with the cleanup chores, we retired to the basement family room where we played Call of Duty on the X Box. I turned in an embarrassingly poor performance; it seemed the real thing was easier than the electronic simulation. Later after the kids were sent off to bed, Sasha showed off her dancing ability which was amazing. After numerous attempts at trying to teach me some of the moves, she concluded that although I was okay at pop and lock, I really sucked at krump.

All the bedrooms were filled, so I would spend the night in Sasha's room. Her mother wanted to bring in an inflatable, but after I saw the cool window seat, I said I would be glad to sleep there. She didn't seem too convinced, but agreed. We stayed up late talking and working on a pop and lock dance routine, however, I wasn't doing well at the sync moves that were necessary calling me a defective robot. Finally she just worked my defects into the routine we later called "Defect", where she would lead and I would follow imperfectly kind of on purpose. We stayed up way too late practicing and laughing about it.

The window seat was comfortable, and the city noises outside were not annoying but reassuring. Next morning seemed to arrive instantly. Cycling everyone through the multiple bathrooms was not as much of an issue as I thought it was going to be. After getting dressed, Sasha had to gangstafy me a little more. I was surprised at the results, not just the very cool look but the added muscle and sun-lightened hair made a pretty nice package it was just too bad that there was nothing she could do about the skanky face.

The dinner chaos from last night was nothing compared to breakfast, it was a kind of rugby match with cereal boxes, but at least I found out, accidently, that Mendelssohn thought I was hot. After breakfast two of Sasha's friends came over, Jemal and C-Dog. Jemal was Sasha's primary dance partner, not really a boyfriend, and C-Dog was the big dog of dance in the neighborhood. We went down to the family room and showed them the defect routine, with Jemal doing the synced part with Sasha. C-Dog soon stepped in and started choreographing; smoothing some rough spots and helping me with some moves. Although I couldn't get everything right he said the important thing was to go through the complete routine with a totally blank expression. "That makes the dance," I assured him that I had no trouble during blank expressions.

After a while, he was standing back with his hand on his chin, nodding. Sasha later indicated that was a good thing. After running the routine two more times, C-Dog announced that we had to take it to the yard. Sasha, Mendelssohn, and I packed into the back of C-Dog's tricked Hummer with Jemal in the front, and Mendelssohn in the middle, enjoying the tight quarters with his hand resting on my thigh. Before long, we were cruising sections of the city that I would never have been brave enough to venture into during my previous life.

We parked next to what looked like a war zone lot now packed with brightly colored human chaos splashing hot life over the cold stone. Like urban wild plants that push through the cracks of old concrete, these people would not be denied their place in the sun. I was not the only white girl, as matter of fact it was amazingly multi-cultural. It seemed that Sasha knew everyone, and everyone was very glad to see her. She introduced me as Skank, but somehow just because of the way she said it, it wasn't a bad thing anymore and I was immediately accepted as if I'd always lived there.

We watched as Sasha and Jemal did some phenomenal krumping together. Then C-Dog spoke, and everyone paid attention. He announced that Sasha, Jemal, and Skank had a routine called "Defect" they wanted to show. We lined up and the boom box started with the heavy Indie beat. Butterflies started, but again I needed to remember nothing but the training. I became machine focused as we started. At first there was some laughter with Jemal and Sasha's perfect sync and my defective follow. I was supposed to remain expressionless but there came a point when the true meaning invaded my concentration. Knowing that my defectiveness had more to do with just the dance, tears started to leak from my eyes. The laughter faded and it became deathly quiet. The dance ended with Jemal and Sasha still perfectly together and me behind, a quarter turn off, pretty much as planned. There was a second of total silence until we came out of character, stood in a line, and bowed.

There were cheers and tears as C-Dog came towards us, tough looking guys I'd be afraid to meet telling C-Dog the routine had ripped their hearts out and touched their soul. There was a guy in a wheel chair who rolled himself up. At first I thought he was angry. "That it, that's exactly it!" he shouted, "You told my story in dance, thank you, thank you!"

C-Dog said "Thank you wheels, but this comes from Sasha and Skank." All the eyes turned to us, and Sasha pointed to me.

"This is your story and my story it's just that some defects we hide in our hearts." I said.

Back at Sasha's house, it was pizza for dinner. We gathered around grandfather Jeremiah, and I sat on the floor leaning against Sasha, listening to him tell of the family history from slavery to triumph and pain to pleasure.

12

Three weeks later, as we lined up in the hazy predawn light, it was hard not feel both sad and excited knowing that this was our final official day with DI Cochran.

In his clean, powerful voice, he said, "I have done all that I can, you are now soldiers in the United States Army. The rest is up to you, you have everything you need, use it." He went down the ranks as if to review each one of us individually. He stopped in front of us. "Wells and Willard, you are two of the best pains in the ass I've ever had, don't let anyone give you any shit." Again, that proud, barely discernable smile. The rest of graduation was drills and ceremony. Afterwards, I had a chance to meet with those of Sasha's family who could make it, as before there was much hugging. I also learned that our dance routine made Youtube.

When I graduated high school, there were plenty of speeches about a hopeful future. This time I actually felt that way. I couldn't help wondering if my father would have been proud of me. This was certainly not the future he had planned, but I wanted to think that he was watching, and was pleased.

I was rousted at 06:00 the next morning by a sergeant I'd not seen before. He told me to "be packed and ready to ship out and report to Captain Benforth at HQ by 07:00. You will not be returning to this facility." It was actually plenty of time to be ready, so I took a few minutes to say goodbye. With everything packed in the duffle, I headed for HQ, and was directed to an admin outside a closed door.

"Private Willard, reporting as requested."

"The Captain is expecting you, go on in."

Inside the spacious office were three men, Captain Benforth I recognized, the other two, a Lieutenant coronel, and a civilian in a dark suit I did not recognize.

"Private Willard reporting sir," I said, standing at attention.

"At ease, private." I stood at parade rest. They were reviewing a file on the captain's desk. The civilian was shaking his head. This didn't look good. The captain finally spoke again, "Private Willard, I don't mind telling you that you have an exemplary record with a unique skill that the army cannot afford to lose, therefore, before you report to your CGS school, you will be reporting to Fort Benning for Airborne and Special Ops training." When the DI said we had everything we needed to face what was ahead, I didn't know Ranger training was on the list.

"Permission to speak, sir."

"Granted."

"I'm a girl, sir."

The captain couldn't contain his laugh. "I think we noticed that, private, you will not be doing the complete Ranger training, however there are aspects of the training you will need for your assignment."

"Specifically, sniper training," The Coronel added.

The Captain removed a folder from the files and pulled out 8.5 x 11 sections of the paper weapons qualifications targets, placing one after another on his desk, each with a single centered hit, except one with a hit off by less than two inches.

"Recognize these, private?"

"Yes sir."

The Captain spoke, "Since the change in the weapons qualification in 2008, no one has scored this high. I assure you that we understand and take seriously the rules about women in combat; however there are still situations where we can use your skills and maintain the regulation."

The Coronel continued, "Because we are entering new ground here, we have decided to make this voluntary, it's your choice, private."

Decisions have never been my strong suit, but right now there was enough brass awaiting my answer to tilt the gravitational pull of the earth.

"Yes sir, I will do it." Why the hell can I never take the easy route?

"Good, it's all set then," the colonel said, "Thank you, captain."

"That is all, private, you may go." The Captain said to me.

When I left, the admin handed me orders saying that there was a military flight that I was booked on. The shuttle would be leaving the PX lot at 08:00.

I arrived at Fort Benning on June 29, my 20th birthday and promptly given a five day leave before I had to report back to camp for orientation and training, which quite honestly sucked, because I had nowhere to go. After getting everything settled at the new barracks, I had 4 days and 23 hours left with nothing to do. I went to the PX and called Murdock, who should be out of class for the summer.

"Hello Murdock, how's it going?"

"Hi Millie, I'm doing okay, so you joined the Army, are you calling about the news on your father?"

"Yes, I just finished basic; I have a 5 day pass and, wait, what news about my father?"

"It was on the news last night, you don't know?"

"No, I don't know, what was on the news?"

There was an uncomfortably long pause, "Ah, it said that your father was selling sensitive information. I don't know the details because I just caught the end of it, but you should be able to look it up on the internet."

"What...? How? That can't be right! Those assholes."

"I'm sorry, Millie."

"Sorry, Murdock, I didn't mean to yell in your ear, thanks for telling me, you're a real friend, Murdock."

"So do you think you'll be coming back up here?"

"Ah, I'm not sure, I think I have something else I need to do, but thanks anyway, Bye Murdock, I'll call you later, okay?"

"Okay Millie, bye, you're a good friend too."

Shit, now what? I went to the PX computer section, logged on and looked up news reports on Mark Willard. There it was: "FBI Accuses Connecticut Man of Espionage." Reading though the article, I noticed things like "may have been in possession of confidential information." It also gave the FBI investigator's name as Jonathan Vander Wellin, out of the Washington Bureau. Washington, confidential information, Dad! Shit, dad, why didn't you tell me? I sat there holding my head in my hands, staring blindly at the screen. Fuck that does it. I looked up the closest airport and found Columbus Airport, but it didn't seem to have regular commercial flights. I called anyway and found out that, although they didn't have regular commercial flights, I could get a ride on a charter flight going to Washington, especially as I was military. Many charter pilots would give me reduced rates to ride along if they were going there anyway. She said if I could get to the airport, she was sure that it would not be a problem getting a ride to Washington. To be honest, I'd never hitched a ride in a car before, let alone an airplane, but what the hell.

Seeing that my civvies had been ganstafied, I bought some Washington-worthy clothes. I also booked two nights in a hotel in Washington near the FBI building. The clothes selection wasn't great, but I got a dark A-line skirt, a matching short jacket, and a pastel blue fitted shirt. The skirt was a little short, so I had to break down and get a pair of dark hose that would go with the pair of black boots. The person at the register said there was a shuttle to the Columbus airport, but it left in about 10 minutes, so I also bought a small bag to put everything in and was still packing the new clothes in it when the shuttle arrived.

13

The Columbus Airport was small compared to commercial airports, but large for a private airport. It serviced a lot of government and business customers. Going into general aviation, I asked at the closest thing I could find to an information desk about flights to Washington. The guy checked a list on a printout, "No I don't, wait, Washington, yes, there's a plane at gate 6, a government agency, should be leaving in, well, about now. If you run, you could catch them, that way." He pointed.

"Thanks!" I yelled, already running in the direction he pointed. Luckily the concourse was short, I could see out the window a small red and white jet still on the ground. There were two guys just heading for the gate door. Still running, I yelled for them to wait, and the two men stopped and looked in my direction. On closer inspection, the two rugged older individuals looked like they had been through the ringer, I was amazed they were still standing, and I felt bad for bothering them.

"I was wondering if I could get a ride with you guys to Washington, I can pay you." I wasn't sure if this was the correct way to go about hitching a ride on an airplane, but it was worth a try.

The shorter guy looked up at the taller guy with a kind of disgusted look on his face and said, "Don't tell me, one of yours?"

"Never seen her before, honest." he answered. They both looked at me. The tall one said, "Okay, come on- oh wait, you got ID?"

I showed my picture Military ID, "Well, come on then, Millie."

"Thanks, how much?"

"No charge, as long as you're quiet and let us get some sleep."

I followed them up the free-standing stairs that had been rolled up to the plane. The pilot didn't look happy about me being along, but didn't object. True to their word, they slept, and I kept quiet. The plane had only six seats, and therefore was amazingly spacious and comfortable inside. I'm not sure when I fell asleep, but I found myself dreaming about my dad. We had just had that argument about differential equations. I was in my room at home, and was very sorry, and was trying to tell him, but couldn't find him. I was calling for him when I felt a hand slapping my shoulder, snapping me awake. "Dad?" I said, then looked up at the tall man who had given me the airplane ride, who had a funny look on his face. The shorter man looked up at him.

"Is there something you're not telling me, boss?" He shot his friend a withering look, and then said to me,

"Sorry, I'm not your dad, we're here, time to get up."

"Oh, sorry." I said, uncurling from the seat, picking up my bag, and following them out of the plane.

"Where are you heading?" the shorter man asked.

"I booked a room at a Hotel on Pennsylvania Avenue, but I can get a cab," I said.

There were several people who were obviously anxious to meet with the two men. I thanked them for the ride as the others descended upon them, asking questions.

It was about 21:00, and too late to just show up at the FBI building, but I tried calling anyway to see if I could get in to see Vander Wellin tomorrow. The answering service took my information, but I didn't have much confidence that I'd get a call back.

After crunching on a very expensive, rather bland chicken salad, I started dwelling on all that had been said about my father. Too bad I wasn't old enough to get stinking drunk, because I could walk the two blocks to the J. Edgar Hoover Building and start banging on the door, screaming for Mr. Vander Wellin to get his FB-fucking-I ass down here and tell me what the hell he thinks he's doing, saying that about my father. Instead, I ordered a diet coke and some Ben and Jerry's ice cream, and drowned my sorrows in calories.

Next morning, even in the plush bedding of the hotel, I found it impossible to sleep past 06:00. I did what stretching and exercises I could in the room; without having workout clothes, I could not use the Hotel's facilities. I showered, dressed, and went to the breakfast buffet and got cereal and fruit. By 07:45, I was back in the room calling the FBI again. I got a person this time, however, I still could not get a commitment to get an appointment, but was just promised a call back, from what she said it sounded like he was in. That was close enough to take a trip down there.

The morning was already getting warm and humid as I walked the several blocks to the building. Inside, I stopped at the receptionist, and told her that I wanted to see agent Vander Wellin because I had information concerning the Willard case. Okay, that was mostly a lie, but at least getting arrested would get me in. She called and talked to someone, and then told me I could go up to his fifth floor office number 554. I thanked her and started in the wrong direction to the elevators, she pointed the right way. I turned around, found the elevators, and pushed the button.

The fifth floor was a confusing maze of short walled cubicles and glass walled offices. It took a while of wondering before someone asked me who I was looking for, and pointed in the right direction. I found his office without too much more trouble. Inside the glass-fronted office, two men were talking. They didn't look happy. I suddenly realized exactly what I was doing; I was about to rag on a federal officer after getting in to see him under false pretenses. Before I had a chance to chicken out and go running from the building, one of the men saw me and motioned me in.

I pulled the door open and walked inside, recognizing one of the men as the one that interviewed me at Fort Knox.

"Private Willard, out of uniform no less, you seem anxious to see me."

I saw the notes on his desk from the messages I left.

I was here, so I had to do this. I pulled the printout I made at the PX of the news article, "It's about this" I said. "I thought I cleared this up, that my father was not guilty?" I unfolded the page and placed it on his desk. He turned it around, but didn't really read it.

"What we cleared up is that something illegal was going on, and we don't know who was involved and who was not, unless you have more information for me."

"What I have is the same question, if my father was helping these people, why was he killed?"

"Bad men kill each other."

"What! You have nothing! All this time and you still don't know where his computer is, what was on it, and why he was killed, yet you're accusing him of being a traitor, I don't understand, why are you doing this?"

He put his hands up as if to calm me down, "Look, Millie, I'm sorry about your father, if he is innocent he will be cleared, you need to trust us to do this. Please don't get yourself tangled in things that could get you hurt."

That could get me hurt, what does that mean? I wanted to ask the question out loud, but instead paced back and forth trying to work off the frustration.

"Please," he said, "Just let us do our job."

"I just want to know who killed my father and why," I said.

"So do we! We'll update when we can, but let us do our job, okay?"

I stood there shaking my head, trying to take it all in.

"Okay, private?" he said more forcefully.

"Okay," I said, then added, "sir."

14

I was out of the building and heading back down Pennsylvania Avenue before my relief of having this over with started changing to anger. I'd come all the way, actually got in to meet with the agent in charge, and was sent away with absolutely nothing. I was mad at them, and mad at myself for not holding my ground.

Screeching tires snapped me out of my funk as a rooter van pulled to the side of the street directly beside me, and the door was flung open. I was grabbed from behind, and felt a prick in my neck. I instinctively did the two arm escape move that backed off the large blonde man in a black leather jacket, but he was undeterred and started coming at me again. Then it was like an invisible phantom hit him in the head with a hammer. I heard a wet, bone-splitting crack; his head snapped back, and he fell backwards to the sidewalk. Then I heard the van peel away, and turned to see it roar into traffic with the side door still open. I tried to look back to the man on the sidewalk, but as I turned, everything faded to a white mist.

I woke up to the rhythmic beeping of hospital equipment, staring up at an acoustical tile ceiling. I just lay there, waiting for all my confused thoughts to settle back into place. I was in a hospital, in Washington, but the "why" part had not focused yet. I started checking inventory; there was an IV in my arm, an uncomfortable plastic thing in my nose, and a little blue box on a pole beeping next to the bed. When I tried to sit up the white mist returned.

When I woke up again, a man in a cord jacket and blue denim shirt was staring down at me with a half smile on his tough but kind-eyed face.

"Good afternoon Private Willard, had kind of an interesting day today?"

Not really the adjective I'd use for it, "Yes, I guess so, what happened? What day is this?"

"Don't worry, it's still Wednesday June 30, I'm Thomas Jackwell, NCIS." he showed me his identification. "Perhaps you can tell me what happened?"

NCIS, how do I rate NCIS? "I was leaving the FBI building, and was walking down Pennsylvania Avenue, a van pulled up in front of me, and a big guy grabbed me from behind. I pushed him back, then something happened to him like he was shot in the head, but I didn't hear a gunshot."

"Is this the man?" He showed me a picture.

"Yes, that's the man."

"Have you seen him before?"

"No, who is he?"

"Igor Totlanik, not a very nice man, called Ivan the torturer."

"Why was he after me?"

He seemed to ignore the question, and instead asked, "Why were you at the FBI?"

"Mark Willard is my father, and I was trying to find out why they were accusing him of spying."

"Did you have information on the case?"

"No, not really, although I did lie to the receptionist and told her I did just so I could get in to see Jonathan Vander Wellin, the agent in charge."

"Who was the receptionist you spoke to?"

"Her name tag said Nikki, I don't know her last name."

"Describe her." he said, then said, "Wait." He peered out the door and called to someone named Thorson. A younger man with a flat top haircut entered. Then he said," Go on."

"She has a thin face like a model, blonde hair pulled back in a ponytail, and a long, thin, straight nose and pointed chin, I'm not sure how tall because she was sitting down."

Jackwell told Thorson, "FBI receptionist, Nikki, go check it out."

"Yes, boss." he said, and left. "Did you talk to anyone else?" He asked me.

"No, just Vander Wellin, and there was another man in his office. Why would this guy be after me? I didn't tell anyone I was coming."

"That, we don't know." he started to leave.

"Wait," I said, "What happed to that guy Igor? It looked like he was shot, but I didn't hear it or see anyone."

"Sniper, now you rest up, private." He left the room.

Sniper, wow, this was making no sense at all. How big is this thing my father was mixed up in? A nurse came checking things and typing on a laptop computer.

"When can I get out of here?" I asked.

"You need to be here overnight." she snipped, and left the room.

I fell asleep with a myriad of questions floating on a sea of uncertainty. Heavy weight Russian torturers and non-existent corporations, this couldn't be real. I woke up sometime in the night with a bunch of medical people fiddling with me, and trying to give me a sleeping pill. They wouldn't leave until I put the pill in my mouth and drank some water. After they left, I took the pill from between my lip and gums and tried to toss it into the garbage, but missed. Then, I went back to sleep.

The next morning, I felt a lot better, the beeping machine was gone, and when I tried sitting up it didn't cause any white mist. I got up and went to the bathroom that was shared with the next room. While I was still doing my thing, someone came in and peered around the door. "What are you doing?" the nurse asked.

I thought that it was kind of obvious, especially for someone in the medical field, but answered, "peeing."

"Yes, but you're not supposed to be out of bed, and you need to call us when you need to go, we need to measure your output."

"Huh? When can I get out of here?" I asked, not understanding what measuring my output meant.

"You'll need to talk to the doctor."

"Could you call the doctor please?" I asked, she didn't answer, just left the room after I got back into bed. After staring at the ceiling for about an hour, the door opened and the doctor came in.

He looked down at me and said, "Well, private, you seem to be good as new, so I guess we can let you out of here."

"Thank you," I said.

"I'll get the orderly to help you sign out." He wrote on a clipboard and left the room. I stood up, looking around for my clothes, finding them hanging in a shallow closet.

I was just about finished dressing when the door opened. Instead of the orderly, it was a man in a dark suit, and it took me a minute to recognize him as the civilian that was in the captain's office the day I received my orders to go to Fort Benning. I involuntarily stood at attention; at least I was able to refrain from saluting.

"Private Willard," he said, "Nice to see you're okay. You know, you're a valuable government asset, so it's important that you take care of yourself and be more careful."

"Yes, sir." I answered.

The concern drained from his face, "That means you need to stick to your training and leave investigating to those who do it for a living. Understand, private?"

"Yes, sir." I answered again,

"Good." he answered, and left the room before I had the nerve to ask what was going on.

I was a lot more attentive to my surroundings, leaving the hospital and getting a cab back to the hotel, where I washed up and changed into my uniform.

15

I arrived at Fort Benning at 09:00 on July 2nd, and was very glad to be back in the Army's tender loving care. I went to the PX, ate, bought workout clothes, and spent the rest of the day at the workout center trying to sweat away the last three days. I couldn't do anything about what others thought about my dad, but I knew he was a hero.

When I returned to the barracks, it was half filled with people and duffels claiming bunks. I had been stationed in a separate, smaller room with six bunks; three besides mine had been claimed. By evening, there were three other women in the room. I'd gotten a chance to talk with one of them; a nicely shaped 5'7" Californian named Morgan Troas, with dark brown wavy hair and golden brown eyes, from Long Beach, a district of Los Angeles. I began to think that everyone west of the Mississippi were nonstop talkers, because before lights out, I knew her family history almost back to the Spanish missions.

The smell of the army bunk was a fragrant aroma, and the 05:00 wake-up call, sweet music. Is personal freedom overrated, forcing us into individual cocoons of stubborn loneliness? We were assembled in the sweet smelling humidity of a Georgia morning, standing at attention while we were given the rules of life at Fort Benning, then calisthenics and obstacle courses. After breakfast, the now five women were separated, and told that we will go through some of the training with the men, which included airborne, tactical situations and weapons training. With that, we were issued M4's, the Army's latest replacement for the M16, and told weapons qualification was a requirement for continuing in the program. We were dismissed for the next hour for breakfast.

There is an Army rule that says, before you sleep, eat, or go to the bathroom, you maintain your weapon. So that was the first thing that I did. I took Morgan with me to an available table to review the manual, then strip, inspect, and clean the M4A1s, which were equipped with ACOG 4X optics.

What I found, however, was that the one that I was issued appeared to have a broken firing pin. Comparing it with Morgan's, I verified that to be the case. I went to the DI with the broken firing pin. At first she appeared annoyed until I showed her the part. She asked me my name, marking it in a logbook, taking the broken part, and giving me a replacement. I took the replacement back to where the rifles were disassembled, and then, after comparing the part with the one in Morgan's rifle and finding them identical, I worked with her to complete the cleaning and reassembly.

"What was that all about?" She asked.

"I think that was a test, because she put the broken part back into the parts bin." Morgan raised her eyebrows.

"We may want to tell the others to make sure they check theirs." Morgan said. After securing the weapons, we headed to the mess hall for breakfast. Okay, maybe I was being little selfish, but I wanted to give Morgan the edge over the others because I liked her. Even more amazing, she liked me. She was telling me about her friends and family in Long Beach. It took a while for me to figure out that Scutter was a person, and I had to ask what a rice rocket was. She was a little surprised I didn't know, and wanted to know where I was from. I told her Winfield, Connecticut, but added not to blame Connecticut for my being clueless. That caused her to ask about my family, and I had to tell her of my sorted past. It was a little scary thinking that, if she knew who I really was, she wouldn't want to talk to me anymore. Instead, she put her arm around me and said, "I knew you'd been through a lot of shit, I like you, you're not all only about yourself, you listen to people and hear what they say."

"I see you," I told her.

It took her a second, then she smiled and said, "Yeah, I see you."

"Are you spiritually connected anywhere?" I asked, kind of a strange way of asking, but I didn't want to appear to have a Christian bias if she were Buddhist or Wiccan or something.

"I was going to Spirit Fellowship," she said, "It's a kind of street based emerging church." Seeing my confusion, she continued, "We are moving away from the main stream big production Evangelical Church to more of a free form, Spirit driven worship. What about you?"

"That sounds cool, I'm Catholic." I said.

"That's heavy," she said, "Do Catholics know Jesus?"

"I think I do, at least I know he loves me, I saw him when I was crying my eyes out sitting on a shelf in a Wiccan Magik store. He was holding me in his arms, telling me everything would be okay."

"I see you," she said, giving me a hug. By the time we got to the mess hall, I was telling her of my personal theory of why we had not made contact with intelligent aliens.

"It's not that I think they don't exist, or because of a Starfleet prime directive, but that we are at the center of the forbidden zone, because we are the ones who released sin upon the universe, causing it to be cursed by God."

She laughed then added, "Not only that, later we tried to kill God, there's probably yellow police tape around the whole solar system." By this time we were laughing so hard that I was having problems getting oatmeal on my plate.

We regained enough composure to finish and walk back to the tables. The two other women were sitting together talking; the newest woman was sitting by herself. We came over and sat with her and introduced ourselves. She was actually a little intimidating, close to 6 feet and 160 pounds of solid female muscle with as little hair and as much ink as regulations would allow. I started telling her, "I found a broken firing pin on the M4, so it might be a good idea to-" that was as far as I got.

"You two are a disgrace to women, giggling like a couple of school girls, you better straighten up and start acting like real women. Look at me, I'm going to be the first female ranger, they call me the Steel Dragon, and what do they call you?"

Morgan didn't miss a beat answering, "Barbie." I almost laughed milk out of my nose. Steel Dragon gave me an evil look.

"And I'm called Skank," I said.

"Fuck you two," she said getting up. "I'm going to laugh at your washout." She walked away. We went back to giggling like school girls.

The other two women came over, "We see you met the Dragon Lady."

"You mean Steel Dragon." Morgan said, "Yep, we met her all right."

"Maybe we should call her Merrimac or Monitor." I said, one of the women got it right away and started laughing, Morgan and the other woman looked puzzled.

"Iron clad," the girl who was laughing added, "You know, Civil War naval battle."

Morgan looked at me, "Must be an east coast thing."

The woman who got the iron clad joke was named Maggie Fenworth, from Virginia, nicknamed Psych, and the other woman was from Montana, named Marion Redland, called Cowgirl. Morgan confessed that she really wasn't Barbie, everyone called her Cali.

So it started out the five of us, Cali, Psych, Cowgirl, Steel Dragon and Skank. After the "Defect" dance routine, it no longer felt like a bad name.

We needed to qualify in three days before airborne school started. That meant two days for range practice. We switched off pairs; the first day I was with Cowgirl. She'd grown up on a ranch and was no stranger to firearms, and put in a respectable 5 of 5 showing at 300 meters. The M4 is a shorter, lighter version of the M16, with some sighting and rail improvements. The optics helped it shoot like a ray gun, and I was able to erase the center number on the 300-meter target. Cowgirl was a little peeved that some New England suburb girl could out shoot her. She challenged me to the 500 meter target, the limit of the point target effective range, according to the M4 specifications. Cowgirl let me go first; I zeroed and got 5 of 5 kill shots, she did 4 of 5 kills. I explained to her that it was because the M4 was made in Connecticut. She gave me a "what the fuck" look, then I explained marksmanship, the reason I was here and sucked at everything else. She said she was glad we were both on the same side.

That afternoon I went with Cali, she was struggling and I spent all the time getting her to relax and find her inner machine. I found out that she was here because she was a video game goddess and was trying for special weapons duty, meaning drone surveillance and other high tech toys. By the end of the session, she improved, but was still in danger. Day two, Steel refused to go with me or

Cali, so Cowgirl took Steel and I went with Cali and Psych. I did my required qualification shots quickly at 300 meters, and spent the rest of the time working with Psych and Cali. Cali improved a lot more after we changed the approach from machine to Zen, I don't think I really understood the difference, but it helped her a lot. Psych was a good solid expert level at the required 300 meter. I had both Psych and Cali work until they could get 5 of 5 kills at 300 meters.

At the end of the day, the DI collected our weapons to be returned for qualification the next day. That night, before lights out, Steel caught me in the hall.

"I hear you didn't even push for the full ranger training, are you afraid of combat, Skank? You're an embarrassment to women, and I am going to love to see you fail."

"You're right, I'm not "man" enough for the rangers, but I'm going to make sure that I'm "soldier" enough to do well at whatever I'm given to do, so they won't have to worry about me not having their backs, whether male, female or even you, Steel."

The next day, after morning maneuvers, we were given the M4s a half hour before qualification. Cali and I immediately stripped, checked and cleaned the weapons. Cowgirl and Psych saw what we were doing and joined in. I noticed that I did not have the same rifle that I'd practiced with, so I was extra careful.

At the qualification test, we were lined up at the range while the DI explained the requirements.

"You will have 20 shots for 15 kills at 300 yards, you are responsible for your weapon, if it doesn't fire, jams, or any sighting problems will count against you." This was tighter than the 15 in 30 requirement in BCT. We lined up at the range, "Not you Skank, you line up with the men at the sniper course, your requirement is the same but at 500 meters." Steel gave me the "I'm watching you" sign with a big grin as I moved over to the sniper range parallel to the course the others were shooting from.

Three men who were qualifying for the Ranger sniper program stood at attention, these were the guys I would be backing up, the ones who get the hardest missions and take on the most dangerous assignments, the General's 911 responders. I felt a little out of place, kind of like a gifted child, but a child none the less. I expected to get some teasing, at least an eye roll or two. But that didn't happen. They stood respectfully and attentively as I was told to go first.

The laser-like M4A1 performed flawlessly, I ended with 15 of 15, and then stood as respectfully for the men as they had done for me.

Later, I found out that Steel had a weapons failure. She was unable to clear within the time limit, and was the only one of us who failed to qualify.

Airborne training started with classroom and moved to the 34 foot swing tower for landing practice. Learning how to absorb impact was harder and more painful than it looked. The 250 foot canopy practice tower was a nightmare, I'd never thought of myself as afraid of heights until I was looking over the edge, seeing how unbelievably steep the zip line angle was. However, after the first jump, the next ones no longer caused me to pee my pants. Cali thought it was a blast, Cowgirl and Psych just did it.

The airplane jumps were a completely different story. For some reason, I was more excited than scared. I think it was because, unlike the tower, if something went wrong, there was virtually no chance of a long, lingering, and painful life to death transition but a quick ejection into the afterlife. Cali was a little freaked, but managed a Zen assisted leap. As usual, Cowgirl just did it, but Psych had a meltdown on the first try and needed our reassurance that parachutes hardly ever failed, and if it did, we would be sure the complain to the company on her behalf.

After airborne, the CGS and sniper cross training started for real. Cali and I spent the most time together; she was switching between CGS and special weapons. I was doing CGS and sniper training. After spending so much time doing physical training, sitting in a classroom for the first part of CGS was outrageously boring. The sniper training was almost all field training with the Special Forces units. The two primary sniper rifles that we trained on were: the Barret M107, a 50 caliber monster that when equipped with SLAP rounds could take out light armored vehicles, and the Knights Armament M110, a lighter weight 7.62 mm antipersonnel rifle.

The instructors were no nonsense types, and Cowgirl and I were treated no different than the guys during training. We expected to take a lot of shit, but the opposite was true. They were respectful and helpful. As the DI explained, we may be the one to have their back some day, and they wanted to be sure we were well prepared. One day after field maneuvers, a particularly grueling combination of forced march, running, and shooting, the guys took us aside to tell us that they trusted us as much as any man. If everything I'd done up to this point was for that one moment, it was all worth it.

Once CGS moved from classroom to field practice, it was much better. During that time I found that, besides being a video game goddess, Cali was also the consummate multitasker, and would splice her life stories between mapping and surveillance data. This habit would drive Cowgirl and Psych crazy. I found that, in my head, the philosopher and the machine could coexist simultaneously, and therefore had no issue interpreting Cali's data while listening to her tell of her latest letter from home. It also became obvious that Psych was so named because it seemed she could tell what you were thinking. This was amazingly useful in high stress situations. If there was any one person who should be the first female ranger, it was Cowgirl. No flashy, pretentious super power, just one touch chick who could be counted on.

In the final weeks of the 20 week Advanced Individual Training, we started working together as teams. The special weapons techs, Cali and Psych, would be paired with Cowgirl and I. Again, I had no issue with Cali's motor mouth tendencies. I assisted her with remote weapon systems, where I would do the rough mapping and backup, and she would operate the remote systems maneuvering. Part of my duties would be to provide protection for our placement, as she operated the equipment. Our final operations were cover ops in conjunction with Ranger squads. We would provide surveillance data and cover for a ranger team that would run search and destroy or rescue missions. They would have to trust our data to complete the mission, one mistake on our part could be disastrous.

Graduation was a cause for much celebration, the problem was, all of us except Cowgirl were under the legal drinking age, so the celebration was held at a local all night diner, where we over indulged in French fries and milk shakes. Before long, we were buying a round of shakes for the whole place and toasting to a future where we would no longer be needed in our chosen occupation.

16

I suppose it was a little ridiculous to think that just because the US government spent all of that time and money training us together as a team that we would actually get deployed together; we weren't. Cali was going to Kuwait, and I was going to Afghanistan. I was leaving first, loaded like cargo onto a C-130 with a stop in Germany, then off to Kabul. The trip took 28 hours, counting the stopover, done mostly in a state of half sleep, not enough to feel rested, but enough to feel dysfunctional.

As usual, I was having a delayed reality attack as we stood in formation in the cold, dry, mid December afternoon sun on the tarmac of the Kabul airport. Standing in someone else's country, I could sense the tension between my Christian feet and the Muslim ground.

When I was in high school, our senior class trip was to the UN building in New York. We were supposed to go to Washington, but New York is closer to Winfield, and therefore the trip was cheaper. But I remember being very impressed with the building and the people. But thought at that time that with so many intelligent people talking out their differences, how could they have failed so badly? Well, now I get to pay the price for that failure.

After what seemed like several hours of standing in the freezing cold, we were divided into companies, then units, and squads. I was loaded into an armored personnel carrier with 7 other soldiers, all men, and rolled out of the airport. Sitting on long benches, facing each other, not one person spoke, all newbie's just like me, trying to get reality to mesh with their internal world model, and so far I was

105

having little success. The inside of the carrier was utilitarian metal painted light beige, noisy and stuffy, with no windows. It was impossible to see where we were going. To control freaks, I suppose it would be maddening, for me, it helped add to the deniability.

We stopped, and everyone was rousted out to stand behind the carrier, where I was slapped with reality once again. We were standing in a town of sand stone buildings and dusty streets, men in traditional dress, and even a few women standing across the street staring at us. Actually, at me mostly, maybe they knew what I was thinking, or maybe it was because I was the only woman. All during training I never once thought about what we were actually training to do, but it was an utter shock to be standing out in the open with the people whose country you were occupying staring back at you. This was no longer a picture in National Geographic. The fact that this was real started seeping into every crack of my brain.

Four of the men were separated out, and the rest of us were motioned back into the carrier. There was a little part of me that was hoping we would get hit by a rocket, and this was as far as I would make it, but I tried to push that thought away because I didn't want the others in the carrier to die. After an hour, we stopped again. This time we were in open desert. I was relieved, but this was just a potty and stretch break. Trying to find suitable cover for that activity in the open desert helped me understand why women were not made for combat. Finally, I had to settle for half canceled half honor system, but I was not getting back in that thing with a full bladder.

It was at least another two hours before the next stop. The four of us got out in another town; again, men standing around staring at me as our safe haven drove away, leaving us alone. A sergeant came out to meet us, herding us into a large, three story, gray stone building that bordered the open square where we first stood. Inside, the building had a wide center hallway that went front to back with rooms off to the sides. The personnel inside were a mix of soldiers and natives in traditional clothing. There was a woman at a desk in the wide center hall, her burqa concealing every bit of her, except the hate for me in her eyes.

The men were ushered down the hall towards the back of the building, while the sergeant marched me into a large room on the right that had been converted into makeshift office cubes, and planted me in front of a lieutenant. I saluted, and he gave a quick disgusted salute back as he was trying to get someone on a radio phone. He must have gotten through, because he shouted into the receiver, "Turnboch, what the hell are you doing sending me a woman, yes, *woman*, we are front lines here, we can't use her, what... Fuck!" He slammed the headset down. He looked up at me, "So you're the crack shot they call Skank, huh?" He didn't really want an answer. "Well find a bunk and get some sleep, you've got roof duty tonight. Dismissed already."

"Yes, sir." I saluted, exited the room, and turned left at the scowling woman, assuming that the bunk room was where the men were going. I found a room where several men were unpacking, and others were asleep in the large room filled with bunks.

"Women are across the hall," one of the men barked at me, I quickly turned and crossed the hall. This one was mostly used for storage, but there were several bunks in the far end along the inside wall. One of the bunks was made up, and the others were completely stripped. I assumed that the made up bunk was taken, so I took one of the others, shedding my pack and other gear at the foot.

Found a blanket on one of the shelves and more like passed out than fell asleep.

I was awakened by a slap on the arm, "Get up. Duty change, 10 minutes." I got up, dressed, and started looking for a bathroom; there was a primitive latrine at the back of the building. I met another woman as I was coming out of the door.

She laughed, "That's the men's room, we use this room over here," She showed me a smaller but cleaner room down a small left side hall.

"Sorry," I said, "Do you know where I report for roof duty?

"Here, I'll show you to the sergeant," She said, and led me towards the front of the building and motioned to the room opposite the lieutenant's room.

"Private Willard reporting, sergeant," He didn't say a word, just looked at his watch. 10 seconds later, a man entered.

He opened a cabinet and handed the other man and myself an M4 equipped with night vision. I started to inspect it.

"Skank!" he barked, "That is not your weapon, regardless of what you were told, you do not maintain it, you do not clean it, you do not strip it. You only pull the trigger and give it back to me when you are done, do you understand?"

"Yes, sergeant." I replied.

"Hawk, you will take the west and south walls, Skank, you have the north and east walls. That's this one," he pointed to the front of the building, "and this one." He pointed to the side wall of the room. "Understood?"

"Yes, sergeant."

"Dismissed."

I followed the other man down the hall and up a set of narrow back stairs that bypassed the second and third floors before opening onto the roof. There were three people on the roof, two snipers and one spotter.

Once they descended the stairs, Hawk pointed out the north and west walls, "If you see anything, let me know, but don't wait to fire if it is a threat." He pointed me to a fat corner post where my two walls met. "Get comfortable, but stay alert, this is the most boring job in the world, but you need to find a way to stay sharp. We haven't seen any action for several weeks, but don't take that as a guarantee. Oh, and don't stand up and make yourself an easy target."

Getting comfortable on this flat roof behind the low walls was not going to be easy. I looked over to the opposite corner. Hawk, who looked as if he had some Native American blood, was sitting cross-legged, diagonal from the corner post, facing out with his rifle on his lap. I tried the same position for a little while, until my joints started to complain. The sun had gone down, and it got cold and dark quickly. I backed away from the corner post and started checking the street and buildings through the night scope. For the first few hours, nothing happened. I began to worry that something was going on that I could not see, I feared there would be a major attack and I would miss the signs until it was too late. But no matter how big that fear was, or how uncomfortable the rooftop was, in a few more hours I was getting drowsy.

Then, on the front wall in a building across the square in front of our building, I saw movement in a second floor window.

Shit, what do I do, I need to report this. "I got movement, two men, RPG." I said, giving a quick play by play. I couldn't believe it, as plain as day in front of me, two men were hunched together pointing an RPG at the top of our building. Shit, this can't be happening; don't these guys know about night vision? Don't they know I can see them as clear as day? Shit, you guys, cut that out. They're not stopping, oh fuck, this is it, I have to do something. Oh God, please tell them to stop. There was a familiar kick but the high picked hypersonic crack was accusingly loud as it echoed off the building; the man with the RPG fell backward, pulling the launcher up, the man next to him could only turn his head before he too was down with another shot. By this time, Hawk was beside me. "RPG neutralized." I said.

"Shit." Hawk said, more dumfounded than anything. He called down for backup, seconds later I saw four soldiers rush out, cross the street and go into the building. A minute later, he updated me, two men were found with RPG and rockets, both dead with head shots. I was still staring into the building. According to all the westerns and war movies, I should be going off the deep end right now, but I wasn't feeling anything at all. Was I really a psychotic killer and just finding out now, or was it going to hit me later?

The next morning we reported to the sergeant, he stripped the rifle, removed the magazine, and verified the number of rounds fired. I was given a form to file a report of the incident. We were then called to formation and mandatory exercises, after which I was free for breakfast and a sleep period before night duty. The men could go into town, however, women were not allowed to. Instead, breakfast was MREs and water that tasted like a swimming pool.

This time, sleep did not come that easy; my high humidity Connecticut nose and eyes did not like the dust and dryness. I spent some time reading my pocket Bible; I had broken the one commandment I thought I could keep and needed to talk to God. What was it about this picture that didn't seem right? We all called on the God of Abraham, but were killing each other. During my reading, several times I thought I saw the central hall woman peeking around the corner at me. Sleep finally came in the late morning. I was awakened early in the evening, earlier than the previous day, allowed five minutes to dress before I was to report to the sergeant.

The lieutenant and two other soldiers were in the office, the sergeant called me to his desk, on which was a rather mean looking curved knife.

"Do you know, Private Willard, that you almost lost your life today?" the Lieutenant said.

"No, sir?" I answered.

"Our receptionist was very close to slitting your throat while you slept, she would have succeeded if Private Billing here had not stopped her."

"Why would she do that?" I asked.

"We were hoping you could tell us, she'd been working here for months without incident, now you show up and she goes off the deep end? What do you think would cause that?"

"I don't know, I can't think of what I've done unless it was about the insurgents I shot last night."

"Well you may want to learn how to sleep with an eye open, now get something to eat before reporting for duty."

I sat in the storeroom eating alone, used the correct bathroom this time to clean up as best as possible, and reported for duty.

Back on the roof, I sat in my corner, under the bright moon light, scanning with the night scope every few minutes. In hazy Connecticut, that moon and stars never seemed as bright as they did here. The night vision hardly seemed necessary. Less than three hours in, I caught three men with what looked like AKs doing a squat run across the roof on the east building next door. Not again, why couldn't last night be a one-time incident?

"Three men with assault rifles on the east roof." I said.

"Acknowledged." Hawk responded, "Take them if you need to."

I skittered into the northeast corner where the corner post was a little higher than the wall around the rest of the roof, it was clear that they could see me in the moonlight. Their roof offered less cover than mine, but they did not seem concerned that half their body was clearly exposed. They just took up positions and aimed straight for me, but never got a chance to fire before I was able to take them out.

What was going on? This made no sense at all, it was like they didn't think I was armed or couldn't hit what I was aiming at. What was the alternative, should I let them just kill me? If it were just me, that was a serious consideration, but what about the people in the building counting on me to protect them? It's not just me anymore is it? Maybe it *was* just me, after all, the woman tried to kill me, and no one else in all this time. Maybe I should just stand up and let them put a few bullets in me, would that satisfy them?

Two hours before dawn, I got my chance as a pickup truck with a machine gun mounted charged the building, firing at the roof as soon as it rounded the corner from the north. Even as bullets skipped off the top edge of the front wall beside me, I took aim and took out the gunner, the second shot through the windshield took the driver. The truck rammed the low wall in front of the building, leaving the truck leaking coolant onto the dusty ground. My pampered middle class girl brain accepted the surrealistic scene much too easily.

"Gun truck neutralized." I reported. For the second time that night, the squad from the building fanned out to investigate, reporting both the driver and gunner were dead.

17

That morning, my debriefing was in the lieutenant's office. I reported the incidents from the night before as he paced behind his desk, blowing out a sigh, rubbing his hands over his bristled scalp. Hawk backed up my story adding that I made the shot despite being raked with machine gun fire. Everyone snapped to attention as a Marine Captain entered the room.

"Lieutenant."

"Captain."

The lieutenant started, "Something's going on here, and I don't know what it is. We haven't seen attacks like this in months, now it's happening every night. I fear there is an offensive happening, or this is some sort of diversion."

"We're not seeing any kind of movement indicating anything in the area, this is all local, do you have anyone checking locally?" The Captain replied.

"Yes sir, but so far, no information." I was dismissed while the meeting continued.

I was unable to sleep with an eye open that day, and was awakened from a deep sleep that afternoon. The person who woke me told me to report to the lieutenant's office in 10 minutes. I washed, dressed, and then reported. When I got there, the Marine Captain was still there with the Lieutenant. I stood at attention, and saluted. The captain saluted crisply, and the lieutenant gave his usual disgusted version. The Captain asked, "You are called Skank?"

"Yes, sir."

"Any reason for the name?"

"It's what I was called in high school, I was not very popular, sir."

"I would say not. However, you seem to be the problem." He showed me a crumpled piece of paper with a picture that looked like it had been reproduced on a copy machine. It was a picture of me, with what looked like a form of Arabic writing.

"What is that, sir?"

"It seems that your name "Skank" was translated into Persian as "cheap whore." Such a name is very offensive to the local people; they would prefer that you not be here."

"I'm sorry sir, but…"

The lieutenant cut in, "I understand that, sir, but how did they get this information?"

"You have locals working here who know English, it is not hard to guess how they would get the information. The question is, what can we do about it?"

"Reassign her, of course, she should not have been assigned here in the first place."

"That will not necessarily stop the attacks, now that the animosity towards her has grown to this level. Whose idea was it to assign her to a combat post?"

"What else could I do, I needed a roof sniper and they sent her, I didn't like it, but I had no choice." the Lieutenant answered.

"You would have been better off going with a short crew; I don't think you understand how serious the situation is. As long as she is here, the attacks will continue. More than that, even the friendly locals no longer trust us, these men will never accept feeling subordinate to a woman. She cannot be on the roof tonight."

My father is a traitor, and the first day I'm deployed I destroy the entire American effort in Afghanistan.

"If I may speak, sir?" I asked.

"No!" the lieutenant barked.

"Lieutenant, you understand this is not her fault, let her speak." The captain motioned to me.

"If I were publicly punished, would that help the situation? Even if you have to take me outside, tie me to a pole and set me on fire, if …"

"This is serious, private." The lieutenant snapped.

"No, I think she has a point." The Captain answered.

"We can't light her on fire, sir."

"No, calm down, I don't think it needs to be that drastic, but it needs to be humiliating to her in their eyes. Are you sure you are up for this, private?"

"Yes sir, I signed up to defend our country with my life, so whatever it takes, I will do it."

"Very well then, go pack your equipment and be prepared to ship out; someone will come get you when we are ready."

"Yes sir, and thank you, sir."

Five minutes later, someone came to roughly drag me to the front office in front of the local staff. Once in the room, the door was slammed shut.

"You're sure about this, private?"

"Yes, sir."

"Okay." there were two other soldiers there who looked pretty scared. The Captain continued, "I understand your apprehension, men, but you have to make it look good. You understand I hate doing this also, from what I have seen she's an excellent soldier."

"I understand sir, do what you have to do." I answered.

"Please take your hair down, private." I obeyed. The lieutenant came and stood before me and yelled.

"You are a disgrace to the Army and our country." He tore open my jacket, tore off my expert marksmen and airborne badges. My hands were tied behind my back with plastic ties. Then the soldiers took each arm and dragged me roughly out the front door past the low stone wall and into the street. They dumped me on the ground; I stayed there in a heap, left alone in the dust of the street as a group of locals gathered. Soon they started jeering as I lay there face down in the street, as clods of dirt and rocks started pelting me. Strangely I was filled with an unexplainable peace and contentment hoping this would be enough to restore what I'd damaged by being here. A Humvee drove up; I was picked up and dumped in the back, then driven just outside of town, not far enough to be out of sight. The captain in the passenger seat turned and said to me.

"Okay, Millie," I was a little stunned to hear him use my first name, "This is the final act necessary to make this work." He said, "You have to make it look good." The driver got out, came around, and opened the back; he dragged me out by the arms dumping me on the ground. The captain got out and came up to where I was. "Stay on the ground, but turn and face me." I think I understood what he had in mind, and flipped over sitting on the ground. He pulled his gun and I tried to skitter away, he fired, I jerked, and then fell flat. He returned to the front seat, the driver dragged me back to the truck by my feet, staying completely limp as he dumped me in the back.

When we were miles out of town, we stopped and I was pulled out of the back, the bonds were cut, and I got in the back seat. Before we got to the next town, I was told to cover myself up. I stayed hidden for the rest of the trip until we were inside a base motor pool building. Opening the door, the Marine Captain said, "You have a great future in MI, you will find your new uniform and equipment in that side room, get cleaned up, changed, and report to the assembly pad marked area B for transport at 21:00. Oh, and here." He handed me my expert and airborne badges. I saluted. After saluting back, the captain and the driver got back in the vehicle and drove away.

I went through the door, stripped and washed away the bad memories. After drying off, I found a locker labeled "SKANK", inside the locker was a new uniform in desert camo. It had my name on it, and my airborne patch, and an MI patch on the sleeve. It's good to be dead, I said to myself, checked the time, and headed off to what I hoped would be a better life.

18

The plane was a jump equipped C-130, there were four men, and one other woman on board. The rest of the cargo area was filled with drop rigged equipment. These people were more talkative than my last flight, and two of the men seemed to know each other. They introduced themselves. They were Pollux and Castor, the others group members were Jarvis, Markley, and Georgia, then there was me, Skank, but I said "Please don't tell anyone, because it got me "killed" the last time."

"Well, welcome to the undead, Skank," Castor boomed, squeezing my shoulder.

"You look pretty good for being dead." Markley said, a huge African American with a face that looked like he laughed a lot.

"Thank you," I answered, "As it turns out, being dead is not so bad."

"Here here, dead like us," Castor called out, raising his arm as in a toast.

"Dead like us." Pollux repeated, we all laughed about it, but the proclamation of being dead seemed to worry Jarvis. I found out during the flight that Pollux and Castor were nicknames that came from two impish brothers in old 1950s SciFi stories. They'd known each other as boys, and got the names from Castor's grandfather. They were team leaders for the infiltration and attack teams. Jarvis was the real last name for a geeky college type kid who, like Cali, was a special weapons expert. Georgia was a nickname; she, like me, was a map reader and shooter.

Our heading told us that we were not going to Iraq. After several hours of flight time, we were called to jump readiness. There would be two passes, the first would be for the equipment, the second for us. The huge cargo door opened, revealing nothing but blackness outside as the cool night air swirled around the plane's interior. A warning buzzer sounded, the ramp started, and the cargo slid into the darkness past the opening. The plane banked, we linked up, the order was given, and we marched out of the plane into the cold night sky. Off to the right at the extreme horizon, I could see tiny pinpoints of light. After what seemed like several minutes of floating in space, I sensed more than saw the ground rapidly approaching. Readying for landing slightly too late, I went tumbling like a weed in a ghost town, but hit only soft sand, and was quickly on my feet dealing with the canopy. I heard the others landing around me and saw red moving lights to the left. I could hear the others moving in the direction of the lights. "This way, this way!" voices were calling. We were gathered together, and names were called off, making sure we were all accounted for. Then, we headed off with the red LED flashlights our only illumination besides the vast dome of the Milky Way overhead. I was indeed dead, and this was heaven.

We were guided into what at first looked like a very large tent, but inside the stars were not completely blocked.

"Skank, Georgia, this is your place here, get some rest, tomorrow comes early." He lifted the flap to an actual tent with six cots, some were occupied, and we took two that were not claimed. "No loud noises, and absolutely no lights," our guide said, then closed the flap as he left.

Our wakeup call came just before first light. We lined up on packed sand, still too dark to make out faces, but I could see that there were a number of people standing around between large vehicles and equipment in a very unmilitary formation. Someone walked up in front of us and addressed us in a low, but strong voice.

"Welcome to Zombie unit, we do not exist, and we are not here, when you write home you will tell everyone how boring being stationed in Kuwait is, you will send fake pictures we have available and you will pine away about not seeing any action. Also do not, I repeat, do not go out from under the netting during daylight hours. Because what you are about to do did not happen, do you understand. DO YOU UNDERSTAND?"

"Yes, sir."

The voice continued, "Castor, Pollux, welcome back, you may take your seats, Markley, you're with them. Jarvis, Georgia, you're with Cowgirl and Psych, and Skank, you're with Cali. We're not moving out today, so plan your targets, now get to work. That is all."

I looked up at a silhouetted figure, and knew it was her.

"Skank, that is you, you gorgeous hunk of girl meat, I'm so glad to see you, what happened to you?" She jumped on me so hard we both almost ended up flat on the sand, we hugged, cried, and jumped up and down, completely unashamed that we were acting like a couple of girls.

"Cali, hi, well, I got "killed" on my last assignment, but I feel much better now."

"You need some work to look like a zombie," she said, putting her hands around the back of my head, undoing my hair, smoothing it with her fingers over my shoulders.

"What are you doing? That's not regulation."

"We don't exist, remember, things are different here, come on, we got targets to plan, boy, I missed you."

By this time, the sky was turning a deep indigo blue in anticipation of the sun. It was light enough that I could see that the large tent like thing we entered last night was camo netting over the entire camp being held up by protrusions from the vehicles parked underneath.

She led me to the back of one of the vehicles, lifting off a panel, revealing the familiar flat panel displays. Within seconds, we were scanning satellite images and terrain maps. "We're searching out terrorist camps?" I asked.

She looked at me, "You're getting as bad as Psych, yes." she brought up a screen, "This is what we are tracking." We spent some time searching through the maps. "We're after this big guy here tonight; we need to plan our station point and planting sites for the gophers. First, you will protect our site as I place the gophers, then I will defend our position as you search out and neutralize anyone who looks like a leader, lastly we backup the rangers." It took only a few minutes to plot and save the results. That completed, she said, "Come on, I'll give you a tour."

She explained that everything was attached in some way to the vehicles, and the entire camp could be uprooted and moved within minutes. The guys slept in the vehicles or on the ground, and the girls had the tent, the one I slept in last night. She took me around and introduced me to the guys. First, the ranger attack crews led by Castor and Pullux; they were the ones that disrupted the targets after we got done with them. The idea was not to completely destroy the camp, but to take out equipment with the gopher smart bombs. Eliminate as many leaders as possible, and make it appear that they were attacked by other terrorist camps.

The dress code was evidently pretty loose, especially with these guys, there were bandanas, baseball caps, and muscle shirts. To my amazement, they were not all men, there were some women that made Steel Dragon look like a skinny model.

"Are you Skank?" One of the women said, she had her shiny black hair covered with a red bandana and tied in a ponytail down her back. She picked me up like a child would her favorite teddy bear. "Let me get a look at you, girl, I heard so much about you."

"I think Cali exaggerates," I said as she held me half a foot off the ground.

"Cali, hell, Cowgirl said you whooped her butt on the range."

"I think squeaked by is more like it." I answered.

"Cali, you got to feed this girl, she's wasting away!" she said.

Cali said, "Skank, this is Barbie. She's from Australia."

"Hi, Barbie." I said as she landed me back on Earth.

Next was the defense crew, three guys that manned the tracking radar and surface to air missile systems that would welcome any unfriendly air craft that got too close. Then the other gopher and sniper teams, Cowgirl now paired with Jarvis, and Psych with Georgia. Finally the brains, Captain Carver and sergeant McGrath, kept us honest and pointed in the right direction.

After the tour, it was time for chores and maintenance. I was given an M110 to become familiar with. Finding a spot out of the sand, I stripped down the 110, inspecting every piece. For such a harsh environment, the rifle had been well maintained. I cleaned everything up and reassembled it.

Sergeant McGrath called all of the snipers to a low place under the netting that looked out over a valley. The edge of the netting had been propped up on boxes. "This is our shooting range, kids, you will lie on the ground two feet back from the cover and fire at that buff over there. Your first shot will be your sight zero shot; you get one to make adjustments. Your second shot is your marker shot that will be your target. Every shot after that must hit at that same point or you fail the practice. You will continue until you pass."

"Yes, sergeant."

"Good, Skank, you go first."

"Yes, sergeant."

"Cut the crap, Skank, on the ground and start shooting."

I plopped down on the sand, and, finding a suitable blank space at about 1000 meters, I squeezed off a shot. The site was low to the left. I zeroed and put the next 9 shots in the same location.

"Well, nice shooting, Skank, but you didn't listen to a fucking word I said; you were shooting at the wrong area, none of this rapid fire cowboy stuff either, one shot in the air at a time during practice to confirm hits. Now if you please, that bluff right there, and try again, or do you need a time out?"

"Sorry, sir."

"Sorry sir, my ass, showoff, I should send you to bed without your supper."

It really was a mistake; I zeroed on the 600 meter white sand hill and took 4 shots, replaced the magazine, and completed the next six, letting him note each hit.

"OK, Skank, you're in, but next time no grand standing, got it?"

"Yes, sir."

"Yes, who?"

"Yes, sergeant."

"Like I need another wise ass punk around here, Georgia, you're next."

Georgia had no problem following orders or qualifying. Cowgirl was next with a 107, did ten at 600 meters, then McGrath had her do 10 at same 1000 meter bluff I used.

"Cowgirl, Georgia, you're in, you can go." McGrath said, and waited for them to walk away, "Skank, I heard all about you, no hot shots here, we're a team."

"Yes, sergeant."

He handed me another 2 mags, "Here, now, empty these in the 1000 meter bluff." He turned and walked away, not staying to verify hits.

While I was still on the ground unloading the second mag, Cali came up and straddled me, sitting in the small of my back, and started straightening my hair while I continued to shoot. "McGrath can act like a prick sometimes, but he's really a good guy." She said.

"I know, I really did screw up, I didn't see which hill he pointed at, I know it looked like I was being a show off, but it really was a mistake."

"He'll forgive you, don't worry about it."

"I just don't want everybody to think I'm an asshole." I said as I finished the second mag.

"Well, that's going to be hard," she said, "because I already told everybody you are."

"You bitch," I said pushing myself up, flipping her on to the ground. I sat on her stomach and pinned her arms down beside her head.

"Ladies?" We both looked over and saw Captain Carver standing next to us, we jumped up quickly saluting. "No extracurricular activities until you put your toys away." He said, pointing to the M110 that was still propped on its bipod on the ground.

"Yes, sir," we both said in unison. The captain saluted back with a sly smile.

It was siesta time. Most of the women were sacked out in the tent, except for the rangers, who preferred the sand. We were rousted by early evening for final planning. The captain gathered us around a single large flat panel display. Sergeant McGrath brought up all of the morning's data.

"As you can see," Carver began, "There has been very little movement since this morning," there was an overlay showing the difference between then and now.

"We are going to put our tech teams here, here, and here."

"Tech teams are us." Cali whispered to me.

Psych and Georgia, I want you here, it's 600 meters and a good vantage point, but it's close, so be watchful during gopher planting. Cowgirl, Jarvis, you'll be here, 800 meters, you'll have the Berret Cowgirl to take out this row of vehicles. Cali and Skank, I want you here on the north side, it's 900 meters, but the closer hill loses site of the west flank, can you handle that, Skank? Make sure, because our people are going to be in there."

"Yes, sir."

"Good, I want the three disruption crews here, here, and here. They have large numbers, so hang back until the snipers take out as many leaders as they can. That's it, go pray, pee, or whatever you need to do, we mount up in 10." I did both.

19

I was suiting up for the night op, tied my hair back, and then put on my jacket, eye protection, com link, and helmet.

"Here, you may want one of these, also," Cali said, handing me a thin gauze scarf, "It gets very sandy on the ride." I took it from her and wrapped it around my neck. I followed her to the one of the vehicles that did not look anything like a normal truck.

"Where are we, Tatooine?" I asked Pollux who was overseeing loading.

He laughed, "It's a hovercraft" he said.

"Nice, but aren't they terribly noisy?"

"Not these babies, turbine powered, the motors buried in here, same tech they use on the stealth plane." I helped Cali, handing up her base station, and the case with the gophers inside. I slung my M110, and was helped up onto the narrow deck by Pollux, "Right here, Skank. Cali, you're on the other side, tech team goes in towards the middle, grunts on the rail." The craft looked like a catamaran top sitting on a black rubber hotdog bun. There was a raised hump from front to back down the center for the engine, with a trough on either side where Cali and I sat, one on each side. On the outside, the deck sloped up to a wide flat walkway that Pollux called the rail, where the rangers or grunts, as Pollux called them, sat.

"Hang on, Mommy's driving." Pollux said as he sat down up front behind a low windscreen.

The sun had just dipped over the horizon as the gentle whine changed to the sound of rushing wind, sand billowed from the side and the whole craft lifted, drifting sideways slightly before heading off to the North West. Castor was driving another craft beside us as we headed towards the fading light, skimming over the sand like we were in a fast speedboat over water. Soon, the light faded completely, but we did not slow down. It was an eerie feeling going this fast in total darkness, Pollux having only the night vision screen and radar to navigate whatever the desert put in our path. I sat crouched in the small trough; hanging on to a hand hold, finding it very difficult to believe this was real.

I thought back to that first night that I killed those two men that were about to attack the building I was protecting. The first two people I ever killed, what was wrong with me? I was supposed to be having a hard time dealing with it, but the event came and went just like all of the other events in my life. Now I was a killer, but nothing was any different, as if I'd always been a killer. Was there something deeply wrong with me? If I was really all that intelligent, why couldn't I see this coming? I could have avoided it by just barely passing weapons training. Then, I could be spending my tour of duty making coffee and stapling papers for some colonel in DC. But I was lost in the praise of my superiors, like a little child wanting adult approval. Now, here I am, screaming through the dark, enjoying the ride to another killing field. My feelings of self-loathing all through high school are finally justified.

The craft began to slow. I could feel it slipping sideways as we settled gently to the sand. I was tapped on the shoulder, signaling this was our stop. I got out and was handed the control base as Cali came around to help me. The gophers would stay with the ranger crew to be released closer to the target camp. We stepped away from the craft as it lifted and slid away. I brought down the night vision to scope the area, and found that we needed to head a few steps south, up a slight rise, to get to our vantage point. There were some dim lights on in the target camp, but not enough to work without the night vision. Cali and I secured the control station, powered it up, and made a systems check. Cali continued readying her equipment as I scanned the perimeter. My job at this point was to protect our position and possibly clear a path for the gophers if need be. Soon there was crackling in the headset, Castor checked in, Pollux checked in, Psych checked in, Jarvis checked in, and Cali checked in. Everything was a go. Our gophers were released first because they had a little farther to go. I continued to scan for trouble. I noticed that there were two people in the camp, possibly sentries that were in a lighted area around a building where Cali needed to plant a gopher. I whispered to her that they could be trouble. It was light enough for them to see the little self powered bombs. They were about the size of a microwave oven, low and flat, but definitely could be seen even in the low light. We waited until the gophers got close, hoping they would move, but they didn't.

"I think I'm going to need a path," Cali said to me through the communication system so that everyone would know what we were planning.

"Are you good with that, Skank?" Pollux asked, "There are two of them; can you get them without making a scene?"

"I'm good," I answered.

"Your show then." Pollux said.

I lined up, the problem with two targets at 900 meters and a muzzle velocity of 2700 feet per second is that there would be a second delay between firing and striking the target. Therefore, I would need to put the second round in the air before confirming a hit on the first. With the heavy-duty suppressor on the 110, they would not hear us; however, I knew from personal experience that one would hear the hit on his buddy. Therefore, they both needed to go down quickly. I put myself in the machine like trance and squeezed out two shots, aiming at the one behind first. He went down; his friend turned, and went down less than a second later.

"We're clear." I said. Cali lined up her last gopher.

"Set." she announced.

"In ten, kids, hide your eyes." Castor said.

Even with our heads down, I could see the flash. Our jobs changed, Cali would protect our position with her HK417, and I would search for anyone who looked like they were in authority. Through the scope, I could see the chaos develop as men came from tents like ants, rushing to the blasted buildings and equipment. They didn't seem to realize that they were under attack yet. I looked for those surveying the action, but not participating. Those would be the highest ranking people.

"Oh, Skank," Cali said, "I didn't tell you, I just got a letter from my cousin Shari."

Two more were talking together directing the others.

"Shari in Santa Barbara?" I asked.

"Yeah," she continued, "She said she just got a new puppy."

The remaining fighters scrambled to defend their camp.

"Really, what kind of puppy?" I asked.

They lined up with their AKs, firing blindly into the desert. The AK47 is known all over the world as the best assault rifle, it's rugged, reliable, and very easy to use. However, for all that, its accuracy quite frankly sucks, falling off drastically after 200 meters, so they were just wasting ammo.

"It's a shiatsu, or at least part shiatsu."

With no obvious high ranking targets the strategy turned to randomizing hits to create more confusion. As their comrades fell, they dropped to the ground for cover.

Cali continued, "But she said it's the cutest thing, it runs around the house following her everywhere."

Dropping for cover didn't help; they were smaller targets, but now stationary and actually easier to hit. The last phase of the attack went underway as the rangers would swarm the camp, firing their AKs into the fray to make it look like they were being attacked by another camp.

"Ready for grunt crew in five, four, three, two, go!" Castor announced. This was the scariest part for me. It would take several minutes for the rangers to get to the camp. In that time, I would keep taking out enemy fighters.

"Funny thing though, she can't seem to get it to play fetch." Cali said.

When they reached the fighting, it was my job to back them up, providing cover to make sure they didn't get caught by stragglers. In three minutes, they arrived. Each of their uniforms had friendly detectors that would show clearly in the night vision to identify them as friend.

"Are shiatsus supposed to fetch? Maybe they're just not retrievers," I asked.

I watched them come in the scope, making sure I could see all of their markers, and then covered their advance. Within minutes, the defenders scattered. I continued to scan keeping the stragglers away from the rangers.

"Actually, I don't know, anyway, she posted pictures, it's so cute, and you've just got to see it."

I heard Castor call for evac. Three more minutes, and they all made it back to their base as Pollux and Castor called in the all clear. I helped Cali pack her station, and she helped me pack my trash, casings, in other words, we did not want to leave a bit of evidence. Five more minutes, and we thumbed a ride back to Zombie land. Pollux even ran the hovercraft over our position to erase the footprints.

As we were heading back, Barbie found me, squeezing my shoulder, "Thanks for taking out that asshole," she said, "I didn't even see him until I heard his head explode. You're the best." At the time, I didn't know it was Barbie that I'd saved. Had I really saved someone's life? But I did it by killing someone else. So what am I, an evil monster who should burn, or a rescuing angel that deserves praise? It's not like I enjoy killing people, it's what I am trained to do; someone has to be sacrificed to do it. So why not me, after all, it's not like I am good for anything else. How much did I take this for granted, as I enjoyed a safe warm place to sleep when I was back in Winfield?

20

Letters from home didn't come on paper, but were posted on our link systems with the command communications. I cuddled up next to Cali as she showed me the pictures. It was nice to be included, and I wasn't aware that I was crying until Cali stopped and was looking at me. "I'm sorry," she said "what's wrong?"

"No, it's okay," I said "I like it that you include me like I was part of your family, thank you, but I'm just having a hard time with not having any friends back home. I think it's my fault."

"How can it be your fault? You didn't cause your father to die."

"No, it's not that, I think there were a lot of people back home that really did like me, but I wasn't able to accept it, I was expecting everyone to hate me, because I think I hate myself."

She gave me a hug, "How can you say that, you're one of the most amazing people I've ever known, you're so open and honest, you accept me as I am, I can be me around you and not have to worry about proving myself."

"I think you're the first real friend I've ever had, it's like you don't care that I'm so screwed up."

"I see you." She said.

The planning went the same as before. This time Cali and I would be taking the position to the west of the camp. It was an 800 meter location, not as high as we would have liked, but the best location on that side of the target. We loaded up the hovercraft and headed northwest towards the next target. This camp was actually smaller than the last one, but we assumed that they would be on alert because they would have heard of the attack on the last camp. I was sitting in the same place on the deck on the left side of the hovercraft, skimming across the desert with only the billions of stars lighting the darkness. I wondered if there was life up there somewhere else. Were they smarter than us, able to live in peace with their own kind? In the SciFi movies, we were always the good guys, fighting the nasty creatures that populated the galaxy, but my guess is that it would really be the other way around; we were the evil bad guys and all of the alien races were praying that we would never find the secret to interstellar travel.

Cali and I were the first off, and went about setting up our station; I checked the perimeter, and then the target area. Inspection through the night scope did reveal a lot more people on guard than the last camp, just as we thought.

"These guys look like they are on high alert. They may have their higher ups sequestered, but be careful, and let's make this quick. Get the gophers where we can, don't spend a lot of time making paths. Instead, if you see a shot at a leader, take it." Castor advised.

Cali got her smart bombs off, and was able to sneak them in without incident.

Caster announced, "In five, kids, five, four, three, two, cover." The detonation of the gophers lit the desert; I brought up the scope and started searching for targets. Again, people started flooding from tents.

"I don't know that much about Islam," I told Cali, "but I think they are told to kill us because we are evil, and they are rewarded if they die fighting us because they die in service to God, do you think that's true?" I found a man who looked like he was directing others in setting up defenses.

"That we're evil?" Cali asked.

The others hit the dirt as another man stepped in and tried to get them organized.

"No, do you think that the people we kill go to heaven?"

"I think that's a different issue, they would go to heaven because God forgave them, not because they kill us." Cali said.

"I hope they do go to heaven" I said.

Another man was rousting people from the tents.

"Well isn't Allah the same God, He's the God of Abraham, right?" Cali asked.

"Yes, I think so." I said, "Why?"

"Well that means we are all going to the same heaven, don't you think they're going to be a little pissed at us when we get there?"

"I'm hoping things will be different there, isn't it supposed to be a place of peace?" I said.

The men that were left leaderless started firing blindly into the desert.

"I'm thinking," I continued "That it's like God has three sons, Israel, Islam, and..."

"Wait," Cali said, "The Bible says that Christians are the Bride of Christ, so..."

"Okay," I said, "God has two sons and a daughter, and God loves us all the same, and we love him, but we hate each other, and are always asking God to give us the whole inheritance and cut the others out. I mean if God's a loving God, what's He supposed to do with a bratty bunch of kids like us?"

Their confusion had the desired effect, bringing out the higher-ranking commanders who tried to mobilize them. The rest started to retreat to more defensible positions. That was the cue for the rangers to attack.

I searched our guys checking night scope markers, all good.

"I don't know," Cali said, "I never thought about it that way, but it's a good thing that I'm not God because I'd probably get rid of us all and adopt the Buddhists, at least they seem to be able to get along."

I kept watch, but with the low vantage point, there was not much I could do because the fighting was too close.

"Castor, I can't get clear shots around our people, I'm not much help here." I warned.

"Thanks for the heads up," he answered, "Let's pack up and go home, guys, we did what we came for." They pulled back and I covered them as they pulled out, firing to keep the hostiles from advancing. We packed up and pulled out quickly before the remnants could regroup.

The night was cold, and there was a lot of sand kicking up as we headed back to base. I wrapped myself up tight in the scarf as the desert flew by. My earlier conversation about Winfield popped into my head. There were a lot of people who'd been very helpful and kind. What about Stacy, and Robin, and even Murdock, I should write to them and let them know that I'm okay, even if I couldn't tell them what I was doing. But what would they think of me if they knew? I had to almost laugh, what would Reaper think if he knew I was actually doing what he was always talking about doing? I don't think he really wanted the reality of death and killing, he only wanted the shock value, and the power that came with talking about it. Was what I was doing really helping? Were the people in Winfield really safer now than they were an hour ago, before the terrorist base was attacked?

21

I would not get a chance to write home.

"Everybody up, we need to move, it's getting too hot here." Sergeant McGrath announced.

We were up and packing, taking care of our tent first. Emptied, pulled up and packed; everything was loaded on the central large hovercraft, a conversion of the Navy's LCAC. It resembled a large flat bed trailer with a cab on the front right corner. In the back there were two large propellers.

Captain Carver and Sergeant McGrath roved the camp directing traffic. Each group handled their own stuff as Cowgirl directed Georgia and me, making sure that all of the sniper rifle ammunition and maintenance equipment was accounted for, working with the dim red LED lights and lanterns. As we secured the packing crates, Sergeant McGrath ordered each of us to equip ourselves with an M110 and 4 magazines for the trip, in case we needed firepower. We were given 5 minutes to ready the weapons and zero sites at 600 meters. Georgia was assigned to the LCAC, while Cowgirl went on Castor's craft and I went with Pollux. By this time, the rangers were pulling in the netting, the last thing to stow on the flat bed.

"Bundle up," Barbie told me, "This is going to get messy." I tied my hair back in a ponytail, secured the com set, eye protection, gauze face and neck protection, then helmet. Looking over at Barbie, I said,

"I feel like one of the Tatooine Sand People."

"Well, up on your bantha then, princess." She picked me up, tossing me like baggage to Markley who was already on the hovercraft, my feet never touching the rail. He carried me on his hip like I was a child.

"Hey, Markley," Pollux said, "If that's Skank, I want her in the saddle."

"Got it, boss," he said, walked aft, and tossed me up to a perch atop the engine hump.

"Buckle up, Skank. I don't want to lose you in the dark." Pollux said. There was actually a small seat and foot pegs. I situated myself and got buckled in. Markley handed up my 110. I held it vertical with a stock between my legs, rather unladylike, but I wanted to make sure that I didn't swing around and whack anyone with it. Pollux called roll, making sure we were all accounted for, then called it into Carver on the LC. "We're a go for launch." I felt the turbine wind up underneath me, then the pop and rumble as the burners ignited. Another few seconds, and we lifted off. We drifted around the LC, seeing only the indicator lights and one or two red LED flashlights as they readied for liftoff. Once we were in front and to their left, they started their props. The LC was by no means stealth technology. We heard the huge fans spin up over our quiet whine.

"Skank and Cowgirl, keep your eyes on, you're our early warning for ground troops. Stay alert." The Captain said as we started moving. Barbie showed me how to release the swivel lock so that I could get a 360 degree view. Shooting at moving targets was one thing, shooting moving targets from a moving vehicle... that, I'd never tried before. I did an NV scan of the horizon. Everything looked clear. I felt our speed pick up, and, looking around, I could clearly see the other small craft to our right with Cowgirl in the saddle looking very much like the Tusken Raider I joked about earlier. Behind and to our right was the LC moving between us in formation. It was hard to guess our speed, but it looked at least 30 if not 40 miles per hour.

I'm not sure why, now that I made my living by killing people, life was so much more fun, was I really that sick? Was it that I secretly enjoyed it, and I was deceiving myself? I didn't think so. To be honest, I think it was the other way around, the fact that I could die at any minute, made life that much more adventurous. As I scanned into the darkness with the NV scope, I began to fantasize about what it would be like to be shot, feeling a twinge in my nether region as I imagined a bullet going through my breast and into my heart. What would it be like to come home in a box, would people say nice things about me? I wondered if I would get to see it.

After another hour, the sky to the east began to lighten. Satellite imaging showed possible regular army activity close by, and radar picked up possible aircraft. It was decided that the best course of action was to tuck ourselves into the wall of an eroded riverbed, cover with the netting, and wait out the daylight instead of chancing travel. We all helped spread out the netting, hoping we blended well enough to not be seen. Breakfast was MREs and sleep was wherever it could be found under the netting. I found Cali in the LC, asleep on a storage locker, and decided not to disturb her. Instead, I found my own box and tucked myself into the jail cell position. Just watching her sleep filled me with joy that I could have a friend like her, someone whose eyes light up just because they see you.

I was awakened in the early afternoon by Sergeant McGrath, "We picked up a possible contact, a lone vehicle about 2000 meters west, heading this way in the riverbed." He wanted me awake and alert in case my services were needed. I did some jumping jacks and gathered my 110, switched to daylight optics, and climbed to the highest point on the LC where I could find an opening in the netting. I scoped out the oncoming vehicle. It was an ancient land rover. After a minute, I could make out the occupants.

"Single Land Rover, three occupants, they appear to be European, two men, one woman." I reported.

McGrath climbed to my vantage point, "Are you kidding?" he asked. Using his own optics, he checked, "Shit, you're right, what the hell are they doing here?"

"I don't know, but I'm sure not going to whack a bunch of archeologists who are just out looking for the lost ark."

"Well, we can't let them find us, it's not like the US Army is supposed to be here."

"How quickly can we look like mercenaries?"

"Too long," he said, looking through the scope again, "But it wouldn't take too long to make some of us look like mercenaries, stay here, keep us covered, oh, and could you take out a tire from here in..." he looked at his watch,"2 minutes?" I checked my watch.

"Cake, sergeant, I hope they have a spare."

He climbed down and gathered Barbie, Markley, Castor and Pollux. I watched the Land Rover come. I could tell they were talking, or arguing would be closer to the truth. I was about to make their bad day a little worse. Times up, I took aim at the right front tire, ticked off a lead, and felt the kick. A second later, dust burst from the tire, and the front of the vehicle took a dive. The younger man who was driving was clearly not happy as he stepped out, walked around the front to inspect the tire, throwing his hat on the ground in frustration. It was clear they did not know they had just been fired upon. Two minutes later, I saw him look up, and checked what he was looking at as the four McGrath picked approach, their outfits modified, not four people I'd like to meet in a trackless desert. There was a conversation. The short of it was, they were our guests at a decoy camp for the day; in return we gave them food, water, and fixed their tire.

Later that evening, they were driven blind-folded past our hiding spot and told to continue on their way, with the warning that the same person who shot out their tire from a kilometer away would be watching that they went in the right direction. I watched them go in the scope. They had no interest in turning around to check us out. When our four mercenaries returned, we were ready to head out.

An hour later we turned northwest away from the river valley. Captain Carver came on the comm. "Things are getting very hot around here, but there is one more base we would like to hit, therefore, if everyone is in, we are going to try to do the hit tonight." I heard the confirmations come in from the Zombie crew; I actually wasn't sure if I would get a vote, but after hearing Cali give her affirmative, so did I. "Good," Carver continued, once all the votes were in, "We will stop at 21:00 do a quick survey of the target, if all looks good, we will go, if anyone has any reservations, it's off. If we go, the LC will turn south towards the extraction zone, we will take the stealth craft to the hit and catch up to the LC afterwards, planning session in 45 minutes, out."

The meeting was held on the deck of the LC. Tech crew hills were chosen; Cali and mine was 900 meters northeast of the target. It looked rocky, but useable. There was concern on The Captain's face, but we were all in. The attack craft were fueled and loaded; Cali and I went on the craft driven by Pollux.

22

It took less than an hour to get to our site. In reality, it looked worse than the imaging showed; the top of the outcrop was not large enough to provide cover, so we had to position in front of it, blocking our retreat to the rear. We set up and checked the base station. The systems check indicated everything was good. A scan of the target base showed normal nighttime activity, a few lights and sentries. All the tech teams checked in, and the attack crews checked in. "Gophers away," Cali confirmed, as I continued to scan. No contacts showed outside the camp. 8 minutes later, the gophers were placed without incident.

"Caster's worried," Cali whispered, "He's not his usual self; he thinks something is wrong."

But he started the countdown, "In five, four, three, two, down."

I went to work looking for likely targets. The usual chaos was not happening, only a few people running from the destroyed buildings.

Castor came on the com, "Stay put, guys. Something looks wrong."

I continued to scope the camp.

"Shit!" Cali yelled, "Shit, shit, shit, shit, shit."

"What Cali, what's happening?" I said. I heard Cali start firing.

"We're under attack; there are a lot of them."

I didn't want to give up on the primary target, but asked "You need help, Cali?"

"I'm not hitting them, they're still coming."

"We under attack, defending our position." I announced over the com, and started backing up Cali.

"Cali! Breathe, think Zen, Cali, think Zen." I heard them open fire.

"Zen? These are people, not paper."

I didn't want to use the machine analogy on Cali again. Bullets started hitting the sand in front of us and pinging the rocks behind us. I could feel her calming down breathing like she was giving birth.

Psych came on the com, "We're taking fire, Georgia's been hit, we need help."

"How you doing, Cali? Do you need me? If not, I want to back up Psych and Georgia, I can see their hill from here and Cowgirl can't."

Rounds continued to hit around us, the Gopher controller took a hit.

"I'm good, Skank, help Psych." Cali said, continuing to fire, seemingly less panicked.

Psych and Georgia's hill was more to my right, so that I had to reposition to get a clear shot at the men who were fanned out in front of their position.

Castor came on the com, "Abort the attack, go help the tech crews." he was telling the rangers. "Cali, Skank, what's your status?"

"We're taking fire, but so far so good," I said still defending Psych's hill. "Get Psych and Georgia first."

Soon I could see our guys flank the men attacking Psych's position, getting them in crossfire as they closed in. I had to back off. Turning my attention to help Cali, it was worse than she had let on, they were close less than 200 meters, within effective range of their AKs.

I could feel my heart beating and hear Cali breathing, telling me that we were both still alive. Together, we were doing better until I emptied my last clip for the 110.

"Cali, I'm out" I said, "can you hold out?"

"Shit, Skank, can you take over? I'm still not hitting."

"Okay," I said, rolling up next to her. I could feel her panic as she passed me the 417. One rifle was not going to be enough to hold out for much longer.

Pollux was on again saying. "We have Psych and Georgia, and are heading for Cali and Skank."

Castor answered. "We have Jarvis and Cowgirl, how's Georgia, do you need assistance?"

"Georgia's bad, don't take the time to come around, we should have Cali in 2. Cali, are you guys still okay?"

"We have only one rifle, but holding our own for now, they are coming from the south and southwest slopes, in two groups, so be careful." Cali informed them.

"Got it, just hang on."

A few tense minutes later, I could see our guys advancing towards those who were attacking us. Once the attackers saw they were being surrounded, they quickly retreated for the camp.

"All clear," I heard Markley report, "Meet you at Cali's position." Cali and I collapsed with relief. Soon, we heard the rushing whine of the hovercraft as everyone congregated on our hill. We quickly packed up and boarded the craft, knowing that it would not take long for the attackers to regroup and be after us again. Once everyone was accounted for, we headed out.

Pollux informed us that Georgia was gone, I felt bad that I'd never really gotten to know her. I didn't know what she was like; I didn't even know why she was called Georgia. I felt sure that somewhere, there was someone on the planet that loved her, and was going to miss her. Was she in that same room with all those people I just killed, waiting to see God? Was God on our side, or on their side? Was he grieved for what we've all done, or just happy to welcome them all home? The stars continued to shine overhead as we met with Castor's hovercraft, traveling together, chasing the LC towards departure point.

Castor reported in to Captain Carver, "Mission aborted before completion, Georgia lost, all others accounted for and safe. Inflicted heavy damage, covered our tracks, heading to departure point ETA 4 hours."

"Castor, what happened?" Carver asked.

"Men were hidden in the sands around their camp; they must have heard what was happening to the other camps and hid people away from the main camp. They attacked two of the three tech crews after the gophers were detonated. We diverted the rangers to rescue the techs." Castor answered.

"Continue to coast departure point, we will meet you before we get there. The ship will meet us past the twelve mile point." Carver replied.

"We may not have the range to meet the ship."

"If we have to, we'll drop the stealth craft in the ocean. We're pushing daylight, I don't want to stop for refueling."

"Aye, captain." Castor answered.

I sat in the saddle, scanning the horizon, still holding the empty 110. Georgia was lying covered with a survival blanket in the spot on the deck where I usually sat. Do killers like me have any right to feel sad? Didn't the people I killed have anyone who loved them also?

But it was not like we were attacking schools, airplanes, or office buildings. They viewed us as so evil that even our children deserved to die at their hands. We used that for proof that they were evil, giving us the right, or responsibility, to go into their country to stop them. Are either of us correct?

Look at Mr. Fallow, his bank has billions, and he probably has millions, and I'd lost everything except the $5,000 I took so long to save. Yet, he took it as his right to have that money, with no thought of what happened to me. I'm a citizen of his own country, what would he do to these people if given a chance, sell their children into slavery? Are there Mr. Fallows doing that right now? Is that the real reason why they hate us?

What would I do if I were asked to do an assault on his house, to take him out through one of his windows from three blocks away? Would I feel anything then?

Why do I find it so easy to trample on the 6th commandment? Do Muslims even have the same commandments? If I'm killing them, perhaps I should at least look that up. We can justify anything, but is God convinced?

At least the parking lot bullies and Mr. Fallow make no attempt to slide their behavior by God, for them, it's their right to take what they can. Is their pure Darwinism, survival of the fittest, unburdened by excuses and mental calisthenics to wash the blood from their hands better than us, who come whining before God? Maybe hell for Mr. Fallow is a place where his clothes are no nicer or his house no more opulent than a skanky girl like me. Maybe God has the last laugh with all his bratty children by making us all live together forever in a place where it is impossible for us to kill each other.

23

Carver came on the com link, "Latest navy recon shows activity on the coast road that we need to cross to get to our departure point, we are going to have to detour about 20 clicks to the east, what is your fuel status?"

"We won't make the coast with that much additional travel." Castor replied.

"Then we will need to do a fueling stop and hope we don't get caught, we can't leave the stealth craft where even a hint of them can be found."

"I have an idea that may minimize damage." McGrath said.

"Let's hear it," the captain said.

"We stop and refuel as soon as we meet while still in darkness. During that time, we transfer all of the incriminating technology and equipment to the stealth craft, they are faster and lighter, and have more chance of getting out undetected."

"That leaves the LC exposed with a good chance of getting caught." The captain answered.

"Yes, but it would be less incriminating, seeming more like illegal naval recon on foreign soil than an attack using secret technology, an embarrassment, but not a disaster."

"Not much better, but let me clear it with the navy to make sure they can get a cover story if they have to."

There was silence for a while as we changed course to make the detour. The possibility of being a female prisoner in an Islamic country while government officials in cushy offices haggled the finer details of saving face didn't sound very appealing. I was sure that in my case, torture would be in my future. I was still contemplating the specifics when the answer came back. The sacrificial plan was accepted, we would rendezvous in 20 minutes to make the change.

The perimeter was verified clear, and then the craft were powered down for refueling and transfer. The gopher tech, sniper, and foreign rifles were loaded onto the stealth craft along with all the supporting equipment and maintenance parts. The camo netting and the empty fuel bladders were going to be the biggest problem. The bladders were divided between the stealth craft. The camo netting was just too large and would have to stay with the LC. Even so they were both overloaded, with no space for any crew besides the driver. The only other passenger would be Georgia. The surface to air missile system would also remain with the LC. Although not standard issue for a navy LC, it was not secret technology.

We watched the two stealth craft fade into the darkness, and then converted ourselves back into regulation military with standard issue M4s. With Sergeant McGrath driving, the LC erased our tracks and we headed south east towards the new departure point. The last hour of darkness passed. So far, so good. There were contacts, both ground and air, in the area, but they did not seem to be showing any interest in us. The eastern sky began to lighten while we were just under an hour from the coast. Captain Carver relayed the message that both the other hovercraft had crossed the beach, undetected, and had met the ship for pickup. That part of the plan had gone well. Now, it was up to us. The sky turned from indigo blue to pink as the sun peeked over the eastern horizon, setting the desert sands ablaze in red. We were maddeningly close. I could smell the salty ocean mists in the air, reminding me of morning camping at Hammonasset State Beach on Long

Island sound when I was 16, with dreams of finding a summer romance. Now, I was hoping that our flight to freedom would find more success than I had that summer.

Captain Carver announced that there were vehicles showing on the radar along the coast road. He was not sure of the type, although it looked like small vehicle traffic, and not a heavy Army convoy. There were also military aircraft, uncomfortably close, that, if redirected, could reach us before we would be under the protection of the Navy destroyer. So there was a risk either way; be seen by some locals who would have a story to tell, or be engaged by military aircraft. We unanimously chose to get out quickly, therefore, the plan was to turn south at the next available slot between obstacles to the coast.

We guessed wrong. The vehicles were not local civilians on the way to Starbucks before work, but the ubiquitous terrorist pickup truck with mounted machine guns in the bed. We crossed the road in a storm of blowing sand, right in the middle of them. Their tire-screeching, truck-swerving confusion lasted only a second before they bounded over the shoulder onto the beach, spraying us with machine gun fire. Everybody hit the deck. I was happy to see Cali make it safely behind the heavy left engine mount. I crawled to the stern between the two large fans and started to return fire. We were now over water, and I could feel the craft pick up speed over the less resistant surface. I continued to concentrate on the lead trucks, mostly just keeping them pinned.

Cali screamed, "Rocket!" I felt a weight slam down on top of me, and then Atlas slipped and dropped the world onto the hard concrete floor of the universe. Everything went dark and silent.

It was such a beautiful morning; the sun sprinkling gold flecks on the wave tops of the dark blue water. The sky was clear, and the desert, a painted backdrop of colored bands. When I looked down, I could see the LC sitting on a bright white cloud of sea spray, safely out of range of the men on shore, still forging ahead despite the wounded left fan. The trailing smoke blending into the clear sky, I knew in my heart the people that I'd come to love would soon be safe in the Navy ship. They were congregating in a semi circle around two people lying on the deck. I could feel Cali here with me and was joyful, thinking that we would both see God together. Suddenly, I was yanked away, back into darkness.

I opened my eyes to jumbled chaos, seeing Castor's face, feeling his hands on me like he had just reached into the dream and pulled me out. I was angry at him because it had been so peaceful and safe. There was still a deathly silence, and I was beginning to panic, knowing something was terribly wrong, but not knowing what it was. I became aware of a growing sound; it started low, then increased. Soon, it sounded like an endless field of angry crickets sawing their legs in mad abandon. More faces materialized, all showing concern as they looked down at me. I wanted to help, but I didn't know what to do. As my mind cleared, I realized I wasn't breathing, I had forgotten how to breathe. I didn't know what to do to start up again, it was like the air was stuck and wouldn't fit into my lungs. Castor reached down and restarted me. I coughed and gasped back to life, desperately trying to get enough air, the concern in the eyes all around me changing to relief. Pain started filling my body. My chest hurt, my joints hurt, my leg hurt, like a volume control being turned up to unbearable levels. I tried to tell them, but I still couldn't hear because of the crickets. The white mist returned, and everything faded away.

150

I woke up in the Washington hospital, the crickets melding into the rhythmic beep of the blue box on the pole. Was that all just a long, strange dream? No, this wasn't Washington; the ceiling was white metal and pipes, not acoustical tile. There wasn't a nurse in the room, but a sailor in a light blue denim shirt. He was checking stuff, facing away from me at first. Then he turned, saw that my eyes were open, "Well, good afternoon, sleepy head, glad to see you are back with us." I'm not sure if it's correct to call a man beautiful, but this guy was; young, clean, very well groomed. Even in his navy work uniform he looked well dressed, his white navy hat at just the right angle on his head. His voice was soft spoken and gentle.

"Where's Cali?" I asked.

"I'm afraid I don't know what you mean," he answered.

"Morgan Troas, where's Morgan Troas?" I repeated.

"I'm afraid I can't tell you, you will have to ask the doctor," he said.

I was getting the idea that the dream that I could still remember quite clearly was not a dream at all. I had a bad feeling that I already knew the answer to my question, I just didn't want to face it. My eyes were clouding up, and it was getting harder to breathe.

"Hey, hey, no crying," the sailor said, coming over to me, "Tough army women aren't supposed to cry."

I could tell he was getting very uncomfortable. He started to leave, but I didn't want him to go. "Wait!" I said, "I'm sorry," He turned to look at me.

"Could you at least tell me if I still have all my body parts?" I asked, struggling to get myself back under control.

He smiled and walked towards the bed, "Yes, all your body parts are just where they should be, you had a bad concussion, and there's a pretty nasty gash on your right calf, but you're all sewn up now, and you'll be as good as new. So, what were all you poor lost souls doing way out in the ocean on that hovercraft, anyway?"

"I'm afraid I can't tell you that, you'll have to talk to my boss." I answered.

"Touché." he said as he gathered up some items and left through the curtain that closed me off from the rest of the room.

Maybe I did know the answer, but I needed to hear it from somebody anyway, and this lying here was going to drive me crazy if I had to do it for very long. I pulled up the sheet to get a look at my leg. My toes and feet were still there, but my right leg was bandaged from knee to ankle. How bad could it be, then? I tried to lift my leg to get a better look, and a searing bolt of lightning went from my foot to my butt... Pretty bad, I discovered. I gently rested it back down, deciding that getting up and trying to find someone was out of the question.

I suppose it really wasn't that long in normal person time before the doctor came in; it just seemed like half a semester. He looked up from his clipboard, "How are we doing today, specialist, that leg hurting some?" He said, seeing that the covers were pulled up.

"No, not too bad," I answered.

"You didn't try and move it, did you?"

"No, well yes, maybe a little," I answered.

"Army people, they can never leave anything alone. There's going to be plenty of time for us to torture you back to health. For now, just enjoy the bed rest."

"Where's Cali, I mean, Morgan Troas?" I asked.

"There are some people here who want to see you, more Army people, I wouldn't let them in if I was you, but if you really want to see them, I'll send them in."

"Yes, please, send them in." I said anxiously.

The doctor opened the curtain and the Zombies started coming in; Castor, Markley, Cowgirl, Pollux, Psych, Captain Carver, even Jarvis peeked around the corner, but no Cali.

"McGrath wanted to be here, but he doesn't do the hospital thing." Castor said. "You know, you gave us quite a scare."

I really did appreciate them being here, but my heart was hurting.

"Hi guys, thank you, is everybody okay, no problems?" I made the mistake of making eye contact with Cowgirl. I don't know anyone more clear-headed and stoic than her, but I could see the corners of her eyes start to glisten with tears.

"The doc says you're going to be fine, they had to stitch you back up a little, but just do what he says and you'll be back in no time." Captain Carver said.

"We want you back," Pollux said "So you get better."

Everyone nodded in agreement and tried to smile, but I could see the rain clouds gathering. I turned to the Captain, "Please tell me, sir, where's Cali?"

He motioned the others out; they all waved and smiled as they left through the curtain.

"Listen, Millie," he started, "there was nothing they could do for her here; she was airlifted back to Kuwait." He paused, "Cali didn't make it; we got word that she died on the way."

"But what happened? She was okay, she was behind the motor."

"Even if she had stayed there, that was right behind where the RPG hit, she would have been killed."

"What do you mean, even if she stayed there?"

"You need to understand, you would have been killed also."

"Why, what happened? Please tell me."

He took a breath. "She threw herself on top of you to protect you from the blast."

"But why, didn't she understand?"

"Understand what, Millie?"

"That I don't want to live without her."

"Would you let her die, if you could save her?"

"No, but, she had friends, and family, people who love her, people waiting for her to come home, I don't, no one waits for me to come home."

"But she loved you too, Millie."

"But there's a whole group of people in southern California, all woven together, and she was a part of it, now because of me, there is a hole in their community that can never be filled."

"First of all, it is not because of you, Millie. She, of her own free will, knowing she was dead anyway, decided to sacrifice herself so that you might live, and you know very well you would have done the same for her."

"BUT I DON'T DESERVE IT!"

"How could any of us ever deserve it? That's not the point, now is it? She gave you a chance to live because she was your friend, now it's up to you to use what she gave you in a way that honors her."

I had no answer for that, but I'm not sure I felt any better, "I'm sorry, sir."

"Now you just rest up and get better, we're all here for you, okay?"

"Okay, thanks, sir." He put his hand on my shoulder then left the room.

"I miss you, Cali," I said out loud then cried myself to sleep.

24

When the doctor said they would have plenty of time to torture me back to health, I thought he was kidding. The physical therapy revealed the truth in what he said. It took three days to get to Kuwait. By that time, I was, still not allowed to put weight on my right leg. I was transferred from the ship to a Kuwaiti civilian hospital that had space reserved for US servicemen. After two days there, I was taken to the US base in Kuwait. After another week, I was given light duty and regular upper body exercises. The light duty was going from building to building delivering files, which I imagine was quite comical to watch, me trying to operate crutches and carry files. Only the Army could think up such a recovery program.

At 23:30 the next week, I was awakened by Cowgirl, Psych, Castor, Pollux, and Captain Carver coming to visit.

Castor said, "Sorry about the late visit, but we wanted to get a chance to visit before we left, we are all being deployed, going off to places unknown for other duties we can't talk about." Although judging from the latest news reports I was pretty sure I knew where that was.

Cowgirl gave me a hug. "You know, you're okay for an easterner." she said, as Psych hugged me.

"Yeah," she said, "not bad for a Yankee."

"Sorry you can't come with us this time just get better." Said Pollux.

Captain Carver said, "There's something we wanted to share with you before we left, if you would come with us." I gingerly got my crutches and started after them down the hall to what looked like a small sitting room with a large

155

flat panel monitor. There was a tech person there who had just got things working. There were a few other people in the room watching. On the screen was a view of Arlington National Cemetery.

"This is Georgia and Cali's burial," the Captain whispered to me. We watched as a the procession slowly moved through the gathered crowd, past the Westboro protesters and onto the grounds. I stood there in silence, not caring that the crutches were uncomfortable. At one point, a man in civilian clothes offered me a seat, but I refused. I watched as the Vice President offered a eulogy for those who gave their life for their country. Then, a list of at least a dozen names was read, and nothing could keep from crying when he said Morgan May Troas. When he was done, I realized I'd never known Georgia's real name.

After it was all over, they started to leave, but I stopped the captain, and asked, "Will her family ever know how she died? That she gave her life for me?"

"They know that she's a hero and gave her life to save another, but they never knew about you, I'm afraid."

"What, but why? She wrote letters about me." Another man walked over to us. It took me a minute to recognize him as the same marine captain who "shot" me after my last assignment. He motioned to Captain Carver. I got a chance to say goodbye to Castor, Pollux, Cowgirl, and Psych. The two Captains saluted and Carver departed. The Marine Captain had everyone else clear the room. He closed the door after everyone left.

"First, I'm so sorry for the loss of your friend Cali, I understand she meant a lot to you." He said.

"Thank you, sir." I answered.

"But the problem is, Millie, that we couldn't have her saying anything about you to the people back home," he slipped a DVD into a player that was connected to the monitor, "Because, as you will see, you're dead. We intercepted this from Al Jazera three weeks ago." The DVD started playing, it was a little jerky at first, then settled down, but it clearly showed me with my army jacket torn open and hair down, being dragged from that gray stone building that I defended in Afghanistan. I was dumped face down on the ground where I stayed amid the jeers of the crowd gathered in the square. A Humvee drove up and I was dumped into the back. Then the view shifted to a grainy scene shot from a distance that showed the driver dragging me out of the vehicle, then the Captain getting out and shooting me as I tried to scuttle away. I was surprised at how realistic it looked. He shut off the playback.

"I have to commend you, Specialist Willard; you are a very good actress. During the hearing investigating the incident, the experts staked their reputation on it being real."

"But you didn't tell everyone it wasn't true, that I wasn't really dead?"

"Oh no, big embarrassment to the Army too, your old Lieutenant tried to tell everyone it was faked, but you know, the Army just couldn't seem to find you anymore. There are still investigations going on, but everyone is convinced that you're dead."

"But why?" I protested.

"And your old home town was all up in arms that one of their star daughters was treated so shamefully."

"Huh, they all hated me when I was alive."

"Oh yeah, some attorney, a Mr. Fallow demanded restitution."

"What!"

He laughed, "Winfield is getting a brand new courthouse, with Mr. Fallow, as the new chief prosecutor, getting a rather lavish new office out of the deal."

"Chief prosecutor?"

"Yes, seems he got fired from his old job, something about losing $25,000 of the bank's money. Anyway he's making out like a bandit over your death."

"That fucker, are they going to name it after me?"

"No." he said in mock disappointment, "You get your name on a plaque to be installed at a later date."

"What about you, aren't you up for killing me?"

"Well, no, it seems they can't find me either. Believe me, we didn't plan it this way, we had no idea it would come out on video, but seeing that it did, we didn't want to pass up the opportunity."

"Opportunity, what opportunity?"

"Go ahead and watch the rest of the video, there's a lot more on there, seems you're the most popular dead girl since Marilyn Monroe, we'll talk later. " He turned and left before I had a chance to ask any more questions.

It's too bad I wasn't really dead, if I were I could be with Cali right now instead of in this strange limbo. Some strange non person to be used for whatever some shadow organization sees fit. And what "opportunity" would that be? Isn't it obvious, I have only one real skill. I can kill people from a long ways away. Is this why Cali died, so I could go on killing people? I hope Cali doesn't have to wait too long to see me again.

I pushed play on the machine; the next section was an NBC news broadcast.

"A disturbing video was intercepted from Al Jazera yesterday that reportedly shows a US Marine officer shooting and killing a female US soldier. The video shows the woman, an Army E4, being dragged from a building, and dumped into the back of an Army vehicle. A second section shows her pulled out of the vehicle, thrown to the ground, and shot execution style by what appears to be a Marine officer. The Army denies that the incident is real." They didn't show the video.

The next was from CNN, "Now, more on the reported execution of a female US soldier." They actually showed the video. "The US soldier who was shown executed in the Al Jazera video has been identified as SPC-E4 Millicent Willard from Winfield Connecticut. The Army indicates that there was a Millicent Willard stationed in Afghanistan, but was reassigned to Kuwait, and that she is very much alive."

CNN again this time, with a "Where's Millie" backdrop, "Three days after the reported executed soldier was identified, the Army has yet to locate her." It went on with an interview of an Army Coronel, "Obviously, we do not go around executing soldiers on the spot, no matter what the reason." I felt bad for him, he was a victim of some secret plot, and I felt bad that the Army, that had treated me so well, was now being trashed on national television. They certainly did not deserve this.

There was even a nightline panel discussion between a bunch of talking heads who didn't know anything about any part of what really happened, pontificating on the guilt of the American Military and how these kinds of things probably happened all the time. It made me sick to watch it, none of these people knew me, and if they did, they certainly wouldn't have given me the time of day. Now that everyone thinks I'm dead, all of a sudden I'm a hero? There are real heroes lying in graves that gave their lives so that others could live, and they're blathering on about me, a cold-blooded killer. The announcer went on, asking,

"Will we ever know what really happened to Millie Willard?"

I couldn't take any more and started to fast-forward, but stopped when I saw a familiar face. Backing it up, I started at the beginning. It was Mr. Fallow, standing in front of a vacant, snow-covered lot.

"Millicent Abigail Willard was one of our own, who, after the unfortunate death of her father, went to serve her country. She trained hard, did her job well, and believed in what she was doing. She went off to war trusting in those who sent her." I wonder how much it pained him to say nice things about me. "But that trust was betrayed when her life was taken from her by the very people who sent her, so we dedicate this new courthouse in her memory, and the memory of all the great men and women who have been nurtured by our wonderful community."

I felt sick; probably the only thing he felt bad about was missing the opportunity to pull the trigger himself. I turned it off and ejected the DVD. Was I really worth all this trouble?

25

It wasn't long before I was back in training; formations, marches, running obstacle courses, and there was shooting practice, only this time it was with all different types of sniper hardware. Besides the familiar M107 and M110, there was a German Heckler & Koch PSG1, a British Accuracy International AS50, and a Russian Dragunov SVD and SVDS.

On the morning of March 9, 2011, exactly 11 months after my father was murdered, I was told to clean up and report to the HQ of Camp Arifjan. I was directed to the office of the base commander. Waiting for me there was Coronel Martin Hothmeyer and the Marine Captain in civilian clothes.

"Specialist Millicent Willard?"

"Yes, sir."

"I'm sorry to say that you will be leaving us, you have been of great service to the Army and to your country, but you are being reassigned to another branch of service that has a greater need of your services."

"Thank you sir, but what branch is that?"

"I will let Mr. Ted Haal explain, but I will need to collect your identification tags and card."

"Sir, but...?" It was in the Army that my life really started, now it was hard to give it up.

"I can understand your reluctance, Specialist, but you will still be serving your country in a much more important role."

"Yes, sir." I reluctantly handed over my tags and ID.

"Mr. Haal, the office is yours." The Colonel left the office.

"I hope you're ready to say goodbye to your old life," Ted Haal said, handing me a document envelop, "Go ahead, open it, it's your new life."

I pulled out a Canadian Passport, a birth certificate, a driver's license, and a Canadian social security card, along with other booklets and a DVD.

"You are now Laura Peddington from Vancouver BC, Canada. Nice city, there's some information about it in there and on the DVD, get to know about yourself. It even shows where your family's house is located. Don't try to call home, however, because they don't really exist, house burned down last year, very tragic. You're now a cultural anthropology student taking some time to study other cultures. Did you take any anthropology, Laura? Laura?"

"What, oh yeah, just biological anthropology in junior college, I needed a science lab class, it was supposed to be the easiest," I answered.

"Good, remember any?"

"Huh, oh yeah, just that we're primates."

"Good, close enough."

"What, wait, what do you mean new life?"

"Well you can't be Millicent Willard anymore, she's dead, remember?"

"Yes, but who are you, and who am I working for?"

"I am with an organization that has been following your Army career with great interest, and is very pleased with your progress. As to who we are, let's just say that we're a well known intelligence organization and we are very involved in protecting our nation."

"But then, why am I Canadian?"

"People don't like Americans, we would have preferred British or Dutch, but you can't do the accent, can you?"

"No, but…"

"And I'm afraid German is out, people hate them too. Come on." he handed up a duffle bag, "Get dressed. You have a plane to catch, if you don't like the clothes, you can go shopping in Ankara."

"Ankara…"

"Ankara, Turkey, we have a little job for you there, real easy, then it's on to our field office in Bonn. You'll get to meet the rest of the crew, you'll like them."

He opened the door to a back room where I could change.

"You know," I said as I went inside, "I think it's pretty nasty what you did to the Army, I mean, they've always been good to me." I left the door open a crack so I could hear his answer. "I hope I'm worth it."

"Don't worry about the Army, they can take it, most of those guys you heard on the video know all about you, except for your old Lieutenant, that is, and he was kind of an ass anyway. And you, my dear, from what I've heard, are worth your weight in gold. We haven't had a shooter like you since that guy Karr retired."

The bag contained jeans, a white cotton button-front shirt, and a high-wasted copper colored jacket. There was also tie-front brown leather boots, underwear, and accessories, including a small outdoorsy backpack with 2008 Winter Olympics patches. Peeing and dressing, I began stuffing my new identity into the backpack.

"I'm going to Turkey dressed like this?" I asked, walking back into the larger front room still looking through the backpack that also contained another change of clothes and a small portable video player.

"What's wrong with that? You look great."

"Isn't Turkey a Muslim country?"

"Don't worry about the clothes, Turkey is very westernized. You didn't put your identification in the pack, did you?"

"Yes, why…"

He took the backpack from me, pulled out the ID then undid the belt from around my waist.

"Because you have to put it in here," he showed me a pocket in the belt, "If you want to keep it." He said as he tucked them into the opening. "Oh, and here," he said, handing me a Master Card, "Now, there is some discretionary leeway, so go ahead and do a little shopping, but this is not chart blanche, you do have to account for your expenditures. We'll talk about it more when we get to Germany, but for now you need to make your plane, I'm not traveling with you because we can't be seen together."

I followed him out of the room onto the base grounds. Watching the troops go about their duties made me sad to know it was all ending for me.

"Will I ever be buried anywhere? I mean, Millicent Willard; will she ever have a marker or anything?"

I followed him to a dark-colored, official looking car, "You know, maybe we can talk about that too, I think you- I mean, she, deserves one."

An hour later, I was sitting in the large commercial Lufthansa airplane, looking out the window, bound for Ankara, Turkey. When I was in junior high, the thing I always wanted most was a new life. I would look up places on the map and go onto the internet to find out everything I could about them, wondering what it would be like to grow up there instead of where I was. It wasn't that I didn't love my father, I did, but I still always wanted to be someone else. Now it was happening, but my old life

164

had disappeared much too quickly and I was given no chance to say goodbye.

During the flight, I watched the video that was made like a home movie of my life in Vancouver. There was also a cell phone with text messages, telling me to look for someone at the airport who would be carrying a sign with my name on it. It was a short flight, and I barely got through the information before I had to stow my electronic devices for landing.

After the plane pulled into the gate, I waited patiently for the mad crush of deplaning passengers to subside, then walked from the plane into the terminal. Sure enough, there was short, dark man with a large mustache waiting for me at the gate. He had on a mixture of western and Arabic clothing. Most everyone else was dressed in completely western styles, including the women.

"Ah, you must be Laura Peddington," he said as I walked tentatively up to him, he continued, "Hello, I am Faruk Zala, so happy to see you, come this way please," shaking my hand vigorously as he spoke. We took a taxi from the airport into the city of Ankara. I was expecting another dry desert with sand and palm trees, but instead it was more European looking, with trees everywhere, just budding for early spring. By next month, it would be a beautiful, lush, green city of light adobe colored buildings and red tiled roofs.

"Beautiful city," I remarked.

"What, were you expecting more desert and sand? You Americans, all the same, and don't say you're Canadian, don't insult me, I know better."

"Sorry, I was only trying to say it's nice, that's all." I said, neither confirming nor denying anything about my nationality.

"Ah, come, we are here." We walked along a street of older buildings, with street level shops, until he found a door to a stairway next to a shop displaying musical instruments. At the top of the stairs, there was a front to back hallway. He knocked on the second door to the right. A European man answered and let us into a room that looked like it was set up for giving guitar lessons.

"Good, Faruk, so nice to see you, and you brought Miss Peddington, welcome to Ankara, Laura, I am Frank." He said it like he wasn't even pretending that it was his real name.

"Hi Frank, pleased to meet you," I said.

"Well then, let's get you outfitted." he spoke with a kind of a British sounding accent, but then, in my new life, it seemed that was hard to take at face value. "Here is your Dragunov SVDS, you should be familiar with it, much like the SVD but shorter and lighter."

"Ah, good for a woman," Faruk added.

"Yes," I said, "I've fired these."

"Good, good, and this is your iPod, if you turn to the menu marked "techno," you will get a picture of the target with firing and sighting instructions. Don't play it until you are set up and ready, because, once run, it will be erased."

"Okay," I acknowledged.

Faruk spoke to Frank, "Ah, if all is good, I will be leaving you two." Faruk was quickly out the door.

"Don't worry, he will meet you at your next stop." Frank answered. I was wondering if it was time to panic yet when Frank brought out a guitar case with a peace sign on it.

"Put the rifle in here, the combination is 615, same as the apartment number where you will meet Faruk." He set the case down on the table and opened it. Inside were cutouts that the Dragunov fit into.

Frank looked at his watch, "Wait here for thirty more minutes exactly, then leave the way you came in, turn left two blocks, then left again for three blocks, enter the first apartment building and find apartment number 615. Knock on the door. Faruk should answer. If you forget anything, there are instructions on a text message on your phone. Good luck." Frank left me alone in the small practice room.

Thirty minutes later, I was walking through the streets of a foreign city, carrying a powerful Russian made sniper rifle in a guitar case with a peace symbol on it, of all things. I'm about to whack some hopefully very bad person in Turkey where, if I get caught, it means a very long sentence in a very bad prison, or a very short prison term followed by a firing squad. I think the time to panic passed a long, long time ago. A year ago, I was worried about how to tell my father I was flunking math; now I have a job being paid by the government to assassinate people. The really strange part was, I was more afraid then than I am now, somehow this all seemed dreadfully normal.

So this is me, Skank, a traitor's daughter, 20 years old, born and raised in the sleepy bedroom town of Winfield Connecticut, occupation assassin. I wonder if I get to put that on my W2. The good news is that people in my line of work don't usually live long, therefore, I won't have to wait long to see Cali again.

26

The directions took me to a fairly modern looking apartment building done in light beige stone and red tile. I took an elevator up to the 6th floor, and knocked on the door to 615. Faruk opened the door to a contemporary styled apartment with a mix of Western and Middle Eastern designs. A slim, dark haired woman came up behind him and greeted me as Faruk made the introduction. "Please, please, come in and meet my wife," He said, taking the guitar case from me, setting it on a bench next to door, clicking the combination and opening it. His wife smiled like she didn't even notice the rifle; instead, she started touching my hair and talking to her husband.

He laughed, "She wants to know if that's your real hair color."

"Huh, ah, yes, yes it is, but what about the…"

"Ah, yes," he said and spoke to his wife; she helped him pull a table over close to the window. "Here, use this."

"But this is your apartment?"

"Yes?"

"You want me to do it here?"

"What, the view is not good?

I looked, I could see the gathering on the steps of a large square columned building off to the left."

"That's the place?"

"Yes?"

"Well, the view is fine, but do you want me to do this from your home, in front of your wife?"

"Ah," he finally seemed to get it "Don't worry about her, she hates the guy as much as I do." He spoke to his wife in Turkish and she laughed.

"Well, that's a little too close to the window then."

"You don't want to get closer?"

"No, after a kilometer, one more meter isn't going to matter much, you don't want people to see the barrel or the flash, do you?"

"No, I suppose not." They moved the table back and I set the gun on top, opening the support legs, and sighted. It was a kind of an uncomfortable position, so I borrowed one of his chairs to kneel on and could sight perfectly.

"Who is this guy?" I asked.

"Ah, really bad man, uses the religious zeal of the fundamentalist to line his pockets. When he goes to Salah, he faces north towards his Swiss bank account instead of towards Mecca." he answered, "He would destroy our whole country just to line his pockets."

"Yeah, I know people like that, why don't you pop him yourselves?" I pulled out the iPod and put on the head piece.

"Ah, it is not right for a Muslim to kill a Muslim."

"Is it any better for a Christian to do it?" I asked as I found the correct selection and started it. His picture came up on the little screen; I checked the sight to verify the target, and could pick him out.

"Oh, no problem, we Turks have been hiring Christians to do our dirty work for 500 years, you guys will do anything for money." He said. I could have taken that as an insult if it weren't so true.

"You do know he's not the one speaking." I said.

"Aw, do not shoot the guy speaking, we do not want him to become a martyr."

"Okay, just wanted to make sure."

169

I heard someone come on the headphones, "Hello Laura, are we ready?" a male voice said.

"All set," I said into the headset mic as I pointed to it for Faruk's benefit, to let him know who I was talking to.

He made a silent "Ah."

I lined up, "You have smooth, even windage from the west, which would be your left." The voice said.

"Are we go?" I asked.

"When ready," he answered.

"I just hope I don't get caught doing this." I told Faruk. The gun popped and kicked; One second later, the targeted man went down behind the man speaking. It appeared that no one noticed at first.

"Good shooting," the voice confirmed.

"We're done then?" I asked.

"We're done." The voice said.

"That it?" Faruk asked.

"That's it." I said, getting up from the chair.

"Ah, good," he clapped his hands once, "Let's eat. My wife made lamb and couscous." I took the SVDS off the table while he and his wife moved it back. His wife continued to set the table while he took the gun and put it back into the guitar case.

"What about the person I shot, he won't become a martyr?" I asked.

"Oh no, everyone hates him, if they knew you took him out they would give you a medal. Well, they would kill you first, and then give you a medal."

"That's comforting," I answered.

His wife started bringing out hot plates filled with aromatic food. It was spicier than I was used to, but good. We talked freely about religion, women's rights, and politics. The only time he became agitated was when I referred to myself as an infidel. He said that word was offensive and wrong to use it to describe myself as a Catholic. He said that I was Ahl al-Kitāb, meaning People of the Book, a believer in the one true God, but not Muslim.

Later that evening, I took a taxi to the hotel where there was a room reserved for me in a more touristy area. I bought a notebook and created a journal out of what I had learned of Islam and Muslim culture from talking with Faruk. I gave him a date code number instead of a name. I was getting into being Laura Peddington, anthropology student. I told myself it was to back up my cover, but maybe it was a way of denying who I was. It was easier to be innocent Laura than tainted Millie. As I tried to get to sleep, I pretended to be Laura, growing up in Vancouver in a normal Canadian family with mother and father and sisters. In truth, it was a way to keep my mind from wandering back to Cali and what I had done. I tried to tell myself that Millie was dead, but she wasn't, she was still killing people. I should have asked Faruk if the person I killed was going to heaven.

I woke up early, still on army time, but feeling like Laura. I washed, dressed, and went down for breakfast. They had a small but nice buffet set up. There were polite waiters who helped direct me. In the process, I noticed a newspaper with a huge headline and a picture of the two men; the speaker, and the one that I eliminated; however, I couldn't read what it said. I asked the waiter about who the men were and what they had done that they were in the news.

"Oh, very strange," he said, "Someone tried to assassinate Mohammad Fassad, but missed and hit Haikef Hasat instead, his very rich supporter."

"Are you kidding, that's terrible," I said.

"Maybe not so terrible." He answered. I didn't dwell on it, instead I had a nice breakfast and went out to look around, and possibly go shopping as Laura Peddington. There were western style stores and there were also many street venders in an outdoor area. This was the area I went into, thinking that's what Laura would do. I was looking through some beautiful silver jewelry when I was approached by a tall woman with long, straight, dark hair, and a thin face. She said, "You should be more careful, you shouldn't be here."

"What?" I asked, "Who are you, what do you want?" I was trying to walk away from her, but she was following me.

"I'm telling you, you're going to get caught; you need to come with me."

"Why, who are you?"

"Don't pretend with me, you're in danger." I began looking around in panic. Who was this woman, what did she know?

I began to get more vocal. "No, I'm not going with you, just leave me alone" This started to attract the attention of a nearby police officer.

She started backing away, "I tried to warn you." I turned and saw the officer approaching; when I looked back, she was gone.

"What was that all about?" he asked.

"I don't know, she wanted me to go with her but she wouldn't tell me who she was or what she wanted."

"Hmm," he said, "Maybe you should come to the station and fill out a report."

"Do you really think that's necessary?"

"What's your name?"

"Laura Peddington"

"Can I see your passport?"

"Oh, yeah, sure." I pulled it out of my pocket, and he looked it over.

"Ah, Canadian."

"Yes."

"I think you should come with me."

"Well, OK, but she's gone now, I don't think that's really necessary."

"It will be okay." We began walking. They couldn't have figured out what I did already, I thought, but if I put up a fuss it could only make things worse, it wasn't like he was slapping cuffs on me. The station was four blocks away.

He took me into an office, not an interrogation room, good sign, I thought, and he asked me to describe the woman. After listening for a while, he pulled out a book with photos in it, asking me to look through it. "Any of these?" he asked as he began going through my backpack.

"Her, I think that's her." I turned the book around for him to look at the picture as he was still holding my notebook.

"Ah Shalla Zuri, Mossad."

"Who, Mossad, like Israel's spies? Why would they be after me, I didn't even visit Israel, and what would they be doing here?"

"What's this?" He asked, holding the DVD.

"Oh, that's from my family, so I wouldn't forget them I guess."

"Why are you traveling here?"

"I'm taking anthropology in college, so I'm taking a year to experience other cultures."

"That's this?" he asked, holding up the notebook.

"Yes." I said.

"So we are the first place you are visiting?"

"No, I was in Kuwait." I had to be honest, because that was too easy to check.

"So no notes from Kuwait?"

"No, it's very American, I've seen plenty of Americans."

He laughed, "I understand."

"So why take a year off from college? Wouldn't it be better to finish, then view other cultures?"

"Well yes, but I couldn't really decide what to do, cultural or biological anthropology, I wanted to try looking into different cultures first." The expression on his face told me he wasn't buying it.

"Well, OK, you're as bad as my parents, maybe I am running away; I just lost my sister Georgia in a fire. All this time I just ignored her, now she's gone, and I never really knew her." I started formulate Laura's family dynamic in my head, drawing emotion from Millie's recent past.

"I'm sorry to hear that."

"Why all these questions, did I do something wrong?"

"Well, Miss Peddington, if that's who you are, we have a little dilemma. See, we would like to believe you, we really would. The last thing we want to do is to falsely accuse an innocent Canadian, but we have this little problem." He showed me another picture. It was a picture of me, not as Laura Peddington, but as Millie Willard, taken from the Al Jazeera video.

"Who's this?"

"Look closely, Miss Peddington."

"It's, what, that looks like me, oh shit, I mean, sorry, that looks like me, but I wasn't in the Army."

"Not just any Army, but the American Army."

"What, that's not possible, you think I'm running away from the army? That's crazy, that can't be me."

"Not running away, see, she's supposed to be dead, but we know the Americans like to pull this little trick where they say someone is dead, but then they turn up later as agents."

"What do you mean agents?"

"Spies, as you put it." I held my head in my hands, staring at the picture, fully believing I wasn't me.

"Spies? What, you think I'm a spy? This can't be happening, this just isn't happening, but, oh no, are you going to arrest me?" Tears began hitting the table as I sat there, still holding my head in my hands, staring at the picture, "This is not possible."

"So you can understand our problem." He said.

"Those damn Americans." I answered. He was about to say something when someone came to the door and called him out.

I sat there shaking my head, "There can't be two people that look the same." I said out loud, "That's not possible, they must have changed the picture. Oh no, they're going to put me in prison with this evidence and make my parents pay money to get me back.

They lost one daughter, now they're going to lose another one. They can't afford this. How could I be so stupid?" Shaking my head and crying.

He came back into the room, "Well," he said "You're either a very good spy, or you're a very unfortunate victim of circumstances, but everything you're telling us seems to check out. So I'll tell you what we're going to do. We certainly do not want to falsely accuse any of our Canadian friends, so we see that you are booked for Germany this evening?"

"Yes, yes I am."

"Well then, we are going to make sure that you get on that plane, so if you are really Laura, you will be okay, or if you really are Millie Willard, you will be out of our country, but that means that if you or Miss Willard should happen to show up here again, well let's just say you have been warned, how's that?"

"Yes sir, thank you sir." I said, and spent the rest of the day not quite in a cell, but under close supervision, and was personally escorted to the plane early that evening. When the wheels left the runway, I finally was able to think like Millie again, and Mr. Ted Haal was going to get a little talking to about the slight hole in his perfect cover story.

There was a slim red streak left from sunset as the plane gained altitude and pointed towards the northwest. I was sitting in the window seat on the left side of the plane next to a rather large gentleman with a round face and salt and pepper hair, who kept staring down the front of the collarless, long sleeve fitted khaki shirt I was wearing over skinny jeans, the other outfit in the backpack. If I'd had half a brain, I would have gone into one of the western style stores back in Ankara and bought myself a jacket. Knowing that it was cool in Turkey I should have realized it was going to be freezing in Germany. It seemed that Laura wasn't any brighter than Millie. I tried to divide things up between Laura and Millie, let Millie take the rap for everything evil I did, and leave Laura sweet and innocent, but actually, Laura was kind of a spoiled brat, herself leaving her parents at a time like this when they really needed her support. I wished I could just call them up and tell them I was sorry and fly off home to Vancouver to live out the rest of my normal life, but then they didn't really exist, and neither did my normal life. The man next to me decided he was tired of just looking, and laid his hand on my thigh. I decided it was a good time to go to the bathroom. Of course, getting around him meant he needed to guide my hips and butt on the way past.

There is something inherently creepy about airplane bathrooms. I don't know if it's the opportunity for so many germs in such a confirmed space, or just hanging your butt over a hole 30,000 feet in the air, but the restroom trip didn't really do anything to clear my head. It did, however, give Mr. Hands another fondling opportunity; I wonder if he would be so free with them if he knew that I killed people for a living. Maybe I would just tell him, hello, my name is Millie, or Laura, take your pick, do you know I killed a famous rich man yesterday from a kilometer away?

Instead I just smiled and went back to looking out the dark window at the light sprinkled ground below. Soon, we were descending into the Cologne-Bonn Airport, touching down, and taxiing to a stop. With a symphony of clicks seatbelts were hurriedly unfastened, and everyone rushed to be the first to stand and wait in the crowded isle. I smiled at the man next to me, and he smiled back, taking my hand in both of his and giving it a friendly squeeze as if to thank me for making his trip more enjoyable.

27

Inside the terminal, the first order of business was to see if I could find something warm to wear. Finding only one shop, I bought a kind of light blue short trench coat style jacket and a calico scarf. While I was paying, I received a phone call. I let it ring as the clerk handed me the bag. Then I answered; it was Mr. Haal. "Oh, good, Laura, you should be in Germany by now, nice work, I know it's late, but could you come to the address I'm texting you now? It's in the old cold war US embassy."

"Yeah, sure, I can be there, and about that good work stuff, I kind of ran into a little glitch along the way."

"Well, we can talk about that later." I was getting the feeling that when Ted said "we can talk about that later," it really meant he didn't want to talk about it at all. I left the confines of the terminal and was suddenly very glad I got the coat and thick scarf, wrapping it tighter around my neck against the cold wind, as I waited for the next available taxi. I gave the address to the driver, who seemed to have no problem with English. Ten minutes later, he dropped me in front of the large gothic styled building behind an iron gate. I was still searching for some form of call box when the gate swung open. This whole secret agent thing, I was discovering, was a kind of mixed bag. On the one hand, I had a charge card I didn't have to pay the bill on and got to go into cool buildings like this, on the other I had to deal with being a murdering liar. In a previous life I could have enjoyed this, now I just felt cold and empty.

I walked up the wide stone steps under the high stone arch to a massive carved oak door that opened easily.

Inside was a two story high hallway with a marine guard in his dress uniform who snapped to attention as I entered. "Miss Peddington," he said "Mr. Haal is waiting for you in the situation room, down the hall through that door to the right and down the stairs."

"Thank you, Sergeant." I said and headed down the hall. Shit, the situation room, it was getting harder to stay mad at Mr. Haal. The door led to a wide stairway that seemed to end at a blank wall with only two small doors off to the side. As I contemplated trying one of the small doors, the blank wall slid apart, revealing another length of hallway leading to another pair of sliding doors. Those also opened as I approached, double shit, was this real? I stepped onto a landing that revealed a large darkened room that clattered with activity. People were sitting at computers scattered around the edges while the center was open with large screen monitors along the left wall.

"Laura, welcome to your new home, come meet the team." Haal called from the open area. I descended the stairs and walked towards him. There was something about seeing his big, smug, smiling, strong-jawed face that brought all of the anger and uncertainty back.

"They had a picture of me there, they knew who I was, or at least suspected who I was." I said.

"But look, you made it out, and you got the bad guy, that's what counts."

"Yeah, well, I can never go back to Turkey again, and another thing, who was that guy? I mean, he could have been the Walt Disney of the Middle East for all I knew."

"Oh, he wasn't, believe me."

Somehow, I didn't seem to be getting through. He was just minimizing everything. "You turned me into a murder and a liar, importing death into their country. It doesn't matter who he was, you think seeing someone gunned down in a public place doesn't affect people?

"Getting a bit philosophical, aren't we?" he said, his smile fading. "Idealism is for people who don't have to deal with reality. That man you took out would have destroyed his whole nation just so he could sell more weapons. You saved a lot more lives than you took, believe me. This is about survival, ours."

"Well maybe I don't want to survive in this world anymore." I was totally losing control and it didn't have anything to do with him or Turkey, I just couldn't stand living any longer. I grabbed the Beretta he had in his shoulder holster, switched off the safety, made sure a bullet was in the chamber, put it in his hand, and pointed facing up under my chin.

"Why don't you just do me a favor and send me to be with Cali?"

"No!" I heard a familiar voice say. I looked over, and even in the dim light I recognized the golden-eyed girl who was walking towards me with a slight limp. "Because I'm still here." Haal took his gun back and cleared the chamber, putting it back in his holster as I stood there completely overwhelmed.

"Cali?" I became weak in the knees. She had to hold me up as we hugged.

"I told you you'd like meeting the team." Haal said, "I'll let you two get reacquainted."

She led me off to a small conference room. "They told me you were dead, I saw you buried at Arlington."

"I almost was, especially after they said you were dead. They airlifted me from the ship to Kuwait, they couldn't save my leg." She lifted her pant leg showing me the prosthesis, "I'm still getting use to it. When they told me you died in Afghanistan I knew that wasn't true; I made such a fuss they had to tell me the truth. Mr. Haal said he would take me to work here, I can't go in the field with you, but at least we can work together." Joy and pain were mixing together like a heavy metal lullaby, Cali was alive and the choking fog of grief was lifting to reveal the awful truth that I'd permanently damaged the one person left alive that I loved. She would have a permanent reminder of what friendship with me had cost her.

"But what about your family, do they know you're alive?" I asked. There was a pause as she looked down at the conference table where we sat as if trying to find the right words encoded into the polished wood grain.

"I lied to you Millie. I made it seem like everything was just fine with my family. The truth is I was thrown out of my parent's house because I messed up my life pretty bad. I can't blame them they have a younger daughter they were trying to protect. I was hanging with the wrong crowd, getting involved with gangs and shit. It got to the point that it was either jail or military. The church I told you about, it's a street church for troubled kids. They saved me from the gangs and got me into the Army. I'm not sure how they did it because the military won't take people in gangs anymore.

Now my family has a hero for a daughter instead of a screw-up, they will be sad but I think in the long run it will be better this way. But you accepted me as I was, I didn't have to prove myself first, you're the best friend I've ever had, I couldn't just stand there and watch you die. And I couldn't go back home to that same mess that I'd created and never see you again. I'm Kristi Rennier now."

"Do you know how mad at myself I was when I thought you were dead and I lived? I wanted to die with you." I told her.

"I know, I really thought we were going to but this way we kind of get that chance."

Ted Haal opened the door and said, "I hate to break this up, but we have urgent need of Laura's services. It seems someone wants to come in out of the cold and needs backup."

"So please don't get killed just yet," Cali said as Haal led me out the door. He stopped at a cabinet under the entry stairs and handed me an M4, "I think this is all that we will need this time," he said, continuing up the stairs. I ran up the stairs following him toward the back of the building. There was a black SUV already waiting. He got in the back and slid over, motioning me in the same door. The car lunged forward the instant I closed the door.

Once again, events were going faster than I could comprehend them, Cali was back, but I didn't have a chance to process it.

"This job is going to be a lot harder now that I have to try to live through it." I said to myself, unfortunately Haal heard me.

"What? Of course you have to try to live through this,"

"Well, I guess before, I didn't really care one way or the other." I said.

"You have too much of a flirting relationship with death, for the person who is supposed to be keeping me alive, you know that?" he said.

"Keeping you alive is a higher priority than keeping me alive."

"Well, that makes me feel better, I think." Ted Haal continued. "At present, I'm not sure what kind of situation we have, could be very simple, could be hostage, could be a trap, but one of our wayward informants called in wanting to come home. However, I don't know if we can trust him. I need you to cover my butt for any of the possibilities." He explained as he activated the SUV's video entertainment system. The first part was an overhead view of what looked like an open field; however, there were indications of abandoned roads and other formations.

"This is just south of Eschborn Airfield. It was used by the Germans in WWII and by the Allies later, but it is abandoned now." He handed me an ear bud, "Cali will be on the headset. She will have overhead surveillance in case we have unwanted company. I want you with me, but you keep listening to her in case she sees something. What's your range with an M4?"

"I've made 600 meters but that's iffy, 400 to 500 is max with kill accuracy on the first shot with good optics."

"That's more than enough," he zoomed in the satellite map. "This is our meeting place right here at this abandoned intersection, so we're dealing with mostly 100 to 200 meters, but there are a lot of them." He was pointing all around the area at several mounds, but mostly at what looked like hedgerows. Next, he brought up a picture. "This is the guy we want, so try not to shoot him if you don't have to. Everyone else, we have to assume are not friendly, so they are all fair game. It's going to take about 3 hours to get there, so it will probably be just getting light. That's why I don't like this; it is the worst possible time, too bright for night vision, and too dark to see clearly without it. That could be on purpose to hinder our defenses, but I have confidence in you."

I couldn't keep my mind from wandering. Maybe that was the problem. Well, not Haal, but Cali. I'd always been confident in the fact that Cali was a compete person; she had her family and friends back home and would be returning to that life, and I was just a temporary friend, we could enjoy our friendship during the army, but then it would be all over. Now I find that she is making decisions based on me, she chose to leave all that she knew behind because of me. Now I'm obligated to stay alive because of her. I guess I never realized there was a certain freedom in the fact that there was nobody left on the planet that would care one way or the other if I lived or died. This was going to take some getting used to.

I woke up snuggled against Haal's shoulder, "Good morning Laura, glad to see you're not nervous about this at all. You sleep like a stone, you know that? That could get you killed someday."

I slowly came awake, looking around. We were stopped, and it was just barely getting light, "Yeah, I know. Someone else told me that." He opened his door and got out, and I got out my side, dragging my M4 with me. The Marine driver was already out, surveying the area with night vision binoculars. I slung the rifle and followed Haal around back. He opened it up and pulled out a 24 inch in diameter flying saucer shaped thing and set it on the ground, then spoke to Cali on the com.

"It's all yours." he said. The device spun up, making a quiet whooshing sound, and went straight up into the air, disappearing from sight.

"Good to go," Cali replied, "Receiving visual and infrared, scanning the area, two targets in the meeting zone, all clear, two hundred meters otherwise." Haal shut the back of the SUV.

"We walk to the meeting point from here. Hanson, you stay with the vehicle, if something goes wrong, report back immediately, Laura, you're with me."

We crossed the narrow country road through a low hedgerow and into the field. It was just starting to get light enough to pick out our footsteps on the fallow field. Soon, we intersected one of the abandoned roads and used it to walk the rest of the way to the intersection. There is something strangely intriguing about what people leave behind as it is slowly retaken by nature, a kind of transition between the two cultures; the ubiquitous straight lines of humans being eaten away on the edges by the fractals of the natural world, made all the more ominous in the colored light of early dawn. As if to remind us that nothing we do lasts forever, while the natural process never gives up. We can only outrun it for a short time.

I just started to make out two figures standing about 100 meters ahead. "I see a man with an AK," I whispered to Haal, "We are already inside its effective range, they have a firepower advantage."

"Let's just hope it doesn't come to that." Haal answered.

We were now at 50 meters and still approaching. The man holding the AK was huge, and had a face marked in both scars and an expression that said he was not at all friendly; wearing a black suit and black turtleneck. And here I was in skinny jeans, a bright blue jacket and calico scarf; obviously, I had no idea of what to wear to a showdown. The other man waiting was the one from the picture. I hugged my M4 to my chest military style for comfort.

"Hey Jim," Haal said, "Long time no see."

"Hey Ted, this is your backup?" the man laughed. "You guys have got to get off this volunteer army kick."

"Short notice," Haal answered, *thanks a lot, asshole*, I thought, "But she does alright." Haal added.

"I need some guarantees," Jim said, "and protection."

Haal was about to answer when Cali came on, "Car stopping south bearing 175, two men getting out, armed."

"Take that." Haal said to me. I turned and knelt, bringing up the night scoped M4. The image was bright, but quickly adjusted, and I could see the men running for cover. Both carrying rifles, found cover, and started to take aim.

It took three rapid shots to down only one man; I missed the first shot completely, but wounded the second man with the second, so it took the third shot to put him down from only 200 meters. I was missing; this wasn't good. The first man I missed was at first stunned, then dropped behind cover. "Shit." I turned back to Haal and the other two men. The big guy had his AK pointed at us, but a confused look on his face.

"I hope those weren't yours," Haal said to Jim, "Because you'll be needed to write to their families."

Jim motioned for the big guy to lower his gun, "What the fuck was that?"

"Some unfriendly people trying to interrupt our meeting, now, you were saying?"

"Yes, as you can see, I need protection."

"Your new friends not like you anymore?"

"It's not like that, honest, I can give you stuff, good stuff, just let me back in."

"What stuff?"

"Arms deals, big arms deals, very dangerous contents, if you come with us I can show you, I have proof, but it's going down soon."

"How soon?"

"We need to get out of here, come with us."

Cali was back on. "The remaining man is approaching bearing 179, he's taking cover." I turned again reading the heading in the scope. He was on the ground behind a hedge. I lined up the shot.

"Down!" I yelled as he was already firing, seeing the flash an instant before I fired.

"He's down." Cali confirmed.

I turned back around. Everyone was on the ground, but alright. Whoever he was aiming at, he missed.

Everyone got up, brushing themselves off. "I told you, Ted, we need to get out of here."

"Where to?" Haal asked.

"I'm parked at a warehouse northeast of here. Come with us."

Haal radioed Hanson, "Track us to the northeast, find a warehouse there, but hold back, don't get too close."

We followed them across the field until we came to another abandoned road, and followed it to a large, low-slung building just passed another hedgerow. Haal started dropping back from the two other men until he saw our SUV approaching from the southeast, having followed the roads around the old airfield, and then he radioed Hanson. Jim got suspicious. "What's this?" he asked.

"You think I'm just walking into a trap?"

"It's not like that." Jim insisted.

Haal turned to me, "I don't like this, you stay here with Hanson, he'll get you on that roof. I need you up there covering me."

"What if they want you in the building?"

"Don't worry about it, just cover me."

"Yes, sir."

Hanson drove up and got out as Haal continued to follow Jim and his ugly friend. Hanson came up to me, "Here," he said, "Put this on." He handed me a climbing harness. I removed my jacket and scarf, despite the cold, and climbed into the harness, cinching it up. He pulled more equipment from the truck and jogged over to the side of the old brick warehouse. I followed; by the time I got there, he'd already had a grapnel secured to the lip of the roof. He clipped a carabineer to the harness, then pulled the line tight. "Rappel up the side." he said. Up, I thought, but as soon as I got into position, he hoisted me up like I was nothing, walking quickly up the 20-foot wall until I reached the top and had to flip a leg over to pull myself onto the roof.

"Men on the roof," Cali said, "three on yours, and two on a roof across the parking lot." I crouched down as soon as I was over the edge. I could see all three clearly. They turned, bringing up their UMPs. There was no cover besides the stairway door on the far side. I fired; the first two didn't have time to fire, the third fired over my head before he was hit and went over the side, to the parking lot on the far side of the building. I no longer had surprise on my side. I quickly ran to that side of the roof and found the other two men on the roof of the other building; they were turning from watching their comrade fall to the ground to leveling their guns on my roof position. I took them out quickly, even as they sprayed the low roof wall in front of me. Shattered brick dust was getting into my eyes. By the time I could see again, I saw only Jim and Haal in the parking lot below, not Jim's ugly friend. Jim had a gun on Haal. Still trying to clear my eyes, I took aim.

"You know what a good shot she is, I'd put the gun down if I were you, Jim."

"Skank! Man on the roof! Look out!" Cali said. I was stupidly too close to the roof access stairway. I only had time to turn to see Mr. Ugly as he grabbed my harness and was about to flip me over the side. I kicked with my left foot, finding his knee. I heard him grunt and start to fall forward. Now, most people, I thought, when they start to fall, let go of what they are holding and try to brace themselves. Well, not this guy, he hung on to me and we both went over the edge. He was trying to ride me down like a carpet. I used a bit of Newtonian physics, curling up to speed our rotation, flipping us over onto his back. I felt his ribcage buckle as it cushioned the impact, but I still saw a galaxy of stars as I bounced up and rolled off of him onto the pavement, trying to remember how to breathe.

"What the fuck." I heard Jim say, but the distraction allowed Haal to get the upper hand. Haal and Hanson soon had him down and subdued.

I was still lying on my back on the pavement, hearing Cali talking to me, "Skank, Skank, please tell me you're okay."

"Okay," was all I managed to say. Haal's face looked down at me. "That hurt," I said as I looked up at him.

"I think that move needs a little work." he answered, "Stay still for a minute." I lay there for a few minutes, making sure that everything still worked, with Haal checking me over; hopefully just to see if anything was broken. Then I slowly got up, picked up the M4 I'd taken on the ride down with me, and oozed my way into the SUV that Hanson had brought over.

As it turns out, the big guy was still alive, but in bad shape. Cali called in the authorities, telling them to send medical help, but Haal wanted to leave with Jim before they arrived. On the way back, he sat in the back with our rather disgruntled prisoner, and I was up front with Hansen.

Back at the base, Jim was off-loaded to professionals at extracting data; however, Haal was not very confident that he would be a wealth of information. He paced the open area, rubbing his hands over his flat top haircut.

"Do we know what's going on?" Cali asked Haal.

"It's a mess, that's what it is, anyone who thinks the fall of the Soviet Union was a good thing is naïve, or an arms dealer." I looked at him, a little confused. "War is big business now," he continued as a way of explanation, "It seems that people will pay any price to kill each other, a fact not overlooked by businessmen. All this garbage about politics and religion are only marketing slogans to help sell more weapons. Moscow is now lined with millionaires getting rich from the fallout. You can get AK74s free with the purchase of three or more rocket launchers. Threats now come from every direction. That guy you whacked in Turkey was one of the biggest, wanting the incite Turkey to fundamentalism only to increase sales. The problem is that his body didn't even hit the ground before others were vying to take his place. "

"About that," I asked "What about the fact that everybody knows who I am?"

"You want to know the sad truth?" he answered, stopping his pacing to look at me with a serious expression. "Not only did they suspect who you were, but that you were the person who killed him. Granted, there was that one in a billion chance that you were really a very unlucky student from Vancouver, but do you think that would have stopped them from putting you to death if they really wanted to punish you? No, the truth is, they knew you did them a favor, they weren't happy with the method, but as long as it was done, they'd just accept it."

"You could have told me beforehand." I said.

"Well, there are some things you are better off not knowing beforehand." He answered, resuming his pacing. "But anyway, we need to keep you on a low profile for a while, at least until your YouTube video's popularity wanes a bit, I don't think we need to change your face."

Change my what, I thought, that was a scary proposition.

28

A face came on the large center monitor, "Haal, what's going on out there?" the talking head blared, "The German authorities have 7 dead men, and another severely injured, what am I supposed to tell them?"

"Tell them, Mr. Harfax, to find out who they are, it appears we have warring factions looking to take over the weapons trade, and they all want us out of the way. Apparently they're not content with the small stuff anymore."

I realized that Mr. Harfax was the civilian I'd seen in the Coronel's office at Fort Knox and in my hospital room in Washington.

"Just keep a better lid on things out there, Haal, you're attracting too much attention."

"Yes, sir." Haal answered.

"Miss Willard, or is it Miss Peddington now, how are you liking your new assignment?" Harfax said.

"Very much sir, thank you." I answered.

"Keep up the good work." The screen went blank.

"Cali, Laura, you're off duty for the rest of the day. Cali, why don't you show Laura around a bit?"

"Come on," Cali said, "We'll use the tunnel." She led me to a small door on the far side of the room, past some lockers and rest rooms to another door that led to a long hallway with large pipes overhead. I followed her down the gradually sloping tunnel.

"Sorry about scaring you." I said. "When the Captain told me that you were dead and what you did, I didn't want to go on living, now it seems strange that it could be the other way around. I need to get used to people caring whether I live or die again."

"Don't ever think people don't care," Is all she said.

We came to a door that came out in an authorized, personnel-only section of a tunnel that served as a walkway under the rail line of the Bonn train station. We walked out of the railway ramp and into the lunchtime pedestrian traffic. She still had a slight limp, but seemed to be doing pretty good walking. "Does that hurt?" I asked. She gave me a questioning look. "I mean your leg; does it hurt to walk on it?"

"Oh, not as much as it used to." She said, "It's getting better."

She steered us into a little storefront deli where we ordered sausages and chips with a pickle. We found a seat by the window at a tiny table. Cali continued, "The happiest moment in my life was when I landed on top of you, feeling you alive beneath me knowing that I was probably going to die, but praying that you would not. Now, my life is better than it's ever been, I have a job like they make movies out of, with people I love depending on me. It's a good feeling."

I was completely stunned that I could be part of someone's happiest moment, not quite sure how to deal with it.

"You know, I could get killed on any one of these little outings," I said to Cali, "I don't want you to hurt too much for me if it happens; I want to know that you will be okay."

She finished chewing her last bite, and then looked down at her plate. "I know," she said "and of course I don't want you to die, but, if you do get there before me, just save me a spot." She smiled at me.

"I will, and will you do that for me?" She nodded, and we pressed our hands together as a kind of a pledge to each other.

After lunch, we went shopping, picking out more clothes. It seemed that there really wasn't a dress code, but she recommended dark rugged clothes that could stand up to rigorous missions. I also bought a pair of those gloves with the fingertips open, because the scramble over the side of the building was a little rough on my hands.

"What about a place to live?" I asked.

"There are quarters on the third floor, that's where I'm staying, but you can get an apartment if you want, they're expensive, and you have to have a way to get to the base at a moment's notice, it's just easier to stay in the building."

"Sounds good to me." I said.

We returned to our base later that afternoon. I was given a room on the third floor, and Cali helped me get it cleaned and set up after scrounging some furniture. That evening, Ted Haal took us to dinner at a nearby restaurant. The conversation centered on how Cali and I met. It also included how we joined, which led to the case of my father, I asked him if there was some way, with his connections with Harfax, that he could find out what was going on in the investigation. He had no immediate information, but he would try to find out at a time when Harfax was not in such a bad mood.

I was awakened at 01:30 Sunday morning by Cali.

"We need you." She said. I was washed and dressed in the green camo provided. I met Cali, Haal and another man named Corsval in a large high ceilinged main floor room. We were all dressed in similar military style fatigues that were not US Army standard issue. Not a word was spoken as they handed out equipment. Kevlar vests and com pieces all around Haal and Corsval took UMPs and I was given an MSG90 a variant of the H&K PSG1. I followed the two men out the back door into the back of a military transport vehicle.

We were well on the way before Corsval spoke in European accented English.

"We have an unfriendly forced extraction." He switched on a small overhead light, popped a seal off a manila envelope and pulled out a folded map. The map looked like a diagram of a small compound and the surrounding area. "We are one of two teams, this is our entrance. These are the rooms we will secure." He took a picture out of an envelope and laid it on the map. "This is the primary, he must be taken alive. All others are expendable." He pulled out a sat image of the area and turned to me. "You will be here." Pointing out a nearby flat roof to the southwest, "You will cover these two walls. All our people will be marked with this marker." Putting down a picture of a symbol that looked like an ampersand, take out all defenders." His voice grew stern. "Understood, do not hesitate, you must take out all defenders is that understood?"

"Understood!" I answered. I looked at Haal his face was emotionless and he did not say a word.

Two minutes later the truck jerked to a stop the back was opened to almost total darkness. We were hustled into the back of a transport plane guided only by small running lights. Buckled into jump seats I only remembered the takeoff. When I was roughly awakened we were on the ground. The rear door opened and we scrambled out into cool fragrant night air, fallowing the two men into another closed military vehicle. I had no idea where we were or who we were going after.

Ten minutes later the vehicle came to a stop, Ted Haal motioned to me to stay silent, and then opened the door, he guided me to a barely visible stone building fronting a narrow sloping street, and there were two men in unfamiliar uniforms flanking the heavy wooden door. One ushered me up steep stone steps as Haal quickly returned to the vehicle. Without a word we passed the second floor up more steps through a low doorway onto the roof, the man pointed in the direction of a low wall that marked the edge of the roof. The faint smell of earth and pine, the lack of street lights and night sounds spoke of a rural area. An NV scope and survey of ghostly monochromatic dark shaped trees confirmed the assessment. To the east northeast was the target compound, 300 meters away. During the daylight it would have been mostly hidden by trees, but the scopes IR enhancement made the guards stand out. There were three that I could see, one patrolling the grounds, two on third floor balconies. I waited in total silence breathing in the night's cool quiet air listening to the quiet sounds of nature.

"Skank, acknowledge." Haal's voice seemed surprisingly loud in the headpiece.

"In place, three guards visible," I answered.

"Neutralize guards in three, two, one." Despite my rifle's suppressor the hypersonic electric sounding snaps split the still night air like lightning answered by the complaints of a myriad of unseen forest creatures. Being more mobile the roving guard was first. Then the two guards trapped on the balconies. An instant later a blast erased the door to the targeted building; two ampersand backed men rushed into the building. Seconds after that the door to one of the out buildings to the east burst open and armed men with no tags rushed out.

"Looks like he has backup, four men coming from the east, taking them out now," I announced. There was no answer. I didn't hesitate; the first man went down and the second tripped over him. The other two dropped to the ground spraying auto fire in my direction. Because three and four were now stationary and accounted for, I kept my attention on number two scrambling for the house. Man three and four saw the flash that took out the second man giving away may position. Bullets shredded through the trees and chewed at the stone in front of me. Number four continued cover fire as three lunged for the house he only took one step before he tumbled head first to the ground. One more shot and all was quiet. I continued to scan the area.

"Skank, pack your trash, meet in the street in two." Haal said in the earpiece. I used a penlight to collect my seven casings and headed out.

At 08:00 I was having breakfast with Cali back in Bonn, I wasn't even sure that the night's activities were anything more than a dream. Later that morning Cali took me to a nearby church that she'd found that had an English service. Despite that fact I don't think I really understood a word that was said. Instead I was still trying to get God, reality and myself to fit where they belonged and not having any success. I tried talking to God about it, but there was no whirlwind or still small voice that I could discern. At least not until 18:00 when BBC World News announced the capture of a Serbian war criminal, Ted Haal just looked at me without saying a word.

For the next week I was helping the rest of the team with intelligence analysis. We were particularly interested in a certain arms dealer named Vonikov and his connections and customers.

Monday March 21, I was sent back to the Army's Baumholder Training Area. There, I was given my old name back, but with the rank of E5, during the training the mission was outlined to us.

It seemed that our friend Jim really did have some useful information. There was a shipment of possible biological or chemical weapons that was heading through the corridor between the Caspian and Black Seas. The mission was to intercept and destroy that shipment. There would be two Special Forces units involved; the first would be the contact force, and the second, our unit, would do surveillance and sniper cover. There were four of us, however, it seemed that the three men were not very happy to have me along. There was Jacob Johnson, called Hammer; a hard bodied A type with way too much testosterone. He was the mission commander. Terrence Shreve, a wiry skate boarder called Thrash, was the tech operator, and Tony Borillo, a Rambo wannabe weapons expert, was backup sniper in case I choked, as Hammer predicted. If it were voluntary, I would have gladly bowed out until I learned that it was Castor and Pollux who were leading the contact forces, and insisted, quite strongly, that I be the primary shooter. To be honest, it was a good feeling that I was that trusted, and it was worth putting up with Hammer's crew to support people I cared about.

Life seemed to have a strange kind of volume control. If you lived a normal middle of the road life, then good and bad would deviate close to that centerline. If, however, you live more on the edge, the good and bad would deviate a lot more from that centerline. If you wanted the really good, then you needed to be able to survive the really bad.

On the Morning of March 28, 2011, all of the teams assembled at Coleman Army Airfield where the final plans were made. We needed to intercept the shipment inside

Russia before it got to the Caspian Sea for transport to Iran. We had conditional support from Russia. In other words, they would not shoot us down, but if the mission became known, they would deny any knowledge of it. The objective was to intercept a truck convoy with the target tuck in the middle. Intel indicated that the material was biological, but we did not know how it was contained, therefore, the target truck needed to be taken intact. The secondary containment measures, plan B, in other words, would involve foaming the truck as a whole if it were damaged, however, plan B had significantly more risk of release. There were a number of contact points discussed; however, there was one that was clearly the best. Selecting our vantage point was another story. There was a close low hill at 600 meters that looked head on to the road the convoy would be taking. That was the hill Hammer favored, because he knew Borillo could make the shot. The problems were that it was, one, too close to remain undetected, and, two, with the convoy head on, only the first truck would be an easy hit. The rest of the convoy would be hidden behind the lead vehicles. I favored a 45 degree offset hill that gave a good overall view, but was 1200 meters; Hammer was convinced that if Borillo couldn't do it, I definitely couldn't do it. Castor and Pollux settled the argument, much to Hammer's disgust.

The insertion was going to be a HALO jump that I had never done, therefore, I was going to have to tandem with Hammer, and Borillo would take Thrash. I was not at all sure about trusting Hammer, someone who obviously hated my guts. We were loaded onto the plane, and were airborne for the 5-hour trip that would bring us in at about 01:00. Pollux tried to get everyone talking during the trip, but it became clear that the only thing Hammer wanted to discuss was how I was going to jinx the whole mission. So, we went most of the way in silence.

At some point, I went out like a light and had to be awakened to prepare for the drop point. At least I didn't call Hammer dad when I woke up. We were suited and ready. I was harnessed to Hammer, but was pleasantly surprised that even though he hated me he wasn't going to let me die on his watch, making sure I buckled in correctly. The command was given and we were cast into darkness. Once the stomach wrenching acceleration stopped, it was like flying. It was my job to hold completely still while Hammer did the steering. Any movement on my part could put us off course. For what seemed like 5 minutes, we floated in darkness, then the chute was opened and he guided us to a perfect landing on the back side of our overlook hill.

With night vision, we surveyed the vantage point to make sure it was secure. The next step was to get Thrash's drone in the air, which took 10 minutes. He did a complete sweep of the immediate area and verified it clear, and then he was off to find the convoy. I requested permission to zero my 107, which was granted, and I zeroed for the 1200 meters, putting 5 shots in a half meter circle. Thrash tagged the convoy, and I verified our guys in the night scope, double checking their friend indicators.

Thrash started ticking down the countdown; I confirmed visual of the lead vehicle at his mark, then target truck, then the last vehicle. Hammer took over the countdown, "3, 2, 1, go." 2 shots; the first and second trucks were disabled. 3 shots; the last, third, and second to last trucks were disabled. One troop carrier and one supply truck before and after the target truck remained operational, but were halted by the disabled leading vehicles. Men started to boil from top hatch of the carrier.

A SLAP round in the side of the carrier stemmed the flow. The escapees were quickly quelled by the contact force. In less than a minute, the operation was over. The contents were inspected by the resident experts on the contact team. We hunkered down and kept watch. Within 10 minutes the contents were verified; and sterilization could now be done with tedious certainty. The other vehicles were checked; a working vehicle would ease our trip to the Black Sea and extraction.

As it turned out, with a little of Hammer's ingenuity, two of the vehicles could be put into service, but it was still a two day trip to where we could be reached by helicopter for extraction. It was a long, tense, uncomfortable trip. We could still meet some unfriendly characters, but it was nice to see that Hammer didn't complain about me anymore.

We were picked up by helicopter and ferried to the US airbase in Turkey for debriefing. According to intelligence, the operation appeared to be a success, and a major hit to the people dealing black market weapons to terrorists. Pollux pulled me aside after the meeting.

"Hey Skank, nice to work with you again."

"Thanks Pollux, I need to tell you something you should know, even though I could get into trouble for it, but Cali is alive. She was badly injured, but recovered; I'm working with her again."

"Thanks for telling me. I'm actually not surprised, knowing how these people work, but I'm very glad to hear that is it true. By the way, Hammer admitted to me that you did a good job."

"Thanks, it would have been nice to hear it from him, but thanks for telling me."

During our conversation, Hammer entered. "Pollux, thanks for your help with the mission, you have a good team. But, if you could excuse me, there's a call for a Laura Peddington."

"Oh yes, that's the other me," I said.

"Okay?" He looked a little unsure. "It's from the French DST, they have a request for Laura's specific skill. They want you to catch a commercial flight from Turkey to Paris."

"Whoa, wait, what?"

"The DST, the French Anti Terrorist Agency." he clarified.

"Sorry, I can't take a commercial flight from here. I'm kind of not welcome in Turkey anymore." I could see him getting aggravated with me again.

"I believe this is an order, Specialist, you will help our allies or I will personally carry you to the airport."

"The last guy that tried to carry me anywhere is still recovering in a German hospital. Is he still on the phone?" I took it from him, "Hello?" I said.

"Ah, Miss Peddington, this is Inspector Pierre de Jardon of the Direction de la Surveillance du Territoire." He answered in French accented English.

"Hi Pierre, I would be happy to help you out, but the problem is that I'm on a arrest on sight list in Turkey, and I would spend the rest of my life, which would be probably 3 days, in a Turkish prison. So if I could fly into Coleman Airfield in Germany, then catch a commercial flight to Paris, I would be glad to help you."

"Ah yes, that would be perfect, we will have a man meet you there, he will escort you to Paris." He said.

"That would be great; I look forward to seeing Paris."

"Tres bon, au revoir, Miss Peddington."

"Thank you, good bye, Pierre." We hung up, "See?" I said to Hammer. "No problem. Everybody's happy."

"You're serious about being persona non grata in Turkey, aren't you?"

Pollux started laughing, "She can be trouble." Pollux explained.

"Where did you find this girl?" Hammer asked Pollux.

"I can't tell you that, or I'd have to kill you." He answered.

We hitched a military ride back to Coleman where the group split up, and I was reunited with my civilian identity that included my jeans, khaki shirt, and a new denim jacket. I noticed that there was a message on my cell phone; it was from Cali, wanting me to call her right away. I did,

"Hello, Cali?"

"Hi Skank, I'm so glad you called before I had to leave." She said.

"Leave?" I asked.

"Yes, I'm at the airport in Frankfort right now, I've been transferred to Langley, can you believe it?"

"Is that good?"

"Yes, I get to work with the big guys."

"That's great, I'm happy for you, I hope it works out, I will miss you though."

"Thanks Skank, I'll miss you too, but we can stay in touch."

"Yes, we can update our latest missions on Facebook." I said.

She laughed, "Bye Skank, I see you."

"I see you, Cali." And just like that, she was gone again.

29

I closed the phone and noticed a sharply dressed young man watching me being escorted by an Air Force Lieutenant.

"Oh, I'm sorry," I said, "Are you from the French DST?"

"Yes," he answered, with only a hint of French accent. Definitely not Pierre. "I am Anton Goberre, here to escort you to Paris." He was an inch or two taller than me, with dark hair and eyes, impeccably dressed in a dark suit and burgundy shirt with a black tie and a heavy silver chain bracelet.

"Hi, I'm Laura Peddington," I said, offering my hand, and he took it and kissed it.
"Actually, now you are Claudette Babbin." he said, handing me a French passport.

"I'm afraid my French is not that good, I only had one year of it in high school and have a terrible accent."

He laughed, "That will not be a problem. You do not have to speak to get into the country."

"You better get moving, you have a plane to catch," The Airman said.

"Marci beaucoup," he said, and we started towards the civilian concourse. In less than an hour I was back in the air, finding there was a lot of travel involved with being an assassin. I guess we couldn't be like doctors and have our customers come to us.

We arrived in Paris late. As it turned out, getting into the country not speaking French was not a problem, as I was playing the part of his prisoner complete with handcuffs, being marched through the terminal gathering stares from the tourists. I was packed into the back of a police car and taken to a station in the city. After being tucked into an interrogation room and released, Anton outlined the details of the assignment.

The targets, two of them, were terrorist recruiters inciting discontent by defacing local mosques and assaulting Muslims in the guise of French Christians. I was shown multiple pictures of each of them.

"This could be a dumb question," I asked, "But why don't you just arrest them?"

"Actually, it's not that dumb," he answered, "I wish we could, but even if we could find evidence and witnesses who would testify, once they were put in jail it would endanger our people all over the world. Followers and mercenaries alike would be eager to kidnap for their release. And to answer your next question, we chose you for what you call plausible deniability, and you come highly recommended. We do have our own people who could probably do it, but they need to be accounted for at the time of the hit. You're basically our last resort."

"Thanks for answering my questions, I'll do what I can."

"There are stakeouts around their usual haunts, and we are currently awaiting word of a possible hit location." Anton continued.

It was 22:00 before we had a positive sighting. I was rushed to a left bank hotel, taking an ancient elevator to the eighth floor. After a tap on the door, Anton and I were ushered in by the two men inside. The room was dark, with a wide open window on the opposite wall. There were tripod binoculars set up next to the window. I was escorted over and shown the target window 800 meters away, two floors down, across the brightly lit street. There were two men at a table. It looked like they were drinking coffee and talking. One was clearly one of the men we were looking for. The other appeared to be, but was partially hidden. It would be a difficult shot. I did not feel comfortable not having a chance to zero the sight. I lined up. Shit, I couldn't afford a miss. I scanned up until a billboard came into view, showing a model elegantly dressed in a black gown, drinking whatever was being advertised. She was about to have another hole in her head. I took a shot. It was worse than I expected; almost a foot off. I zeroed and focused down at our two friends still seated. The men in the room with me got panicky. I motioned for them to chill. Aligning on the difficult shot first, the Heckler & Koch MSG90 kicked twice, and the first guy went down, followed by the other before he had a chance to react. "It's done." I said to the anxious room, "two hits." They all started breathing again. I handed off the rifle and left with Anton.

As Anton drove back, I just stared out the window. I was a last resort, someone they came to when the legal system failed but the problem couldn't be ignored. Was this a future trend, or was I just the next generation of a continuing underground institution?

He took me back towards the city center, dropping me at a very nice looking hotel, "We have reserved you a room under your Babbin name. Enjoy your stay in Paris tomorrow, on us." He gave me a kiss on the cheek and left. I went inside and received a key card to a suite on the twelfth floor. It was indeed a very nice room. I also found a change of clothes and even sleep wear in a small suitcase that was laid out on the valet stand. I washed and donned the large t-shirt-like sleep wear, however, even though I have no problem sleeping in vehicles on my way to potentially deadly situations, here in a luxury Paris hotel, I just lay staring at the ceiling.

Just like that, Cali was gone again, but this time it was different, more than just the difference between death and Virginia. When she was dead I felt like I couldn't live without her. When I found she was alive she said she couldn't live without me. What changed? There was a new piece of information that she had and I did not have, that she didn't want to tell me about. What was it? I wasn't mad at her but happy for her; I hoped her new life would take her wherever she wanted to go, meshed into her chosen cog in the machine we call human civilization.

Anthropology taught me, or maybe it was Calvin and Hobbes, we don't have the fangs and the claws to survive on our own, we need each other. But what about me? Before, I didn't have a place to fit into, and I ground in the gears of that same machine. Do I now have a place but am I still pretending it doesn't really exist? I need to face reality; I am a last resort, a fix for civilization's failure to deal with its darker side. But am I temporary caulking in the cracks of the justice system, or am I just another in a long line of the unseen, sacrificed to do civilized man's dirty work so he can go on thinking he is civilized?

Who am I, when the phone rings, am I Millie, Laura, or Claudette? Most people, when they get a call, they try to identify who is on the other end. I, on the other hand, try to figure out who I am, what lie to be today. So tomorrow, a cold blooded killer will roam the streets of Paris rubbing shoulders with Parisians and tourists alike, just as if I were a normal human. I will gladly aid wide eyed lovers by snapping their picture in front of the Eiffel Tower. Will that little note make it to the back of the photo? "PS, this photo was taken by a woman who just killed two people the night before."

At some point, I did fall asleep. I woke up as the sun just started peeking through the window. Well, today I would be Claudette, with the terrible American accent, but I wanted to get out and enjoy the sunshine with an early morning breakfast at a French Café. I turned on the TV and searched for an English broadcast, and found BBC world news. The story about the two notorious terrorists being killed in an apartment in Paris came on. The news report made it sound like they had been shot from inside the room. I finished getting dressed in the clothes provided; a pair of faded jeans, white soft cotton shirt, and dark navy narrow waisted pea coat that actually fit pretty well. The case also included 300 Euros; that should at least get me breakfast. I did a pocket check and walked out the door to check out and start looking for a place for breakfast.

There was a small Café on the East end of the block named Le Lorette. I went inside and attempted to get something to eat. In the US, we are well versed in standing in line, and there is a strong ethic of waiting your turn. As it turns out, it is not that way in France. It was more of a survival of the fittest style free for all, and I was getting pushed out of the way by children and old ladies. As I was resigning myself to the reality that I was going to starve to death, I got a call, it was Anton, "Claudette? Where are you now?" he asked.

"I'm in a Bistro called Le Lorette on the end of the block where the Hotel is. Don't the French know anything about waiting your turn? I'm getting trampled to death in here, I guess I'm going hungry today."

He laughed, "Are you telling me that last night you single handedly took out the two most feared terrorists in France, and this morning you can't be assertive enough to get breakfast?"

I guess it was kind of sad. "Well, you guys took my MSG90 away." I answered.

"I will meet you there in 15 minutes." He said and hung up. Anton walked through the door ten minutes later, saw me sitting dejected at a small table off in a corner by itself. "Do you drink coffee?" He asked.

"Café au lait please, oh, and the real French style café au lait, not the American tiny drop of milk in awful tasting coffee style."

He smiled. "I think I like you, Claudette." He put in the order and returned to the table.

I smiled at him, "I hardly know who I am anymore." He smiled, sitting close to me in our secluded corner like we were lovers.

The waitress brought the coffee, and it was actually very good.

"You are not like the other people I've seen who do this job," he said "You have a light in you that I do not usually see in the other Americans."

"What job, professional assassin? How can anyone be human and do this job?"

"I meant counter terrorist, but yes, you seem to be able to do it and still be human, as you put it, it's just business to you, you don't let it destroy you."

"I like to think what I'm doing actually helps, but I'm not always so sure." I answered.

The waitress brought over our breakfast, a broccoli and cheese omelet.

"I have often thought that myself, but if we can save any of our citizens from being hurt, then we are doing the right thing. We are at war, and this war is directly against the innocent. Some of us need to be charged with doing things we don't like so that others can live good lives, free of pain and fear."

"It's too bad it's not about nuclear annihilation anymore. In that one, even the men who pulled the strings would be destroyed, so they had to think carefully about what they did. Now it's the best case for all the leaders involved."

"I don't understand what could you possibly mean by that?"

"Think about it, the leaders on one side get to use God's name to incite impressionable young men to satisfy their lust for blood and power. The leaders on the other side get to decry the horrors of these terrible acts to bolster their own power, by preying on the fears of the people so they give up freedom for security, and it's not the leaders who are in danger, it is the average citizen who pays with their lives. It is the perfect war, as far as the leaders are concerned."

"That is a very cold hearted way of looking at it, but I see your point. However, if that is true, then you can bring the war back to those leaders who believe they are safe. You are the new nuclear weapon." I am the last resort, a post modern nuclear weapon. Maybe that was the moment I let myself fall into my niche in this great machine, be it a comfortable ride or gateway to hell. In the meantime, this thermo-nuclear device was pretty hungry, and the omelet was very good. He watched me eat with a funny smile on his face.

"What?" I asked.

He pointed to the fork in my right hand, "You are very American." He laughed. I watched him eat with the knife in his right hand and the fork in his left.

"Well, why bother with a knife if you don't need it?"

"So what do you do if you need it?"

"Cut it up and then eat it, what's so strange about that?"

"Americans." he said, shaking his head. Then he said, "My boss wants you to come and work for us."

"You mean the DST?" I asked.

"Yes, you come highly recommended and I've seen you in action. You are very good. He thinks we can help each other. We can give you a safe place to hide out, and you can help us."

"You mean with the nuclear thing?"

"Yes," he said "and I've read your file, I think there are other things you can help us with."

"I don't know, I think that's kind of up to my boss, I've already got Afghanistan and Turkey trying to kill me, I don't want the US trying also."

"It seems that Afghanistan already succeeded, and here you are, still doing okay. I think my boss is pulling some strings."

"Okay, maybe, and I may even learn French, but I'm never eating with my left hand, I have to draw the line somewhere." I said, holding up my fork in my right hand with a little piece of omelet on it. He smiled and shook his head, returning to his own breakfast.

After finishing, he left a tip on the table and he guided me out the door, walking down the street. Turning a corner to a side street, he pointed to a small Renault, and I got in the passenger side after he unlocked the door. As he pulled out of the side street and into traffic, I asked him, "So I have a file? What else is in it?"

"It said, and this is an exact quote, it said that you are dangerously intelligent."

"And you still want to work with me?" I asked.

"Well," he answered, "My file says I am dangerously reckless."

"And I'm sitting in a car you're driving?"

"I guess I should have told you that before you got in."

"You should have it printed in at least three languages here on the passenger side visor."

While he was driving, he got a phone call. I was amazed that he was able to dodge the Paris traffic and talk at the same time.

"What!" He looked over at me, "Is he there now?" He clicked off. "I've been requested to bring you to the office." he said.

"What is it?" I asked.

"Please, I do not want to tell you here." He whipped through traffic, living up to what was printed in his file.

We did, however, make it into a parking garage under a modern glass and stone building. We took an elevator up to the seventh floor into an open area of steel and glass computer stations, with intermittent glass walled offices spaced about the room. Anton led me to one of those rooms with two people already inside. He tapped on the door, then opened it for me. The men looked up as I entered.

"Miss Babbin," one of the men said.

"Pierre, correct?" I extended my hand; instead he held my shoulders and gave me a kiss on each cheek.

"So good to finally meet you, I hear our mission was a complete success. This is Mr. Miller from your state department."

"What is it?" I asked

"I will let Mr. Miller tell you that," he said.

Mr. Miller began, "We are closing the Bonn facility and everyone is being reassigned, as you know, Miss Rennier has already been transferred back to the States."

"What!" I said, "And what about Ted Haal?"

"I'm afraid he has been reassigned to lead a different team, Miss Peddington." Miller answered.

He continued, "We believe the Russian arms dealers whose shipment you disrupted are planning to retaliate. This is for your safety. What we would like, Miss Peddington, is for you to stay with the French DST for the time being as a cover."

"Um, I don't mean to be disrespectful or anything, but do you have any identification?" I asked.

He looked a little irritated, but dug into his suit jacket pocket and showed me a US Department of Defense ID.

"Thank you, sir." I said, "But can we get a hold of Mr. Harfax for verification? I would like to get a chance to speak with him about what has happened."

"Now see here…" Miller started.

Pierre calmed him, "Miss Babbin is correct to request confirmation, I would expect nothing less from any good field agent."

Miller checked his watch, "He will not be available for another hour."

"If Miss Babbin agrees, she can tentatively say this is a go, pending confirmation with Mr. Harfax, agreeable?"

"Yes, that is agreeable." I said, Miller still didn't look pleased, but accepted it. He shook hands with Pierre and left without looking at me again.

"Tres bon," Pierre said. "Let us show you our humble home."

I was kind of still in a daze as he showed me around the room, being introduced to the people who were behind the computers. I didn't want to tell him that none of this was sinking in. Next, we went to what looked to be a large conference room, however, inside was a room somewhat similar to the open area of the Bonn office, with a large back wall mounted monitor. We were interrupted by a woman who said it was time to give Mr. Harfax a call. We made the call from the mission planning room on a speaker phone. A receptionist answered.

"We would like to speak with Mr. Harfax, please." Pierre said.

"Mr. Harfax is unavailable all day," the receptionist said.

"Is he in?" I asked, "This is very important, could you tell him Laura Peddington is calling?"

Seconds later, Harfax came on, "Millie, where are you?"

"I'm in Paris, just finished another assignment. What happened, was that true?"

"Unfortunately yes, we believe the Russian dealers are planning something. Could you please go off the speaker for a moment?" I picked up the headset. "We are letting the Russians complete their attempt, so no matter what you may hear do not be upset. Everyone, including Mr. Haal and Miss Rennier, are okay.

"Thanks, Mr. Harfax. Does she know what happened?"

"Yes, she just got in; she will be told that you are okay."

"Thanks"

"Thank you for calling in."

"Mr. Harfax, do you know a Mr. Miller?" I asked.

"Yes, why?"

"He was here in Paris, it was his suggestion that I be assigned here with the DST to keep a low profile for a while."

"Leave it to Miller to give my assets away without consulting me. Okay, but this is temporary, we may have more missions coming up that we will need you for, so stay connected. Let me speak with Pierre."

"Yes, thank you Mr. Harfax. Pierre, Mr. Harfax would like to speak with you."

"Mr. Harfax, this is Pierre de Jardon from the DST, her help will be greatly appreciated. I assure you, we will keep her safe." There was a pause. "Yes, Mr. Harfax, I understand. Au revoir. "

"Tres bon, Miss Babbin, we are looking forward to working with you."

"There are a few details I need to get straight," I said. "First, who am I? Am I Claudette, or Laura? And next where will I be living?"

"I think it's best if you stay Claudette for now during normal working projects, we may at times change your designation for specific assignments. As far as living arrangements, for now, we will put you in a safe house here in the city."

30

The safe house was a nice, four bedroom, town house that was a short metro ride from the DST office. I was also given a Rosetta Stone French language course; they said it was not required, but a good idea.

That evening, I was alone in the TV room, so I switched on BBC World News and found that the top story was of the bombing of our old Bonn office building. There was video of the remnants of the three story stone building that was nothing more than a pile of bricks filling the basement. The report said that all eight people who worked in the building died in the blast that occurred at 10:00 AM local time. I think that's what Mr. Harfax referred to when he said, don't be alarmed by what you hear.

Monday, I started a normal workday at 8:00 AM, introducing them to the weighted mapping style that Cali taught me that she used for Mr. Haal's operation.

It was actually interesting, looking at the big picture; I imagined that this was much like what Cali was doing at Langley. For the rest of spring, this was like a normal job for me. I learned to speak French, a little better, anyway, started taking Pre-Combat Savate classes and was even able to survive getting my own Café breakfast. It was a nice, quiet time of relative stability, a kind of two-month normal world holiday. We hashed over tons of money trails, phone calls, maps, and internet communications, trying to separate out terrorist behavior from the multitude of other shady deals that were part of the lives of the normal citizens. It had a kind of strange fascination, viewing the ugly underbelly of life. If the good citizens only knew how much of what they think they are hiding, we view every day it would confirm their worst conspiracy theory fears.

The month of April was the closest I ever came to a normal nine to five job. There were a few "special assignments" to be sure. They went much like the late night operation in Germany, in and out in the dead of night with no preparation, little conversation, and less information. Two were unfriendly extractions and the other three were plain and simple assassinations. Sometimes I could guess what actually happened from later news reports others I could not.

4:32 AM May 2, I received a call from Cali, it was very short she only said.

"Get to your DST office and call in your people, something's happening." That was it, nothing else. This told me that whatever it was, it was big. I called Pierre on the way in, and had no trouble convincing him. In our business fewer words means bigger event. By 5:15 the full team was assembled, by 5:30 we had a good map of normal activity. A few minutes before 6:00 the announcement came in, stunned shouts of surprise and concern went up around the room and everyone fixed an accusing eye on me. I knew enough French to know that many were cursing.

"Why weren't we told about this?" some were demanding as if I'd known all along.

"I told you what I knew when I knew it." I countered. Pierre calmed them down, speaking in French.

"Be happy we had the warning we did now be watchful." Less than a minute later I got another call from Cali requesting that we sync with the CIA center. Another minute and the communications monitoring supercomputers were linked and recording. The large monitor was pinpointing hot spots. To be sure what we were seeing was secondary activity because the primaries knew to stay away from high tech devices but their activity produced inevitable secondary fallout. The data would be recorded, analyzed and verified, before anything solid could come out of it.

By 8:00 AM things had stabilized and we were watching for any local chatter. I took time out to watch the video of the president's speech to the American people. Then the video shifted to the celebration that was going on outside the White House. At first I started to get caught up in the reaction but the sad reality soon overshadowed the jubilation. I remembered the celebrations in the streets of Palestine as much as the falling towers on September 11, 2001. It was that day that I'd vowed to never wear metal jewelry, something about airport metal detectors, somehow it made sense to an 11 year old girl. From that day until now I'd kept that promise. Now it had gone full circle, but I would still keep my promise because we still live in a world where disagreements are solved by violence. Ten years ago I never imagined that I would be one of the ones pulling the trigger when reason failed.

A week later I received another special assignment call at 10:30PM, thirty minutes later I climbed into the back of a windowless van dressed in dark clothes, fingerless gloves and a Kevlar vest. There were two other people in the back of the van. I recognized one of them even through the dark face-paint. The other man outlined the mission. In the dim light he spread out a map and showed several pictures. The map showed the position and layout of the target house. It was a two story, wood frame storefront below, apartment above. Although it was a wet-works operation the MO was slightly different. We were hitting a bomb making operation; the plan was to hit a completed device with an explosive round setting it off. This would neutralize the entire cell with the added benefit of making it look like their screw-up.

We spent just under an hour on the road before stopping. We silently exited the van, there was enough light to see we were in the loading dock area of a large shop or small warehouse. The first man scrambled up a latter beside one of the loading docks to the roof, I followed, and then the other man came after me carrying the rifle case. We low walked across to the opposite side. The first man started scoping the target shop while the other man set the case down and began scoping the surrounding area. The weapon was an Accuracy International AW50, a 50 caliber bolt action. I didn't like bolt action rifles because it necessitated disengaging the target to chamber another round. But in this case theoretically it should only take one round.

I removed the rifle, chambered a round switched off the safety and took a position beside the man scoping the target. Looking through the NV sight I could make out individuals inside the house through the back door window. The man next to me put a hand on my shoulder.

"Hold," was all he said. I continued to look through the scope. "Hold," he said again. I saw a man inside holding a cylindrical object. "There," he said. "That's it, hit the object." One more second of lining up on the 400 meter distant bread loaf sized object. The gun kicked the rifle report lost in the concussion of the explosion. Bright shrapnel trails streamed from the doors and windows of the bottom floor. For a second it seemed that all had gone as planned. Then the entire target house erupted in a massive fireball, the walls bowing like rubber before disintegrating into splinters and the roof lifting into the air riding on the mushroom cloud. I felt the shockwave all the way to my uterus and heat from the blast seared like sunburn. Windows shattered blocks away. If there was a family living in the apartment they were gone and I changed status from killer to murderer. I jumped up suppressing a scream with my hands over my mouth and was immediately yanked back down.

"Go!" the man next to me hissed into my ear. We scuttled across the roof, down the latter and into the van like bad boys fleeing a broken window. An hour later I was deposited in the alley behind the safe house where I lived. I wondered into the house up to my bedroom still in a daze. The difference between killer and murderer may not seem like much to most people, but to me it's what kept insanity at bay. I had no more excuse, no loophole to hide behind; there was no rationalization and no hope of recovery. I prayed earnestly for God to kill me and send me to hell. The morning came and went, Anton finally found me still sitting curled jail cell style on the window seat holding a loaded SIG P29 that I don't even remember picking up.

After relieving me of the weapon Anton called in and I was taken to a hospital for observation over the next two days. I was told that the apartment was empty but the damage was already done. There was no guarantee that I could prevent an accident that could kill an innocent person. And there was no more fooling myself about my chosen profession.

The next "special assignment did not occur until mid June. Anton and I did a little working holiday to Nice. He donned his working clothes; another sharp Italian suit, and I got an emo makeover, complete with bangs and blue streaked hair. He took along his official documentation to help with the railway police, and I took along a guitar case containing the Heckler & Koch MSG90; a little risky, I suppose, but hopefully his DST ID would keep us out of trouble.

After the explosion incident the plan was to make this more like a low stress vacation as a way to ease me back into my wet-works assignments. Nice was beautiful. We stayed at a Hotel on the east side of the harbor. The evening before the actual business transaction, we did a little clubbing; it seems Anton was a bit of an emo fan. He was the one who suggested my new do. However, the evening ended with a little altercation in the parking lot with three rather well oiled individuals who were overly interested in Anton's flashy rental. We tried to persuade them differently, but it seemed that what they really wanted was to try to steal it. He took two, and I took the other, giving me a chance to practice a little of the pre-combat level savate I'd learned, as a part of DST training. It seemed to work quite well, because they decided they really didn't want to bother us anymore after all.

This was probably not the condition we should have been in to complete our business transaction, however, as we were returning to the hotel Anton got a call indicating that the time table needed to be moved up, because the sheik was not going to make the meeting with our Russian target. They were concerned that he may try to depart early. Anton and I took a drive down Boulevard Carnot, turning off at Chemin des Cretes du Mont Boron, then Route Forestiere du Mont Boron. Turning off on an unmarked dirt road, we stopped in the hillside forest that overlooked the cove on the east side of Nice. Still moored in the cove was Vonikov's yacht that was to be the site of his meeting with the unnamed sheik. Vonikov, the Russian believed to be the instigator behind the Bonn bomb attack, was the target. Anton was checking the boat with binoculars as I was setting up.

"It's not the Sheik, but it looks like he has company." Anton said. "I checked through the scope, and there was another individual on the boat, but it didn't look like it was a friendly meeting. Vonikov was holding a gun on him."

"Well this could be that guy's lucky day," I said. I took a sight zero shot in the water, hoping they were too busy to notice. The other guy turned, but Vonikov didn't. A second later, Vonikov's head seemed to vanish. The other man dove for cover. I hoped he didn't hurt himself, because it wasn't necessary. We watched as he crawled through the doorway to below decks.

"Did you get a picture of that guy for ID?" I asked Anton.

"Yes, I did." He answered.

"Good, I think it would be good to know what's going on there." I packed up the gun, but he continued to watch.

"You know," he said, "We may have messed everything up for that guy, Vonikov could have been ready to, how do you say, spill the beans, to that guy, thinking he was going to kill him anyway."

"You could be right, but at least I didn't wait until just after Vonikov killed him."

"That's true." He admitted.

"Maybe, if we find out who he is, I should send him a card or something." I said.

"Wait, he's back, he's, he's got something with him, looks like he's putting it in a plastic bag and going over the side. I wonder what that is all about?" Anton said.

"Should we try to intercept him?"

"He's going to towards the far shore; we could never get around the cove in time. But I think I'll call it in." Anton said. "It would be nice to have a look inside that boat, also." However, the instant he said that, it exploded from below decks, evidently opening a hole in the hull, because it sank in seconds. Anton put a call into the local police and the coastguard.

"If they find anything, we should be able to get hold of the information." he said.

We packed up and headed back to the hotel. Once back in the room together, things started to get out of control, we kind of couldn't keep our hands off each other. Although it felt good, it got a little awkward and Anton put the brakes on. We sat in an uncomfortable silence for a few minutes. He finally confessed that as much as he wanted me he didn't want this to become a one night stand. At first I was very angry, I thought I was betrayed, but after taking turns in the shower. I realized that he'd actually done the right thing. It wasn't like he'd made any commitment to me; this just happened it was as much my fault as his. I respected the fact that he'd told me before and not after.

The next morning, Anton was up first and kissed me awake, "Thank you for last night," he said.

"What do you mean? Nothing really happened."

"That's what I mean, I was thinking about how dangerous it was to anger a girl who shoots as well as you do."

"How do you know I'm not plotting your demise right now?"

"Because I know you're not that kind of person." He was right. I'm not really a chick flick type girl but I'd seen enough Hallmark channel to know I should have been insanely angry, but I wasn't. And maybe at one level I was, I did want him, I even thought about doing the one night stand anyway. But like eating too much chocolate, enjoying it now and paying for it later was ultimately a bad idea. I guess I'm just too logical.

"You know me too well." I answered. There was something in his eyes that said maybe he was sorry we didn't work out also.

We took a leisurely breakfast, but by late morning we were back on the train heading north. An hour out of Nice I got a call, "Hello?"

"Laura, glad I caught you, where are you?" It was Mr. Harfax.

"On my way back to Paris, I should be back late tonight."

"Good, we have another Zombie project coming up that we will need you to participate in."

"Any details you can give me now?"

"There will be training in Germany."

"What about the DST?"

"Pierre was quite understanding, he wanted to thank us for your service. He seemed to be impressed with you, as we all are."

"Thank you, sir."

"Talk to you soon with the details." Mr Harfax disconnected.

"What was that?" Anton asked.

"I'm afraid Mr Harfax wants me back, he's got another mission for me, and I was just getting good at French." He gave me a funny look.

"What?" I said. He squeezed my hand and smiled.

"Just stay safe." He said. I snuggled up against him, and we sat together in silence, staring out the window as a few more miles of French countryside glided by.

"Shit." I said.

"What?" He asked.

"I don't like this," I said "I don't like getting snatched away like this."

"That's not always our choice, everything will be okay."

"Thanks." I said I'm not sure how he could say that with any certainty, but just knowing that he would want things to work out was nice to hear.

31

It was late evening by the time we pulled into Gare de Lyon. Despite the late hour, we were requested to come into the office. We were ushered into the Director's office, where they were intently going over what looked like site maps and architectural drawings, with about 8 men in the large office.

"Miss Willard, the one I've been hearing so much about?" one of the man said.

"Yes, sir," I answered, a little concerned he was using my real name.

"I am the from the State Department Security Division." He said.

"From the USA?" I asked.

"Yes, we need your help."

"Yes, sir."

"Look at these plans." he turned them so I could see them, "If you were going to hit someone at this location, where would you do it from?" I was suddenly very uncomfortable with the line of questioning.

"Who are you, and why do you want to know that information?"

"A fair question." the DST director said. He had everyone show their identification. Four of the people had US IDs.

"The situation is this; there are some very important people from the States coming to visit, and we are looking for possible shooter locations." George Row, the head of the group said.

I'm not sure I was completely at ease yet, but I said, "I'm assuming this person or persons will be getting out of a car here and walking in this direction into this building. Is that correct?"

"That is correct, Miss Willard."

"Then you look for clear sight ways along this path. May I?" I asked, picking up a pencil.

"Yes." He answered. Outlined what I knew.

Something seemed wrong; most of the information was part of the normal training. It seemed very strange that they would not have already known everything I'd told them.

The next morning, I was expecting a call with the details about the latest Zombie mission; however, it didn't come, so I went into work as normal. When I got there, the State Department guys were already there, and I was called over to the director's office again.

"Good morning, Miss Willard." George Row said.

"Good morning," I said, pretty confused. "What's up?"

"Our problem is that we have a credible threat at an attempt on our people. We want you, Miss Willard, to be a part of our team." This was a scary proposition.

"How is that supposed to work?" I asked.

"We would put you on the roof, and you would watch for a possible shooter."

"How would you hide me on the roof so that I could see all of the likely locations?"

"Why would you be hidden? It's more of a deterrent if you could be seen."

"Doesn't that only work for people who are undecided? If I were the shooter and saw people on the roof looking for me, it would just give me more information as to where to pick my site. And if it's a case of just having someone there as a deterrent, then it doesn't matter who they are."

"Well, it would still be helpful to have you there."

"Also, the information I gave you is only for shooters who are trying not to get caught. A suicide shooter would be a completely different story. The shooter would be much closer, therefore could line up quicker, and could be more hidden until the last second."

"So what's your answer?"

"You know, I was supposed to go on another mission."

"We know. It's been delayed."

"My answer is still no."

"Well that wasn't really a choice, I was just giving you a chance to do the right thing." He stated.

Everything in me told me this was all wrong. I was driven with the rest of the building crew out to the American Embassy. I was dressed an obnoxious black uniform, and given a briefing that was basically a regurgitation of what I had told them the night before. I was glad that he got most of it right, and even more pleased that he didn't point me out as the source of the information. I was also hoping that it wasn't anybody super important, because I still had a very bad feeling. I was given an M4A1, which would be completely useless for any of the sites I pointed out yesterday. Then ushered up to the roof for the next 4 hours to make sure we were bored and inattentive by the time the person arrived. I was surprised that these people seemed to think this was normal. These are certainly not trained security people. regardless I don't think I'll be taking him up on his offer for that job anytime soon.

After the first hour, the guy who did the briefing did a tour of the roof. I was given a ripping in front of the crew for my non-regulation emo hair, and he made me tuck it under the ridiculous looking hat. Funny, he didn't say anything during the briefing. As soon as he was gone, I lifted the hat to let it back out. I began scoping the areas I would have chosen, not that I expected to see anyone yet, but it would be good to get an idea of what they look like now, in case anything changes. Approaching the second hour, I stuffed my hair back under the hat, and sure enough, Mr. Nasty Temper was back. This time, he lit into me because I didn't look attentive enough. After he was gone, I thought maybe I should have left my hair out, maybe I could get fired. I let it out, and continued to sweep the area with the scope. There was now an open window in a 600 meter building that was closed before. I told one of the others about it, and his answer was, "So?"

Okay, I guess this guy really wasn't important, but I would keep watch at that place. I missed my cue for hour 3, and didn't even think about stuffing my hair back under the black painter type hat. He didn't say a word about the hair, but instead hit me up for supposedly standing too close to the edge of the roof. Am I dreaming? These people are just here for pomp, to announce to the world that whoever is visiting is important enough to have guards on the roof. I went from wondering if they wanted him to get whacked to hoping he *would* get whacked. Of course, I knew the real reason I was here was that, if he did catch one, I would be blamed for it. I wondered if this was standard practice. Someone to blame was more important than protecting the person.

It was now getting close to time. I pulled my hair through the hat's size adjustment strap to keep it out of the way, and did another sweep of the area. The original open window was still open. Looking closer, I could see people inside; a man and a woman. It could be just a family. Ten minutes to time zero and our boss was back; he did a sweep of his troops, but didn't leave this time. At 5 minutes, everyone got a little more serious about scoping the area. Two minutes, and the boss started marking time to arrival. From where I was, I wouldn't actually see the person who got out of the car, because he would be under the portico. I checked the apartment with the open window, there was still no interest. If I were the shooter, I would be setting up by now. I scanned the other buildings; nothing looked wrong, no new open windows. It was possible that they could shoot through a window, but that adds inaccuracy, and therefore they would need to be much closer. 30 seconds; the people at the front of the building reported a visual. 10 seconds; the car was under the portico. 5 seconds; the meeting crew would now be going to the car. 3 seconds, doors open, 2 seconds, aids getting out. 1 primary getting out, nothing changing, open window still clear, plus 1 second, the primary would be surrounded, and plus 2, they were inside.

We would stay on the roof for another 4 hours while the meeting was going on. Mr. Obnoxious resumed his normal periodic checks. This was life for these people? Did they ever switch off jobs to be a part of the ground crew? I didn't know, and was afraid to ask; it seemed that one rule that was adhered to was, no talking.

I got an image of a bunch of baboons down in the meeting room comparing penis sizes as they tried to out posture each other. The wars that raged around the planet were living testimony of how ineffective these meeting really were. I started to have a problem, there was no restroom on the roof, and I needed one, so rule number one was going to have to be broken. Finally, I asked. "How do I get relieved so I can go pee?" I asked the guy closest to me.

"You don't." was the answer.

"So you guys never pee?"

"We just hang it out over the side." Yeah right, asshole, I thought.

"Well I'm having one of those heavy flow days, and I don't think the guys down below will like me flipping that over the side."

I saw his eyes scrunch in distain. He checked his watch, "Downstairs, make it quick." I took a quick trip down the stairs, making the mistake of bringing the M4 with me. There was a guard in the hall that heard me running down the steps, he turned, saw the rifle, and fired. The shot hit my Kevlar dead center, in the chest. I went down flat on my back, feeling like I just got hit with a sledgehammer, trying not to pass out. I couldn't move, I couldn't talk, and I hurt. People came running up, but it was difficult to focus on the faces. Somebody was handling me, opening my jacket and assessing the damage. I think he said something about calling an ambulance. It hurt to breathe and I was losing the consciousness battle. I closed my eyes. The next thing I was aware of was being in the ambulance. I was half undressed and my chest was taped. An EMT looked down at me. I wanted to tell him to put me out of my misery, but was still not able to say anything. He faded away.

This hospital thing is getting old, they even have the beeping machine in France, if I'm still in France, I thought. I had no idea how long I'd been out. I wasn't hurting, but I wasn't fully awake either. So I just stared at the ceiling, wondering if whoever it was made out in better shape than I did.

I was kind of fading in and out of sleep for what seemed days. It was probably more like hours. A woman came in, saw that I was awake, and came over. I could tell by her accent that I was still in France.

"We are awake?" I still wasn't sure I could talk.

"Yes," I tried to say, but it wasn't very intelligible. "Yes, I'm awake," I said, a little stronger. At least it didn't hurt.

"Ah, very good, I will get the doctor." she said. A few minutes later, a man I assumed was the doctor came in.

"How are we feeling, Miss Willard?" he asked.

"Like I got shot." I answered, "How bad is it?"

"Not really as bad as it feels, I'm sure, badly bruised, but nothing broken. You should be okay in a few days, just take it easy. No over exertion for a few weeks." The doctor left, leaving the door open, and was talking to someone just outside the room, but I couldn't quite hear what was being said.

Then my roof boss came in the room. He looked down at me and started in on me, "What the hell did you think you were doing? You're lucky you're not dead..." I was so very tired of this guy.

"Shut the fuck up." I said, surprised that I could say it that clearly.

"What was that?" he demanded.

"What part of shut the fuck up was not clear?"

"How dare you?" His expression changed. "What's the matter? Didn't get coddled from us like you were through the Army because of your daddy?"

"My father's dead, asshole."

Mr. Haal walked into the room, took the man by his white shirt and red striped power tie, flung him around, bouncing him off the wall, and then said very slowly, an inch from his face, "GET OUT, and pray that I never see your face again." Then shoved him through the open door. He turned to me.

231

"I need to get you back; as soon as you can get out of here, you're being transferred back to Baumholder, where you will finish your recovery. We can't afford to lose you."

"Thank you sir, but what is going on here? Who are those guys, and what is this all about?"

"George Row and his crew of glory hounds, he's not really State Department, they're a bunch of low level security screw ups. He was trying to make himself look good by disgracing you."

"I guess that explains a lot, but what did he mean by, coddled because of my father?"

He got a pained look on his face, "He was just trying to get back at you."

"Please Haal, I know better, that was about something specific, wasn't it? Was I given a free ride?"
"He closed the door to the room; "I can't be telling you this."

"I need to know, is this all a lie?"

"Please, Laura, Millie, Millie, just listen, okay, it's not like that. Sergeant Bennet was told to do what he could to get you into the service."

"What?"

"Please, Millie, please, just listen, I'm not good at this, so please just let me get this out. It's true that we requested Sergeant Bennet to do what he could to get you into the service. That recruitment center didn't really exist. The real one is miles from there. How do you think he was able to look up your information so fast, or come to pick you up with your test scores? Even Detective Harvester coming to pick you up after the test.

I felt myself losing my grip on reality again. "But why?"

"Why does that matter?"

The tears started as I sat up in bed, "Did it have to do with my father?"

"They saw how devastated you were, so they thought if they could get you into the military, they could help you, you just made their job easy."

"I love our country, but you have to admit, that is not normal behavior for the US government, so there has to be more to it than that."

"They did not know what was going on, but they thought you could be in danger. That's all I can tell you."

"But what about my father?"

"I'm sorry, I don't know anything more, the Feds thought you would be safer if we could get you into the military."

"So this is all a free ride?"

"No, no, absolutely not, they were just supposed to get you in, and thought you'd get some home assignment stapling some general's papers or getting him coffee. All this, the highest test scores the recruiting center's ever seen, the extraordinary service record, the unparalleled marksmanship, the self sacrifice, the unwavering bravery under fire, the selfless service to your country... That is all you. All of it you earned, there is nothing we could do to give you that. Everyone involved was completely flabbergasted at your performance, surpassing anything we could have imagined. So did we help you get in? Yes we did. Was it a free ride? Absolutely not, you earned every bit of it, and don't you ever doubt that. Captain Carver, Castor, Pollux, Pierre de Jardon, even Hammer, they all can't say enough good things about you. That does not come through someone with a free ride."

I couldn't say a word. I sat there with my face in my hands. I didn't know what was harder to process, the fact that I was tricked into the Army, or hearing what people were saying about me. "I can't believe this." Was all I could manage to say.

"I'm sorry, I can't tell you more, but I'm not sorry we conspired to get you into the military, because we need you. Now please get better, and don't worry about that asshole, you won't be seeing him again."

"Thank you Mr. Haal, Sir, Thank you for telling me." He smiled and squeezed my shoulder and left the room.

32

By 8:00 AM that Sunday morning, I was tired of hospitals, and pestered them until I was released at 9:00. Instead of going home, I went to the city center and soon found myself at Notre Dame in time for the 11:30 international mass, and was surprised to see that it wasn't standing room only. To be honest, I don't think I really was as attentive as I should have been; trying to see if God could make sense of who I was, and why I was still alive. I was brought back to reality by a man touching my shoulder.

"Êtes vous bien?" he asked.

"I'm not sure, Je ne suis pas sûr." I answered. He switched to English.

"If you would like to see a priest, I can arrange an appointment for you, but the mass is over, and the next one will start shortly."

"I'm sorry, but I need to leave for Germany tomorrow, so I would not be able make any appointments, but thank you for asking." I stood up and started to leave. It was probably better that I not see a priest, because I would start confessing and create an international incident between the US, France, and the Catholic Church. As I turned to go, the man took my hand and squeezed it.

"Don't doubt God's capacity to forgive." He said. Maybe God was listening after all, I thought.

Monday morning, I took the Metro from the safe house to the DST building for the last time, and met with Pierre. He thanked me for my service, and told me he would welcome me back anytime. I was told that Anton was away on another case, so I would not get a chance to talk to him before I had to leave by train to Baumholder, but there was a person who looked just like him in his office. It was a lonely train ride back to Germany.

Once back at the base, I was given all of my old identification back as Millie Willard, just like I'd never died. I wondered if Mr. Fallow would have to give the new courthouse back. They checked me over, and I was put on therapy, which was not nearly so bad this time. Several days later, the team was called together for a briefing on the mission details. Again, we were going into a country that we were not supposed to be in, to do something we were not supposed to do. The next two weeks were crammed with intensive training. I would be at first protection for the tech crew, in this case, Jarvis, then backup for the ranger crews both in and out; to be headed by Castor and Pollux. This mission would be using aerial drones, plus a new cave crawler device that Jarvis was being trained on. We would be deployed to an existing US occupied zone, then do a covert border crossing. The terrain would be too rough for the hovercraft, but tracks were not an issue. We would start as regular army, then switch to mercenary garb during the bulk of the mission. As usual, we were mostly on our own; we would, however, have extensive access to recon information.

Don't get me wrong, it was good to be back with Castor and Pollux, but it was different this time somehow. I'm not sure if it was the time working a semi normal job in Paris, or if I was just missing working with Cali. Or maybe it was the information that I now had bottled up inside me about my military career. Even though I knew I shouldn't be doing this, I had to tell Cali. So the first chance I got after maneuvers, I found a secure phone and gave her a call. It would be early afternoon there, so I was hoping that she was in.

A familiar voice answered.

"Hello, Cali?"

"Skank? Nice to hear from you, I thought you were on a mission?"

"In a few days, just finishing training, hey, I need to talk to you about something."

"Skanky girl, are you okay, you don't sound good."

"Well yeah, but I found out something about my father's case, about me really, they kind of conspired to get me into the military." There was an ominous silence.

"Cali?"

"Yes, I know something about that. I'm sorry, I found out in Germany, I should have told you, you're listed as NFA."

"What is NFA?"

"No Family Attachments, it means if something happens your family can't be used as leverage against you or against them. They like people like you for missions like the one that they're sending you on."

"Like ones that I don't come back from?"

I could hear the break in her voice. "Skank, girl, you've got to tell me you're going to be okay."

"Yes, Cali, I'm okay, please don't worry, and thanks for telling me. That's not exactly the way I heard it, but your story makes more sense. Listen, could you do me a big favor? Only if it won't get you in trouble, because I think this is a very touchy subject. I found out about me, but I did not find out anything about my father and the case around his death. Is there some way you could find out about that? Without getting into trouble."

"Touchy subjects are my specialty, I'll see what I can do, and please be safe, Skank, I need you back."

"I'll be okay, but remember what we talked about?"

"Yes, but not this time, okay? Please not this time."

We disconnected, and I sat staring at the table. Ted lied to me, AGAIN, but somehow it wasn't important now. Something was wrong with this mission, and Cali could feel it too.

Mail call was always a little painful for me, I enjoyed it when the others would share their letters from home with the group, but it was always a little painful knowing that I would never get a letter. Except one day, I did get a letter, obviously hand addressed by a child. I was completely stunned. I thought being dead would automatically preclude me from receiving mail, except for the occasional credit card offer. But this was a real letter, a card, actually; it was hard to keep the tears away as I opened it. Pullux and Markley came over as I tore open the envelope. It was from Joey Tomlinson. He was in third grade, going to St. Sebastian Christian School in Cloverdale, Kentucky. It was written in the big letters of a child.

"Hi, My name is Joey, I live in Cloverdale with my Mom, Dad, and two sisters, Molly and Danielle. My dad sells insurance. I'm 7. My teacher said we should write to you because you are helping to make the world safer. And we should say thank you. Thank You. I picked your name because she said you didn't have a family to write to you. Remember Jesus loves you. Bye. Joey."

There were pictures in crayon along the bottom that must have been his family on the left side; mom, dad, and three kids. On the other side was a picture of a blue-eyed blonde girl dressed in green I assumed was supposed to be me. I was overwhelmed, and passed it around to everyone to see. We put it up on the wall and took a picture of all of us around it, and me in the middle. Jarvis printed a copy of the picture so we could mail it with the letter. Then I wrote back to Joey:

"Dear Joey, Thank you so much for your letter, your teacher was right that I don't have a family. Your letter was the first one I've ever received, and I can't tell you how much it means to me that you took the time to write. We put your picture up on the wall, where we are training for our next mission. I've included a picture with all of the people in our unit. I'm the brown haired girl sitting in the middle. I hope you are enjoying school. I would like to hear from you again if you want. I pray to Jesus that what I'm doing is making the world safer for you and your family, and I'm glad I can do it for you. Jesus loves you too. Thank you. Millie Willard."

I stuffed the letter and the picture in an envelope and addressed it. It would go to be mailed tomorrow, after we were to leave on the mission.

July 5, 2011a gentle fog shrouded the pre dawn sky as we waited to board large transport plane that would deposit us in the US base, at the starting point for our next mission. All of the training completed, and now as we waited on the tarmac, I was not thinking about the mission, but only about how Germany somehow reminded me of Connecticut, with sweet smelling summer mornings and lush green trees creating shadows in the fog. That made me think about my father, and my home town, and mornings just like this one when I was younger, and how the early morning was full of adventures, back when adventures were fun. When was it that life had ceased to be fun, and got so terribly complicated? I came back to reality with Pollux waving his hand in front of my face.

"Sorry we had to wake you so early, Skank, but it's time to get on the plane." His big smiling face said.

"Huh, oh sorry, I kind of zoned." I answered as I watched the others do an eye roll. I got myself together and boarded. Once on the plane, I went back to thinking about my father, but in the present, hoping that Cali could find out what happened, but being afraid of what that might be. I woke up as the landing announcement was given, snuggled against Markley. As hard as his body was, he was still incredibly comfortable, and he didn't seem to mind.

After landing in the base town of desert scrub, we met up with the other half of the crew that included Cowgirl, Psych, and a new Texan called Walker; a tall, lanky, hawkeyed man that reminded me of Aragorn from Lord of the Rings. They took us to one of the airport hangars, where our final mission briefing was to take place. The briefing was relatively short, telling us only that command had given us a maximum of 4 weeks to complete the mission. If we had not found the target by then, we would be pulled anyway and plan B would be instituted. Suspecting what the target was I didn't want to think about what "Plan B" might be. By late afternoon, we were on our way to the nighttime border crossing.

July 26, 2011 I managed to hold off the attack long enough for Jarvis to complete his work, but I felt bad that I was handing him a losing battle. The enemy would soon regroup and over run our position, and there would be nothing we could do about it. If we both fought, we could hold out longer, but it was more important that I cover the rangers for as long as possible.

Automatic fire was hitting all around us as Pollux and Castor's crew boarded the choppers with the prize the terrorists had obtained from an "ally". I was able to cover their departure until I knew they were safe. Jarvis took a hit as I shifted my attention to our situation. I saw him hit the ground grabbing his thigh. I scrambled to a kneeling position and threw up my hands, expecting to take hits anyway, but it didn't happen. Within seconds, we were surrounded by a mass of AK wielding men; boys, actually, as I looked into their faces filled with youthful zeal and confusion. Most couldn't have been more than sixteen years old. They were shouting in a language I couldn't even identify, thrusting their guns at me, but not getting too close. Others, however, descended upon Jarvis, as if attacking him.

"No, no, please, he's hurt, he's hurt!" I yelled, still kneeling, but waving my hands in his direction, knowing full well they would not be able to understand. I tried to stand to help him, but hands on my shoulders pushed me back down. But they did see that he was hurt, and eased their attack. Guns were lowered as older men approached. I looked around at the two young men who were still holding my shoulders; they seemed reluctant to look me in the eye.

I imagine that when they write the report on this mission, it would be called a success, and there would be someone who didn't participate who would be taking all of the credit. To be honest, it didn't really bother me. I was hoping that in the long run, it would all be worth it. But right now, my wrists and ankles were tied to poles, with me in a standing position spread out between them. My jacket had been removed, and my hair was down. I believed right now my captors were trying to justify what they were about to do to me. I don't know if I was really all that scared; it was kind of like sitting in the waiting room at the dentist's office. You knew it was going to hurt, but everything would be better when it was all over.

I did not realize it then, but now, as I was contemplating my meeting with God, I realized it was faith in the eyes of the young men who had captured me. Whether what they were doing was actually God's will or not, they at least believed it was. Would God honor that faith, even if misguided? I was the one that doubted, the one who was not sure I was doing the right thing. Could I be forgiven?

Three long bearded older men approached, two of the men stood in front of me while the other one went around behind. At first, I kept my eyes down as they looked me over. The third man came up behind me, grabbing my hair, pulling my head up. I heard Jarvis gasp as he watched, but could do nothing to help me. With my head pulled up, I looked the other two men straight in the eye.

It was strange, right now, for some reason, I thought about my home town; I wanted them to know what actually happened to me. I wanted to hear what they would say about me after knowing the truth of what I had done, and how I died. The man behind me pulled out a long curved knife, and positioned it beside my neck. I was actually relieved, it could have been a lot worse. The expression on my face must have given me away, because one of the men in front held up his hand to signal the man behind me to wait.

"You do not realize that you are about to die?" One of the two asked, speaking slowly in heavily accented English.

"Oh yes," I answered "I will be with Jesus very soon."

"Even if Jesus could save you, why do you think he would want to help a whore like you?"

I smiled, then spoke slowly, "Begging your pardon, sir, but I am a skank, not a whore, and I certainly do not deserve anything from Jesus, but because he *is* Jesus, he has already saved me, and even now he is waiting to welcome me home."

"Then you will die deceived, Skank." I was flooded with infinite peace as I heard him say my name. He motioned for the man behind me to continue. He never got the chance. I heard the now familiar wet crack, and something warm and wet hit my arm and shoulder. The two bearded men's eyes widened in horror, watching the headless man fall, and then looked at me as if I had killed him. Finally it dawned on them that they were under attack. There was shouting as the fighters were mobilized. Total chaos broke loose as grossly undertrained soldiers started firing in all directions. It was strange, being on the other side, I could almost picture what was going to happen next. Those who were leading started falling. The two bearded men stood and watched as if they were immune to bullets. I realized that they were clerics, not combatants. Within minutes, the rangers were overwhelming the camp; those defending started throwing down their weapons and either surrendering or just running away. The clerics were captured. I felt strong hands on my arms holding my wrists as they cut through the ropes binding me to the posts. With my arms released, but my feet still tied, I lost my balance and was starting to fall forward. I looked into Markley's big smiling face as he caught me, helping me sit as Walker sliced through the ropes at my feet.

"Did you guys get Jarvis? He was injured," I said.

Walker helped me to me feet, "Yes, he's going to be fine." Castor answered as he came forward.

"How did you guys get here so quickly? Last I saw, you were getting the device into the chopper."

"Well," Pollux continued for Castor, "We decided to join your party because it looked like you were having all of the fun."

"You didn't abort the mission just to get us, did you?" I asked.

"No, our prize is safely tucked away, we just didn't all go for the ride back with them, don't worry, we weren't going to leave you." Castor said.

We had to hold our position for twenty minutes, waiting for the choppers to return. During that time, Jarvis was attended to, and I was reunited with the rest of my equipment. I used the scope to scan the perimeter, verifying that it was clear.

Later, I sought out Cowgirl; I was pretty sure she took the shot that saved my life. The thank you hug I gave her got a lot more emotional than I'd planned. I think I embarrassed her. She tried to brush it off as nothing, but somehow I could tell that it was more than that.

Why do I try to deceive myself? A few minutes ago, I wanted death more than life, I was eager to go through that one-way door, and be done with all this. But now, I was actually happy to be alive, death could wait, for a little while longer. Maybe you couldn't go both ways, but I was loved on both sides. Is there anything better than that? Maybe I could learn to like life after all.

"Choppers in 5," Castor announced, "We can't take all of our new guests, so help me make sure they can't fight back after we leave." That meant destroying their weapons. Castor mobilized us to do just that, disassembling AKs and removing vital parts. We were still at it when our rides arrived. The guns that were not disabled, we took with us as we loaded up, leaving most of the confused captives behind. It was almost like some were disappointed. We took the two clerics and two other leaders.

At the base, I had a chance to talk to Jarvis before the medics dragged him away, telling him that I was sorry that

I got him shot and captured. He said that he thought it was his fault.

"I knew when I decided to backup the rangers that you had no chance of holding out against such an overwhelming force." I said, "So please don't think that it was your fault."

"Thank you." he said. "That was both the worst and best moment of my life. Best because we did everything we could and helped make the mission a success, worst, thinking that I was about to be responsible for your death."

"Then it was the best for both of us." I answered, picking up his hand and hugging it to my heart, before they carried him away. The debriefing was mostly a celebration. Castor could not say enough about the performance of his men as he spoke to the brass gathered, who tried to maintain their objective straight faces, but were having a hard time suppressing their joy. I hung on every detail that Castor recounted about Walker and Markley's bravery, as they took point to search out the tunnels that made up the hiding spot. I thought that just being here and hearing this was an amazing honor. The brass left, and we were treated to officer-worthy food and drink.

This was the first time in three weeks that I was able to get a long hot shower and sleep in an actual bed, however, in the quiet after I'd stopped wallowing in the praise of men, another quiet voice started speaking to me.

When you shoot someone from 1000 meters at night, they show as a green person shaped blob in the scope. At close range, you can tell they are real men, in this case, children, their young faces filled at first with wide eyed zeal, then confusion, not expecting a woman to be able to fight back. When I'd raised my hands in surrender, they had no idea of what to do with me. I was killing children;

God's children. I prayed that they were with him now. God lives outside our universe, we do what we do, and then we come home. A wise man once said it like this; meaningless, meaningless, all is meaningless. Was it time to just say no to man instead of God?

33

The next morning we were divided up again. Jarvis would be going back to the US; his tour of duty over early, complements of his war wound. Castor and Pollux would also be going States side, their current tour of duty over. Walker, Markley, Psych, and Cowgirl would be going to Hammer's crew.

I was going to England. I'd been asked to testify as an expert witness before the Joint Chiefs meeting in London. In the orders I was given by Captain Carver, I was to be personally piloted in a military plane to London for the high level meeting. Its purpose was to provide the definitive report on women in combat. I looked Carver in the eye, "Is this for real?" I asked.

"I think this is about as real as it gets." He answered.

"Shit."

"Is that fear, Skank? I talked to Jarvis yesterday; he told me that you were the bravest person he'd ever seen."

"That was only death, sir; this is a meeting with the Joint Chiefs."

"I see your point. Anyway, your ride is waiting." He motioned to a lieutenant in a flight suit standing at attention. He led me to a ready room where I was helped into a similar suit, complete with gloves, helmet, and the respirator mask, then followed him to a plane that looked like it was a fighter plane's younger brother. There was an Air force WO there at the base of the ladder that led to the cockpit. The lieutenant went up first, then I went up, and the other man followed. He instructed me on how to get into the rear seat. There were so many dials, switches, knobs, readouts, and levers, I didn't think that there was any way that even my 5'5" 130 pound body was going to fit around them, but he showed me where to plant my feet, then the rest of me followed. Once in, the seat was amazingly comfortable. My personal flight valet helped me get situated, plugging my dangling wires and hoses into the plane.

"This is the latch for the respirator. Once airborne, you will want to lock it in place." He showed me how it swung over my face. "And this is the control for your visor; you are going to want it down once you are above the cloud layer."

"Thanks." I answered.

"Ready, Miss." The pilot asked.

"Ready, sir." The turbine wound up, and the plane began to taxi as the canopy lowered into place. I made sure that all of my arms and legs were inside the ride as it came down. I wanted to remain cool, like this was no big deal, but the truth was, this was way too much fun. I watched as we lined up on the long, straight runway. The engine changed from the soft whine to a deafening roar, and the acceleration pushed me into the seat. I did everything I could to keep myself from screaming with excitement.

On the way, the pilot was not very talkative, which was okay with me. I was having a big time "What's wrong with this picture" crisis. I couldn't get my head around me being an expert witness. There were two possibilities; one, I was being summoned under false pretenses and this had nothing to do with women in combat, or worse, I was about to be blamed by history from this day forward as the person who messed up the future of the military, no matter what I actually said in the meeting.

We had to do a refueling stop in Turkey. After a potty break and small salad, we were back in the air. Three hours later, we were landing at a military base just outside London. I was met at the bottom of the ladder by a very official looking woman in a dress uniform, with her hair in a bun. She escorted me into a mid century modern single story brick building. Once inside, the heels of her pumps clopped like a horse on the hard tile floor as she continued her pace though large rooms and down corridors. Without a word, she opened a plain wood door and motioned me inside. She did not enter, but closed the door behind me. There were five older men in the room in dark suits. A balding man with a fringe that stuck out in all directions stood and held out his hand.

"Miss Willard, I presume, how good of you to come." As if I had a choice. I took his hand. "My name is Welford Scott. I will be your escort to the meeting." He said.

"Thank you Mr. Scott, could you please give me the details on the meeting so that I know what to prepare for?"

"In due time, first we must get you out of that suit and into some proper attire." he said. I hoped that didn't mean he was going to assist with the getting out of the suit part. I must have had a confused look on my face because he turned red faced and started to backpedal.

"Well, no, I didn't mean that I, I mean that, well you know. Let me just get you to the haberdasher." He led me out of the room, not bothering to introduce me to the others.

"Isn't a haberdashery for men's clothes?" I asked, looking to the others for assistance, tripping over my own feet as he led me from the room. Outside, in front of the building, he flagged down a driver that had been waiting by the curb and we drove off towards the city. We were deposited on a busy street in a shopping district.

"We need to find you something to wear to the meeting." He said, as he started up at a surprisingly brisk pace for an older gentleman. He turned into a formalwear shop. "Splendid." he announced as we walked down the aisle. I finally got a good look at the row of black pencil skirts, white frilly blouses, and straight waisted black jackets. If I were to put one of these outfits on, I'd look like a tetherball pole going to a funeral. I took this as a definite sign that it was time to put a screeching halt to the whole thing and just say no.

"Here, young lady, why don't we just try one of these on?" Well I not sure about him, but I was not going to put one of those outfits on.

"No, I don't think so." I answered.

"I beg your pardon?"

"I'm not trying one of those on."

"What is wrong with these, they are fine womanly fashion; you can't go dressed in that flight suit."

"First of all, that looks like I'm going to a funeral, most likely mine, and what is this meeting about anyway?"

"We can't talk about that here." He exclaimed.

"Well I'm not going anywhere until we do talk about it, I don't think this is about women in combat."

"Don't get loud." He said, motioning with his hands as if he were trying to push cotton down into a big box. "If you want to go to a different store, we can, we just can't talk about anything here."

I took his hand and dragged him into one of the changing booths. Several of the 60ish women in the store gave us a very scandalous look.

"Can we talk about it here?" I asked.

"No, we cannot talk about it here, or anywhere." He said in a quiet but forceful voice.

"What do you mean we can't talk about it anywhere?" I held my head in my hands to keep it from exploding. "That does it, I quit, I'm going back home." I turned around and walked out of the booth; to be honest, it was kind of an empty threat because I had no idea where home was anymore. He ran after me, grabbing on to one of the miscellaneous belts or flaps on the suit.

"You can't quit, I can't let you do that."

"Well then, shoot me if you have to." He whipped something out of his jacket; it happened to be a cell phone, not a gun, and pushed a speed dial number. The call was answered quickly.

"Sir?" He said, "I'm having a bit of a situation here. It's one of your um, agents, sir, she's in somewhat of a snit, says she wants to quit, and I should shoot her." He looked up from the phone looking a bit confused. "Are you the one they call Skank?"

"Yes, that's me." I answered. He handed me the phone.

"Hello," I said into the offered phone.

"Hi, Skank, it's been a while, I hear great things about you." It was Ted Haal.

"Well, I think they're exaggerating, what is going on here?"

"If I know these people, it's no exaggeration. Look, this is very important, Laura. The world is changing, and you've been there to see it. These people are still living in the past, they need to get jolted out of their spit shined shoes, and I know you are the person who can do it. No bullshit, Laura, let them have it, how do you say, with both barrels. I know you, you're intelligent and observant, you know the score, but you need confidence. Don't hold back, this is your generation's world and they are screwing it up, take it by force if you have to; don't let them push you into their mould. Okay, Laura?"

"Yes, sir." I answered.

"And get out of that frumpy store and find some real clothes, go to SBS in Westfield Shops if you have to."

"Yes, sir." He disconnected and I handed the phone back to Mr. Scott. "We need to go to Westfield Shops." I told him.

"Why, that's all the way across town." He answered.

I turned and took another long look at all the pencil skirts, "The farther from here, the better." I answered, turning back to Mr. Scott.

A forty minute cab ride through London traffic later, we turned down Woods Lane past a subway station sign and up to the shopping center.

"We could have taken the subway, it would have been easier." I said.

"You mean, take the underground." he said in a tone that both pointed to my ignorance of Britain, and his disgust for public transportation. I didn't challenge him on it. Instead, I looked up on the directory and found SBS Point of You, and I dragged him in the direction the map indicated. There was a certain apprehension barking at my heels as I headed for the store. In the past, there was nothing that conjured my innate skankiness than me trying to dress up, but I looked over my shoulder at the man following after me. Between him, me, or the US government deciding my fashion statement, it looked like I was the best choice. We got to the store. At first it looked a little too stark and formal, but the mannequins spaced around showed a style that took cute grunge to a whole new level. There was a little tweak of fear in the fact that Ted Haal knew me so well, but he was a spy after all. At first, Mr. Scott, after viewing the store, seemed relieved; then he got a look at what I was contemplating.

"You can't wear dungarees to a meeting with the joint chiefs."

"That's exactly what I want to do," I answered. The horrified look on his face said it all. To be fair, it wasn't just jeans; it was an abstract, designer print, black, very short t-shirt dress over skinny jeans; a look that I liked, but thought went out three years ago in Connecticut. It also included a tie-waisted short trench coat, and the shoes were over the ankle length tie brown boots. An emo-haired metrosexual glided up to us, looking my US Air Force flight suit up and down.

"Can I help you?" he asked.

"I want this," I said.

"The jacket?"

"The whole thing."

Again, he looked me over, "But I don't think…"

"Don't think, just get."

"But what size are you?" To be honest I didn't know any more, and especially in European sizes.

I took his hand and started pulling him towards the changing room. "Come on, measure me." I said.

Mr. Scott objected, "Wait, you can't be out of my sight, Miss Willard." He said.

"Then come on," I said. We all crowded into the changing area, I unzipped and shrugged out of the flight suit. Mr. Scott was relieved that underneath I was wearing a Go Army t-shirt and fatigue pants. The poor clerk about peed his pants at the sight of the standard issue M9 Beretta in the Galco Classic Lite shoulder holster.

"You will have to take those off," he said tentatively, indicating my pants.

"Oh, sorry," I undid the belt and dropped them to the floor, stepping out. Scott groaned and turned around. The clerk measured my waist, inseam and hip to floor, he seemed impressed.

"Miss Willard, this is highly unorthodox," Mr. Scott remarked, still facing the curtain.

"They asked for me, so they are going to get me." I answered, and I have Mr. Haal's permission to do so, I added to myself. The clerk returned with all of the components, and I tried them on; they all fit perfectly. "I'll take it." I said. Mr. Scott just shook his head. I pulled up my pants and handed him the flight suit. Starting to walk out of the changing room, he cleared his throat and pointed to the now unconcealed M9. "Oh, sorry. I'll wear the jacket." I said to the clerk after paying with the Government issued card.

Mr. Scott made another call, and by that evening a driver had taken us to another building in a car with darkened windows, so that I had no idea where we were. Mr. Scott took charge of my new clothes and the flight suit. I kept the jacket. I was shown into a large room set up with chairs facing a speaker's platform in front, and a line of tables with sandwiches along the back. There were about ten other people milling around; some sitting, some were eating, none were talking. About half of them were in various military uniforms. I went over to the sandwich table and picked out something that looked like a fairly normal roast beef with lettuce and tomato, and then rummaged through the bowl of condiments, picking out a packet of horseradish, first time I'd even seen it in a packet. There was a young man also standing there, picking out a mustard pack. A light bulb went on in my head, and I took another look around the room, everyone in the room was male except me. This was kind of one sided for a meeting that was supposed to be on women in combat.

"Do you know why we're here?" I asked him.

He looked at me funny, then in a heavy British accent said, "Joint American British training exercises, of course." Of course, my ass, I thought; I'd been lied to again, but why should I be surprised? An obviously high-ranking British officer strode into the room, closely followed by two men in black suits. "Take your seats, please, this meeting will come to order." He announced as if giving an order. The military people obeyed almost instantly, but the rest of us, not so much. He stood at the podium, clenching his jaws, waiting. "SIT!" he bellowed. I quickly finished my seat selection and sat.

Before everyone was seated, he continued.

"Whatever you were told as to why you were called here was a lie. You are here because, in one way or another, all of you are directly engaged in anti terrorist actions. There is no need to be secretive within this room, and everything you see or hear is strictly top secret and will be handled as such. I am telling you this now, because everything to be discussed in the meetings tomorrow needs to be done in the most open and honest fashion possible."

A photo of a man covered the screen behind him.

"Frances Grennen, aka Frank, Fran, or Hans, infiltration." I recognized him as the Frank from Ankara. I also saw that he was in the room, glaring at the man up front, because his cover had been compromised. I knew then it was coming for all of us, kind of a covert operative ice breaker. Another picture, "Groden Voord, aka Rude, covert ops." I found him in the crowd. The next picture came up, "Hammel Massa, aka Maus, or mouse, infiltration." The next picture was of a large blond man, "Enrich Kraus, aka Igor, interrogation." Then the one I knew was coming, not a very flattering picture either, "Millicent Willard, aka Skank or Laura Peddington, assassin." I could feel the eyes on me. This exercise continued through everyone in the room.

"Now that we all know who we are, there is no need for any more pretending. Each of you will be called into the meeting, and I expect that you will be cooperative. This is not voluntary, and don't expect special treatment. The meetings will start tomorrow at 9:00 AM, and you will not be late. Rooms are provided for you in the building upstairs, and I know most of you are carrying. You will not, I repeat, will not, be allowed to take any weapons inside the meeting rooms. That is all."

There was still very little talking as we slowly drifted from the room. So these were my colleagues, nice to know, I guess, but I doubted we'd be setting up friend pages on Facebook. When I walked out of the room, I found Mr. Scott waiting for me. I'm sure I looked pretty shell shocked as I walked up to him.

"I trust everything went well?" he asked, with a knowing look.

"As well as could be expected." I answered, and then said, "Sorry to be so much trouble."

"No trouble at all, young lady, you should have heard the stories about the others."

I smiled. I guess us interrogators and assassins can be hard to handle at times, I thought.

The room was relatively nice, except for having the small window blacked out; I was glad that I was not claustrophobic, because it was pretty creepy. I peed, washed, and laid down on the bed in my usual staring at the ceiling meditative position; however, I didn't remember any of it.

The room phone rang. It was our morning wakeup call. I checked the clock: 07:09. Despite the fact that Mr. Scott didn't like them, my new clothes were hung in the closet. I dressed, checking out the trenchless look in case I wanted to ditch the jacket; pretty nice, the jeans showed that I'd added a little shape to my hips and thighs in the last year, and then checked the look with the jacket, very nice. I'm ready, I said to myself. It was a good thing that the jacket had pockets, because nothing was fitting in the jeans. I took the holster and Beretta with me, not wanting to leave it in the room. I assumed they would have safe storage outside the meeting.

I tried the door and found it locked. "What the fuck?" I picked up the room phone, "Miss Willard, if you're ready, we will send a man for you." A man said, before I even heard it ring. It would have been very easy to take that completely the wrong way, but instead I said,

"Yes, thank you." Two minutes later, the door opened, and another older man was there, not Mr. Scott.

"This way, Miss Willard." He led me down to a breakfast buffet, not too fancy, but not bad. I picked out fruit and cereal. There were several other people in the room, but few conversations. I caught the eye of the man I'd spoken to at the condiment table last night. He acknowledged, and then came over after he finished gathering breakfast.

"Millicent Willard, did I get that correct?"

"Yes, and you are Dwight Maxwell?" He smiled and nodded. His specialty was infiltration.

"That's correct, so how did you get a name like Skank?"

I smiled, "That's what I was called in high school. I was kind of a poor dresser."

He laughed, "You look like you've improved a great deal since then."

"Thanks, but a large government charge account helps."

The grumpy Military officer entered. "45 minutes," was all he said.

"What are we, children?" I said to Dwight.

"Some of those guys act like it," Dwight said. We finished, and I got up to get some orange juice as Dwight filled his plate a second time.

"Fifteen minutes," our personal town crier announced. I went to find a rest room, doing business adjusting, washing, and doing a final mirror check. I was just leaving when I heard the five minute warning. My phone buzzed, shit, it was Cali. I love you, Cali, but your timing sucks.

"Cali? What time is it there?"

"Oh, three something in the morning, I'm still up. I found out about your father." Shit, I so wanted to hear this.

"What, Cali?"

"What's a DXF file?" she asked. I rummaged through my head.

"It's a type of CAD file, it was an old standard for transferring CAD data in text file format. I don't think anyone uses it anymore. My dad always complained about them because they never worked very well."

"Well, the company that your dad worked for was sending sensitive information coded into DXF files. Your dad didn't know he thought that, they were just having him make drawings of their own equipment. The confidential data was coded into it through some type of algorithm without his knowledge. The problem was, the equipment they were having him draw as a carrier for the sensitive information was stolen from other companies. He found that out, and assumed they were only stealing the designs of the equipment he was drawing. He told the authorities. They didn't handle it well, and tipped his bosses off. That's why they closed down the company and killed him. It took the FBI a long time to figure out what was going on, but they also found that your dad's company wasn't the only one. That's why they didn't want to say anything to you, or want you to get involved. They didn't want to tip off the other companies until they could get a handle on all of them."

"So he was actually sending information to China with the CAD files he thought he was sending to the manufacturing plant?"

"Yes, exactly, there wasn't even a plant there, they were just decoding the information they'd stolen from area defense contractors. Customs checked for illegal States only technology, but the actual drawings were okay, just the buried encoded stuff was not." I was getting a dirty look from the men guarding the meeting door.

"But my dad's company was all Americans, it wasn't a Chinese company, why would they be betraying our own country?"

"Money, of course," Cali said, "To them it was just a big score. Wave cash under the nose of most Americans, and they roll over like puppies."

"Off the phone now," the man barked.

"Cali, I have to go, but thank you, thank you so much, I'll call you back later." I clicked off.

"What the fuck?" was all I could think. I surrendered my M9 and holster at the door, and was escorted to a gallery behind the main meeting table. We were sitting in mostly darkness while the men around the table were in the light, talking in low tones so that we could not hear. Once we were all in, a man at the end of the oval table closest to the door stood up.

"Attention please, this meeting of the Joint Anti-terror Subcommittee will come to order. You who are in the back gallery are here specifically at the request of the President and the Prime Minister. Your purpose is to provide open, honest, unbiased information on the state of the field. Sergeant," he called, "Close and secure the door." The speaker sat down. The man at the other end of the table took a drink of water, then said, "Shall we begin?"

For the first few minutes, I tried my best to stay attentive; they were discussing past events and their effects on the world situation, however, there seemed to be no interest in us being here at all.

My mind started to wander, big score meaning money. Ted told me I knew the score. The Russian I killed was in it to get rich selling arms. War is business, Ted had said; people are willing to pay anything to kill each other.

I tried to focus back on the meeting. They were talking about Arab extremists; one man began ranting on how easy it was for religious extremists to be manipulated. I thought about the man I assassinated in Turkey, how he was controlling a fanatic, only because he wanted to sell more arms. The big score, what did Faruk say, we would do anything for money. Roll over like puppies is what Cali said. I could see people in my night scope, as Cali talked about puppies. I saw the kids that captured me, and I realized they weren't afraid of me because I was a woman fighting back. I wasn't shooting at them, I was defending the rangers. They didn't know what to do with me because they didn't want to hurt a woman. That was real Muslim teaching according to Faruk, you never kill a woman, and they were conflicted.

One of my colleagues in the back chimed in of how proud he was of their latest tactic of following the arms dealers to the leaders of the warring fundamentalist groups to find out who they were. It seemed like the people at the table were not listening to him at all. One man pounded the table. It's a known fact, they only respect power. The only way to break a fundamentalist is to hit their leaders hard. That's wrong, I thought, he didn't know anything about religious people. That only makes them stronger.

260

Just like 9/11 made us stronger. Money makes us weaker, the big score, I know the score. In a flash, I got an image of grabbing the tail of a big dog, and it all came clear.

"Holy shit!" I yelled, finding myself standing with all eyes looking at me. "This is all wrong, we've got everything backwards."

"Sit down!" one of the men at the table demanded. "I am not wrong about this, force is the only way."

"No, reaching out to the moderates will show that we are their friends..." another man railed.

"STOP!" I screamed. "If you want to flaunt penis size, get a ruler and make a chart. Did you call us here to listen to us or not?"

"What..." The man speaking about power looked into one of the files spread on the table with my picture in it. "...Skank, do you have to say?"

"This is not about ideology; we are killing the wrong enemy, it's only about money. This is not the same war that you are used to. War is a business venture now. It's about making money. The arms dealers are the leaders; they are creating a market for their wares. Ideologies are now only marketing tools. We are all being manipulated, just like you yourselves said about religious extremists. Christian, Muslim, Jew, it doesn't matter to them, as long as we buy weapons. It seems people will pay any price to kill each other. As long as we keep falling into the old trap of thinking ideology, we will lose."

"Then who are these enemy arms dealers?" I pointed to the man who had commented earlier. His face turned ashen white.

"The Russians, sir." He said tentatively. "And the Chinese, and the Germans, and the French, and even our own people." He continued.

"We can't fight everybody," the man at the head of the table said.

"That's why this is so difficult now," I answered. "Threats come from everywhere." I said, quoting Ted. "The enemy is criminal corporations and greedy business men, not nations, the sooner we realize that, the better able to fight it we will be."

"So then, do the others think Miss Skank here is correct?" The distain in his voice poured like molasses onto the table. I gave the other talkative man from our ranks a look that said, "Don't forget I have assassin in my job description" as I sat down.

But it was Dwight Maxwell who spoke up. "I believe she is correct, sir."

"What, you are siding with her?" The man at the head of the table barked.

Frank spoke up, "We have documented cases where that type of activity has occurred, and others where we suspect it may be happening."

"What about the rest of you?"

There was some muffled speaking. "For the most part, we have not viewed it as such, but what she says makes a lot of sense." Another man said.

The man next to him continued, "It could be a growing trend, sir."

Dwight answered again, "I believe you have said it yourselves, the fundamentalists in your own nation are easily swayed by well placed political rumors to vote a certain way. Is it that much of a stretch to believe dealers would do the same thing to sell guns?"

"How can these criminals have that much power and influence to steer whole nations?"

I spoke up again. "You know that to be the case, where drug cartels are more powerful than nations and control whole governments."

One of the men seated next to the man speaking whispered something to him. He stood up, "We will take this under advisement. This meeting is adjourned." Several armed military men quickly ushered us out of the room.

As we were leaving, Frank took me aside and said, "Well you sure stepped in it this time, I'll be surprised if any of us are still standing be the end of the day." He walked away, clearly upset. I retrieved my hardware from one of the guards outside the door. I couldn't help thinking that if he was that concerned, why did he speak up in the meeting, or better yet, why didn't anyone tell me beforehand that even though I was invited, I was not supposed to actually speak? I've obviously got a lot to learn about this whole spy thing.

We were being herded towards the elevators that would take us down to the parking garage below the building. Even on the way down, I noticed that no one wanted to look at me. Great, now I've pissed them all off, and I don't think these are the guys I really want mad at me. We emerged from the elevator, into the garage where the same dark windowed limos were lined up to take us to who knows where. I just wanted to get out of here and survive long enough to give Cali a call back.

"Miss Willard?" I heard Dwight calling.

"Yes?" I turned to him, thinking that he was also going to be upset with me, but instead, he had a huge grin on his face.

"I can't believe you actually told your secretary of defense to get a ruler and measure his penis. The look on his face was absolutely priceless."

"Is that who that was? Shit."

"Where are you off to now?" he asked.

"To be honest, I don't know, I only thought about getting here."

"Well then, come, we'll share a ride." He cut though the gathered crowd and flagged down the lead car. "Kensington Gardens, my good man." he told the driver, and opened the door for me. The driver gave him a "do I look like a cabby" look, but got in and drove us away.

"Where are we going?" I asked.

"Kensington Gardens, it's beautiful this time of year, right next to Fergie's place, you'll love it."

"A nice place to bury the body?"

"What? Oh, no," he smiled. "I thought you were great, did Mr. Haal put you up to it?"

"No, well, yes, in a way, I guess he did, as a matter of fact."

"Well, good for you and good for him, I commend you for speaking up."

The car stopped, and the driver tapped on the window between the front and rear.

"This must be our stop." He reached over me, brushing lightly against my breasts, pulling the handle to open the door. I lingered a bit, enjoying the contact, then stepped out onto the sidewalk. Dwight followed. The car drove away, revealing four stone pillars holding iron gates. I followed him, sprinting across the street between traffic. Just outside the gate, he stopped at a vendor selling ice cream.

"What flavor?" he asked.

"Vanilla," I said.

"I should have guessed," he said.

"What does that mean?"

"Everybody thinks vanilla is plain and boring, but in reality, it's exotic and complex. It comes from the orchid, a beautiful flower, and is very difficult to cultivate and refine. I bet most people pass you by, they label you skank, without understanding the complex intelligent person inside."

"Did it say your specialty was infiltration, or profiling?"

He laughed as he handed me the small cup with a scoop of ice cream and a tiny wooden spoon. He paid the vendor, and we walked through the gates. The park was a beautiful endless field of lush green lawns with tree-lined paths.

"The point is, don't let what other people don't see in you shape your self image. You quite possibly changed the world today, and for the better. The others were too busy worrying about their own arses to notice." I knew that the world was just as messed up now as it was when I went into the meeting, but it would have to get along without me for a while. I just snuggled up to him, putting my arm around his waist, and continued to walk down the tree-lined path with no other thought than to enjoy his company and the beautiful garden.

Ted Haal found us still in the park a half hour later.

"Laura, you were spectacular today," he called, "Although I wouldn't recommend bringing the secretary's privates into the discussion, but that sure got their attention. Hey Maxwell." He added as an afterthought.

"They're taking it under advisement" I answered, slathering it with sarcasm.

"Well, the milk is spilled, they can't ignore it now." Ted said.

"I need a vacation."

"You're still in the military, Laura, you don't get vacations."

"A leave then, I haven't had leave since completing BCT. I want to stay here in England for a while, go to Maidstone, and see where my family comes from without having to kill someone when I get there."

"Do you know any Willards still here in England? Dwight asked.

"No not really, after John Willard and that Salem Witch Hunt thing in 1692, the records got a little muddy. We think we're from the indentured servant side of the family, but we're not sure. But I know that the Willard name mostly comes from Southeast England, I looked it up on ancestry dot com."

"Well, I'm afraid any vacations will have to take place in The States, they want you back there."

"What? Why? Look, I'm not popping any US citizens."

"No, it's not that, it's... Well, you've got yourself in trouble again."

"Oh great, this isn't about the secretary's penis, is it?

He shook his head, "No, it seems dead soldiers are not supposed to write to grade school kids."

"I'm still dead? I thought that was fixed."

"Dead is not something that usually gets better."

"I'm going to be sick." I said, crouching down to the ground, holding my head in my hands.

Ted looked down at me, "You're booked on a flight from London to Washington tonight, I made them spring for first class so that you will be able to sleep on the plane. Your hearing is tomorrow morning in Washington.

"Hearing, what do you mean hearing?" Dwight challenged. I stood up and got between the two men.

"It's okay, Dwight, what are they going to do, kill me again?" I said, looking to Ted.

"Dwight said. "If you want political asylum, I think I can arrange it." It sounded very tempting.

"No, I think I need to do this." I answered.

Epilog: Arlington National Cemetery

Cali and I laid flowers on Georgia's grave. Her real name was Bethany Lynn Harland, she was from Seattle, and no one really knew why she was called Georgia. Then, we walked down to the simple white headstone that read Morgan May Troas, and sat down on the grass.

Cali said, "I had no idea that coming back from the dead was so complicated."

"I wouldn't recommend it." I answered.

"No, I have to stay dead if I want the gangs to leave my family alone."

"I'm so sorry about that, you can't contact them at all?"

"It's better this way, I want them to remember that I finally did something good. So sorry about your dad, they really handled the whole thing very badly."

"The police just went to the company officers and told them my dad accused them of industrial espionage?" I asked her.

"Basically yes, no one had any idea that they were actually sending military designs encoded in the DXF files. It seems Connecticut is full of defense contractors."

"But what about the computer, does anyone know what was on it?"

"They needed to get their encoder back; if the Feds got a hold of it, they would know immediately what was going on, and could read all of the documents from all of the other companies they had set up. They killed your father, and then realized they took the wrong machine."

"My dad," I smiled thinking about him. "He's the only guy I know nerdy enough to hide a computer under the floor."

"So are you going back home, then?"

"To Winfield? Eventually, I have another hearing on Monday; now that I'm alive again I have to answer for everything I did while I was dead. Then maybe I can go.

"So what was the final determination on how you could come back from the dead?"

"They said I was on loan to the French DST, which is partly true. The Army just lost track of where I was. How did you find out all of this information on my father's case, anyway?"

She laughed, "The Company has some pretty cool tools."

"You really like what you're doing now, don't you?"

"Yes, very much, thank you for helping me get here." She looked over at her headstone.

"So is there an empty box down there?" I asked.

"No, they're saving it for when I really need it."

"Oh, I was kind of hoping I could get the space next to you."

Uncorrected Copy

Made in the USA
Charleston, SC
31 May 2011